I0733253

GONE TO TEXAS

A. S. FRENCH

NEONOIR BOOKS

Copyright © 2022 by A. S. French

All rights reserved.

No part of this book may be reproduced in any form or by any electronic or mechanical means, including information storage and retrieval systems, without written permission from the author, except for the use of brief quotations in a book review.

This is a work of fiction. Names, characters, places, events, businesses, locales and incidents are either the products of the author's imagination or used in a fictitious manner. Any resemblance to actual persons, living or dead, or actual events is purely coincidental.

ALSO BY A. S. FRENCH

Crime Fiction and Thrillers

The Astrid Snow series

Book one: Don't Fear the Reaper.

Book two: The Killing Moon.

Book three: Lost in America.

The Detective Jen Flowers series

Book one: The Hashtag Killer.

Book two: Serial Killer.

Book three: Night Killer.

Northern Crime Fiction

Where The Bodies Are Buried

Writing as Andrew. S. French

The Arcane Supernatural Thriller Series

Book one: The Arcane.

Book two: The Arcane Identity.

The Ella Finn Fantasy Novella Series

Ella and the Elementals

Ella and the Multiverse

Ella and the Monsters

Ella and the Dreamers

Supernatural Short Stories

Dead Souls.

Go to www.andrewsfrench.com for more information.

1 WHISKEY BAR

Astrid sat at the table, cradling a pint in her hand. It was only half full since the rest of it was dripping from the head of the bloke opposite her. A gang of four lurked behind him. All their eyes were on her as Bob wiped the booze from his face. She guzzled from a bottle of Belgian beer. It tasted of coriander and orange peel and smelt like the back streets of London, the place she was due to return to in fewer than six hours.

Bob scowled at her. 'Why did you do that? I was only being friendly.'

'By putting your hand on my leg? That's not being friendly.' She finished her drink and put the glass on to the table. 'That's you being a pervert.'

'Where are you from, lady?'

The familiar smell of sweat and spilt beer hung in the air as one of Bob's group tried to stuff a plate of giant onion rings into his mouth. She studied Bob's face as Lou Reed's voice serenaded the back of her skull. His dark eyes appeared to shrink into his head as he hunched his shoulders and leant close to her, but not making the same mistake again: there was no touching the leg this time. She spotted the fear lurking in his face and realised this was all for show and the hulking men behind him were not his friends. That clumsy hand on her leg was from desperation.

'I'm going to London, Bob; do you want to come with me?'

His gloom vanished as he spoke. 'Can we go now?'

She was about to reply when the not so fantastic four stepped back to let a tall man approach her.

'I hope young Robert isn't bothering you, Ms?'

His Armani suit stuck to him like a second skin, and he smelt of fresh jasmine. Long, messy dark-brown hair hung down to his shoulders. If there'd been a remake of Tarzan on the horizon, she would have nominated him for the role.

Astrid stood and took Bob's hand in hers. 'He's going to show me the bits of the city the tourists never see.'

The man didn't move, blocking their exit. 'Oh, you don't want to do that, Ms.' He rubbed his chin and peered at her. 'New York is far too dangerous for strangers.' He transferred his smile from her to Bob. 'And Robert is in enough trouble as it is.'

She let out a long sigh. Did she need this aggravation when she had a plane to catch in a few hours? What did she care about the troubles of the man who'd grabbed her leg? She kept her eye on the new bloke and the four who must have been his employees while glancing at Bob. His hands shook so much, she thought they might drop from his arms.

And then the leader stepped to the side and presented her with a way out. But curiosity got the better of her.

'What trouble is he in?'

Dapper Dan put a hand on his heart as he laughed. 'Don't let that concern you, Ms. You just be on your way now and be careful out there. The streets of New York can be hazardous.'

She was about to reply when the phone pinged inside her jacket pocket. Astrid removed it and read the message.

I need you to go to Texas as soon as possible. Please. It's a big favour for me.

She returned to her seat, surprised George would ask her such a thing. She'd known him for nearly twenty years, the man who was her leader and mentor at the Agency and the only friend she had in the world, and in all that time, he'd never asked her for anything. He'd done lots for her, had risked his life and career to help her untangle herself from the clutches of the Agency, and now here he was asking for something unusual.

Bob touched her leg again. She didn't flinch, seeing a face consumed by fear. Whatever Dapper Dan and his gang wanted him for, it wasn't good. Still, what did she care? She used her phone to check flights from New York to Texas. The earliest was in five hours, a four-hour journey to Houston. So, there was time to kill.

She replied to George.

Why?

His reply was instantaneous.

I'LL SEND MORE DETAILS WHEN YOU GET THERE. ASAP.

It was something serious for him to be using all capitals. But he didn't say when you get *here*, which meant he wasn't in Texas.

She brushed Bob's fingers from her leg as she leant towards him, so close only he could hear her.

'What's the deal with you and these morons?'

His eyes narrowed as his lips shook. 'Grayson hurt my

sister, so I went to the police. Then he threatened me if I didn't change my story.'

She assumed Grayson was Dapper Dan. 'So why are you here?'

He trembled as he spoke. 'I live around the corner, so they must have followed me. When I saw you on your own, I thought they'd leave me alone if I was with you.'

He was as naïve as he was brave. She scanned the rest of the place, seeing what was close to her and selecting the correct map inside her head. Then she stood and went to Dapper Dan.

'How loyal are those goons to you?'

His shoulders shook as he laughed. 'Why?'

'Because if all they care about is money, I'll pay them to go.' She glanced around the bar, spotting what she needed and where she had to be if things turned nasty. 'Or you could just let Bob and me leave and enjoy your night.' She gave him her warmest smile. He returned it with a crooked grin.

'Now, why would I do that?'

Astrid stood six foot two in her bare feet and would have towered over the men around her even without the high heels she rarely wore, but had tonight. This meant she was peering down at Grayson as she pushed her face into his and grabbed his balls; they were small and easily accessible through his thin trousers.

He let out a shrill scream which was barely audible above the sound of The Strokes blaring from the jukebox. The goons were slow to respond, but her expression and clenched hand told them not to move towards her. She continued smiling as she turned to Bob.

'Go home, Robert; you'll get your justice.'

He scampered past her and out of the bar. She kept on

squeezing as she wondered if she could transfer her plane ticket from London to Texas.

I didn't ask George where in Texas. It's a big place.

Grayson gritted his teeth as his lips quivered. 'Let me go.'

She ignored the request and addressed his thugs. 'Did he hire you to protect him?'

They stared at each other, dumbfounded, and she guessed there wasn't a leader amongst them. Then the one in the middle with the blazing skull tattooed on his throat – that must have hurt – stepped forward.

'You better let him go, lady.'

She tightened her fist and watched a flood of tears gush down Grayson's cheeks.

'Sure, in a minute. But I want to know what you lads will do once I release him.'

The blazing skull returned to his colleagues and they whispered amongst themselves. While they did that, she used her free hand to text George.

Whereabouts in Texas?

She slipped the mobile into her pocket as she waited for a reply. Then the blazing skull turned back to her.

'We take orders from him.'

The phone vibrated against her leg. 'So, if he tells you to attack me, you will?'

His face was unmoving. 'That's the rules, lady.'

Astrid moulded the maps in her head into shape. She could let go of Grayson and try to fend off the goons, but that would mean managing the conflict area and finding a weapon. Not a gun or a knife, she didn't want to harm anybody apart from Grayson, but she needed something to defend herself with.

She scanned her immediate surroundings again: the bar

was six feet away, with plenty of glasses or bottles to use. Beyond that was a pool table, and the cues and balls would be handy as weapons, but she doubted she'd reach them before one of the thugs grabbed her.

The only other option was to go on the attack and hope for the best. She could push Grayson into them like a bowling ball and pins. They were close together and only a few feet away; his bulk with her force might scatter them. Then she could grab her glass and smash the closest of the thugs. But that would still leave three of them, and unless one or two tumbled into the floor with Grayson, they'd be on her in seconds.

Or perhaps she could drag him out of the bar, a hostage to help her escape. Then what? Let him go and run? What if one of them had a gun and shot her in the back?

All of this bounced through her mind as she squeezed his genitals. The pain must have been too much for him as he fainted and collapsed into her. His weight promised to take them both into the floor, but she managed to get the proper leverage to stay on her feet.

If he's out cold, he can't give them any orders.

They glared at her, and she wondered if they'd noticed their boss was sleeping. As she did that, the sounds of sirens shot through her head. She thought her internal jukebox had kicked into automatic for one second and she was listening to The Clash or The Beastie Boys. Then she realised it came from outside and was getting closer. Maybe Bob had called the police. The goons must have heard it as their mugs dropped faster than a snitch in a concrete overcoat. That's when she knew what she had to do.

'He's all yours, boys.'

She pushed Grayson at them, then turned and strode out of the bar. By the time she heard the crash behind her, she was outside and lights screamed towards her as she ducked down the nearest dark alley.

Astrid dodged the rats and dog shit as she picked up pace. There was a small bag to collect at her hotel, and then it would be straight to the airport. If they wouldn't swap her current ticket, she'd get a new one and charge it to George.

A cold drizzle of rain dropped onto her as she cut out of the alley and moved in the opposite direction from the bar. Nobody had followed her, so she removed the mobile from her pocket and checked the latest message from her former boss and mentor.

Go to San Antonio, then to Eureka Falls, about a thirty-minute drive away. Let me know which flight you get.

The rain turned heavy and drenched her hair. The phone was in her hand as she walked; it was a longer flight, around six hours, but at least she'd have more time for sleep.

San Antonio instead of London. Texas over England.

Great. I've always wanted to go to the Alamo.

2 WISHFUL SINFUL

Astrid got no sleep on the journey, instead watching some terrible film about a symbiotic alien and two old episodes of *Father Ted*. At least they left her in a good mood when she stepped off the plane. San Antonio was an hour behind New York, so it was eleven o'clock Monday morning when she passed through the gates. There'd been no new messages from George, and there was no point texting him since it would be five o'clock in the afternoon in London and he'd be leading an Agency meeting. Once she passed through security, she headed out and climbed into a cab for the ride to Eureka Falls.

The drive was short and the hotel cheap, enough for her to pay for three days with the cash she had on her. The kid on the desk only ogled her twice as she paid, and then took the stairs to her room. The corridors smelt of last week's food, and the carpet tried to stick to her shoes. The place was compact with a view of a giant office block straight from the grey 1970s. She threw her bag to the floor and her body onto the bed. Her phone lay next to her and she waited for it to ping with a message. She was considering leaving and taking a walk through town when a noise in the corridor made her sit up.

The thump on the door was as heavy as the footsteps that had approached her room. In between the banging was wheezy breathing which, to her keen ears, indicated a heart attack soon if the owner wasn't too careful. She was letting them knock one more time when the words *police, open up* put her on alert. She peered through the spyhole and glimpsed two sullen figures behind the badges they held. They could have been fake, she'd used plenty of her own over the years, but she didn't care. Even though she'd checked into the hotel in her real name, nobody knew she was staying there, so this might be something to keep her overactive brain occupied.

She let them in and gave them her best smile. He was tall, rake thin with a handlebar moustache transported from the 1980s. Her face was so tight, Astrid could have opened a bottle using her skin. She was younger than him, maybe by ten years.

'How can I help you, Officers?'

It was the woman with blonde flecks peppering her dark hair who replied. 'Are you Astrid Snow?'

She didn't see any point in lying. 'I am.'

'Ms Snow, I'm Detective Hudson, and this is Detective Hicks.' Astrid watched them inspect the surroundings, examining the shabby furniture and frayed carpet. Their eyes narrowed as they looked at each other, and she guessed they were making a quick judgment about her based on the room. She scrutinised them, noticing the confident way he held himself and the tiny tic at the corner of Hudson's mouth. The woman spoke again.

'Do you know a man called Adam Church?'

Astrid racked her brain, but that name didn't ring a bell. 'Never heard of him. Has he left me some money in a will?'

Her attempt at humour fell on deaf ears. 'We have him at the station downtown, and he's asking for you.'

A man she'd never met had given them her name and knew she was in Eureka Falls.

'How did you find me here?'

Hicks stuck a toothpick between his teeth as he replied. 'We checked arrivals at San Antonio airport, and then rang all the hotels in town.'

'All the hotels?' Their diligence in locating her was disturbing.

He laughed as he wedged a foreign object out of his mouth. 'There are only two in Eureka Falls, and we got lucky calling here first.'

'So you want me to come with you?'

They both nodded. 'I'm sure it won't take long,' Hudson said.

Astrid followed them from the room, down the stairs and out of the hotel. It was only when she was in the back of the car she thought to enquire some more about this Adam Church.

'What's he done to be locked up?'

Hicks turned to her. 'Two children were found murdered in his basement.'

<hr>

IT WAS a twenty-minute drive to the Eureka Falls police department, and she got no further information from them. They were reluctant to volunteer any details, and she wasn't going to ask. The only thing to catch her interest on the short journey was glancing out of the window to notice something called the Soccer Factory.

A little bit of England. If I get the chance, I might pop in to see if they have the latest Aston Villa home kit.

Astrid thought about her last trip to Birmingham as she spoke. 'Does Church have a lawyer?'

Hudson shook her head. 'Not yet. He made a phone call, and then asked for you.'

They got out of the car and guided her into the station, a small building with more empty parking spaces than vehicles. They strode through reception with its bulletproof window as Detective Hudson entered a code to get them inside. They led her past dispatch and staff hammering away on keyboards while glued to computer screens. They moved down a narrow corridor and turned right. Hudson opened a door and ushered her in. A table and four chairs were in the middle of the room while a uniformed police-woman stood next to the wall. Hicks left them as Hudson sat down and indicated for Astrid to take the seat near her.

Hudson pushed a stray hair from her eye. 'Where are you from in England, Ms Snow?'

'London.' She wasn't interested in small talk.

The detective crossed her legs and placed one hand on the table. 'We assumed you were Adam Church's family lawyer.' Confusion crept into her face. 'Once the captain ordered us to collect you and bring you here, it seemed obvious to us.'

'Who is he accused of killing?' Astrid didn't see the point in correcting the detective for her misunderstanding.

'Detective Hicks will explain more, but two young sisters, Kay and Martha Glick, were found in Adam Church's basement twenty-four hours ago. Church claims he discovered them, and then called the police, but denies any knowledge of the crime. I was the first detective on the scene.' She paused as the colour drained from her face, and Astrid guessed Hudson still saw the bodies every time she closed her eyes.

Hudson took a deep breath and started again. 'The house was locked with no evidence of forced entry. His DNA - skin and hair - was on the girls, but there was no sign of sexual assault.'

Astrid was processing that information as Hudson's partner returned with the suspect. Adam Church stumbled into the room with his face glued to the floor, his shoulders moving like potatoes in a sack with each step he took. When he twisted his head up, he mumbled something under his breath as he stared at her. His face told a story of no sleep, with the bags under his eyes reaching down to the bottom of his nose. There was no life in his cheeks, only a scattering of lines which should have been on someone twice his age. Hicks pushed him into the chair opposite her.

Astrid turned to Hudson. 'Aren't you going to give us any privacy?'

The cop scrunched her mouth into a humorous shape. 'Are you his lawyer?'

'You know I'm not.'

'Then we're staying here.' Hudson nodded at the uniformed officer, and she left the room.

Astrid peered at the man she'd never met before, but who knew her name and where she was staying. She'd sat at numerous tables like this, stared across at hundreds of people accused of crimes they claimed to have no knowl-edge of. For most of them, she never spoke first, always waiting for them to damn themselves with their words or their impatience. She had endless patience, but this wasn't one of those times. Adam Church had a face lacking sleep and eyes which couldn't keep still.

'How do you know me?'

Hicks stood at the side of the room, his gaze fixed on the suspect. Church stopped his erratic finger-tapping and brought his shaking hands up to his chin.

'My uncle told me where you were and to get in touch with you. He said you were the only person who could help me.'

Astrid narrowed her eyes. 'Who is your uncle?'

Church puffed out a long breath of air while running fingers down his nose and across his mouth. 'George Cross.'

Adam put his face into his hands and lowered his head to the table. She'd expected cuffs on him, but there weren't any. While he lay there and sobbed, she removed her phone and checked for new messages, finding none.

What's George got me into this time?

3 TELL ALL THE PEOPLE

Astrid gave Church a minute to purge some of his distress before speaking.

'I didn't know George had a nephew.'

He rolled his head in his hands and lifted it from the table. Shaking fingers wiped the tears from his face and he stared at her like a rabbit in the headlights.

'I've no idea who you are.' He sucked air into his lungs and seemed to gain a semblance of control. 'You sound English. My uncle is English.' Church appeared confused.

'Yes, George.'

He used his arm to wipe the spit from his lips. 'Yeah. I've never met him, but I know he lives in England somewhere. He's my mother's older brother, but they were separated years ago.' His eyes glazed over. 'George. George Cross. It's a funny name, right, because I know a George Cross is a British medal.'

George, you old devil. You never told me you had relatives, let alone any in America.

'He sent me here, Adam.' She let that information sink in. 'Do you want my help?'

He sat up straight, seemingly looking at her for the first time. 'Really, Uncle George sent you here?'

Astrid checked for new texts on her phone and discovered none. 'Yes. Do you want my help?'

He didn't reply immediately, which surprised her.

Maybe he's guilty.

'Yeah, of course, yes. I mean, I need all the help I can get.'

'Did you kill those girls?'

'No, no, definitely not. I was in the basement, checking on stuff, when I found them. I've no idea what happened to the girls or how they got there. The house was locked when I left, and you need a digital code to get through the security, and a key to the front or back door as well.'

Astrid glanced at Hudson. The detective was smiling, a grin which told her she knew something they didn't.

'The police claim there was no sign of forced entry to the house.'

Adam seemed confused. 'I don't know about that.' He sank his head into his hands again, and his whole body trembled.

'Why don't you already have a lawyer?'

He spoke with his face pressed into the table. 'Everything has happened so fast. My head's never stopped whirling since they brought me in.' He lifted his head and looked at her. 'Aren't you a lawyer? Isn't that why Uncle George sent you?'

'No, I'm not, Adam. My skills lie somewhere else.'

She glanced at the blank walls and considered what she could do to help him. She didn't know if he was innocent or not, not yet, but she knew she'd do George this favour.

'So how will you help me?'

She spoke to the detectives. 'Can you share the case file with me?'

Hicks snorted laughter across the room. 'I don't know how criminal investigations work in Britain, but we don't share information with members of the public.' He moved from the wall and opened the door. 'And now you've used up all your time with him.'

She stood, knowing it would be fruitless to argue, but she needed to speak to Church again.

'When you have a lawyer, they'll have access to the evidence against you, and I need to see that. They should also be able to get me into the crime scene.'

'You want to go to my house?'

'I need to if you want me to prove your innocence.'

That's if he is innocent.

'Okay, I'll do all that, but you have to do something else for me.'

Here it comes.

'What?'

He pushed his thumb into his palm, rubbing at the skin so much, she expected it to come away and reveal the blood and bone underneath. 'Will you tell my sister Eve what's happened?'

Astrid's eyebrows arched towards the ceiling. 'Your parents named you Adam and Eve?'

Dark shadows consumed him. 'They were deeply religious.'

'Were?'

'They died in a car crash five years ago. It was ironic, really.'

'In what way?'

'They were leaving an event they'd organised, Christians Against Sin, when a drunk driver drove into them.' A tiny grin crept across his face. 'God does work in mysterious ways, after all.'

He appeared unsympathetic to the loss of his parents, or it may have been the shock of his situation overwhelming him, but she couldn't hold that against him.

'Where is your sister?'

His shoulders shrank into his chest. 'Eve checked herself into a facility when she was eighteen. She can leave anytime she wants, but she's been there for seven years.'

He gave her the name and address: the Tranquil Waters Rest Home. It sounded divine. At least it was something to do while waiting on the lawyer.

'Which of you two is the older?'

Adam's face twitched upwards so he stared at the blank ceiling. 'That would be me by five years.'

'Why haven't the police contacted her if she's your closest relative?'

Astrid was reluctant to say Eve was his next of kin, thinking it implied his guilt, and then the death penalty. She wasn't even sure if Texas executed some of its criminals, but if she had to guess which of the American states did, she'd go for the Lone Star State.

Church looked between Hudson and Hicks. 'I didn't tell them where she is.' He pressed his fingers into his forehead, and she thought he might be trying to drag his brain from his skull. 'Evie was, is, very self-conscious about, well, everything, and it would mortify her if anyone found out where she'd been living these last seven years.'

From the anxiety seeping from his eyes and the way his hands twitched as he spoke, Astrid assumed the Church siblings had some personal issues they had yet to overcome. Still, who was she to judge how families functioned? Her relationship with her sister, Courtney, currently resided below the seventh level of Hell, hanging together by the tiniest margin called Olivia, Astrid's niece.

He continued talking, but she didn't hear any of his words. She pictured where she should have been right then, feeling the frigid blast of her sister's gaze as she handed Olivia the presents she'd bought in America: Mickey Mouse wearing a Ramones t-shirt and the *Sherlock Holmes Children's Collection*. Courtney would likely frown at her daughter reading such books, but Astrid thought a seven-year-old as clever as Olivia, and she was much brighter than either Astrid or her mother were at the same age, should be challenging her mind all the time.

She pushed the image of Olivia back into the shadows of her head. 'What did you say?'

He leant closer to her. 'Be careful when you tell her about this; she's quite fragile.'

She peered at him and wondered what he was hiding. Hicks's scowl told her it was time to leave, so she followed Hudson from the room as her partner stayed behind. She didn't know Adam Church from Adam, but George was the only person she called a friend, and she'd never let him down.

Astrid was moving down the corridor towards the exit when Hudson's fingers landed on her shoulders. In any other situation, she might have broken the detective's wrist but now wasn't the time. She stepped to the side and away from her reach.

'Can I have a few words before you go?'

'Is this a demand?'

Hudson held up her hands and grinned. 'Just a simple request from one investigator to another.'

Astrid contemplated the situation before acquiescing.

There was no point in pissing off the police when she might need them later.

'How about quid pro quo? You share something with me, and I'll do the same.'

Hudson pointed at the desk behind them. She strode towards it, and Astrid followed. As she sat, she examined the clutter there: printed emails and faxes, a half-full cup of cold coffee, three books on policy standards, and a photo of two kids grinning into the camera. There was no image of any significant other.

She's married to the job.

Hudson pushed her face into the computer as if she'd forgotten her glasses and tapped at the keyboard.

'Your name is Astrid Snow, and you're British.'

'I'll give you those for free.'

'What are you doing in the US?'

'Sightseeing holiday.'

Hudson pressed a single key. 'Before coming here, you visited New York and Washington.'

'That's correct.'

The detective sank into her chair. 'So what type of investigator are you?'

Astrid sighed inwardly. No matter how hard she tried to leave her past behind, she could never get away from it. She could lie, but didn't see the point. 'I worked for the British government. I can't tell you any more than that.'

'That must be why I can't find a file on you anywhere. Not with the FBI, the CIA, Homeland Security, or the NSA.'

Astrid shrugged. 'I'm a responsible citizen.'

'Oh, I think you're much more than that, Ms Snow.' She picked up a pen and used it to tap the screen. 'What most

American people don't realise is that each one of them, responsible or not, has a file about them somewhere. Since 2001, every American government has collected personal data on all of its citizens. They can access some of it if they ask, but most of it is off-limits. But, even though you're a foreign national, to have no file at all is quite exceptional.' She paused and waited for a reply. Instead, Astrid asked a question.

'What are you allowed to tell me about the case against Adam Church?'

Hudson dropped the pen on to the desk. 'He called the police to say he'd found the bodies of two girls in his basement. He claims the house was locked all day, and no one else has a key or code to the building. There was no sign of a break-in or forced entry.'

'How were the girls killed?'

'Someone strangled them. His DNA is all over them. His hair and skin were on their clothes.'

'Wouldn't that be expected inside his home?'

'There's more evidence I can't reveal to you.'

'But you'll have to tell his lawyer.'

'Yes.'

'And they'll tell me.'

'That's up to them.'

Astrid stood and turned to leave. 'Is there anything else you want to know about me?'

'The evidence we have is bulletproof, so why are you helping him? He's as guilty as sin.'

She thought again of being back in England and bathing in her niece's smile. 'Because I have a friend who, no matter what I do, I can never repay what I owe them. But this is a start.'

Detective Hudson shook her head. 'It's a start, all right; the start of Adam Church's journey to a lethal injection.'

That answered the question regarding Texas having the death penalty. There was one last thing she needed from Hudson.

'Is there somewhere nearby I can hire a car?'

'Sure. Do you need anything else?'

'Give me the address where you found the bodies.'

4 CURSES, INVOCATIONS

Beverly Shaw hated being called Bev, yet it had happened all her life. It had started with her family, then with the other kids in the street and school, continued with her teachers and co-workers, and even included strangers. But today was the absolute worst.

Her parents and brother were out and she'd taken a day off to work on her plans. When the doorbell rang, she should have ignored the howling of some terrible Led Zeppelin song her brother had programmed into the chimes, but she always worried she'd miss something important if she didn't answer the door.

The bell shrieked again as she rushed to turn the water off in the shower and climb into her robe. In her haste, she whacked her elbow against the bathroom door, and a surge of electricity shot up her arm. She rubbed at the pain and wondered why people called it the funny bone since there was nothing humorous about it. She wiped the steam from her eyes, stepped into the corridor and took the stairs two at a time. The thick carpet pushed up against her bare feet, and she considered how ironic it would be if, in her urgency, she stumbled and broke her neck when she was on the verge of something great. Years of planning were about to reach their fruition, and she might throw it all away because of her impatience and paranoia. Beverly knew there was only one thing that would calm her troubled mind. She whispered the mantra as she approached the front door.

Transfer the pain. Transfer the pain. Transfer the pain. Transfer the pain.

The words swirled inside her skull as she opened the door and stared at the UPS man. There was a large parcel at his feet.

'Is Paulie Shaw home?'

He examined her as if peering at a bug under a microscope. Water dripped from her forehead and ran into her eyes, blurring her vision and adding to her confusion.

Transfer the pain. Transfer the pain.

'His name is Paul and he's at work.' She glanced at the box and cursed her brother under her breath.

It's probably parts for his grubby motorbikes. He gets everything he wants while I'm left with nothing.

The delivery man smirked at her. 'Whatever. I need someone over the age of eighteen to sign for this, and you don't look old enough, little lady.'

His smirk turned into a leer as his eyes grew as wide as his forehead. He put one foot in the door, moving towards her and flashing yellow stained teeth. He smelt of stale pizza, and she wanted to throw up. She controlled her breathing, the mantra invisible inside her head.

Transfer the pain. Transfer the pain.

'My name is Beverly and I'm twenty-five years old.'

She knew her voice sounded like a teenager's, but she couldn't help herself. Her legs shook as she realised she was only in her gown while she dripped water onto the carpet. She turned her hand into a fist and forced the fingernails into her palm. It was that little stab of pain that brought her enough pleasure to ignore his foul presence. He ogled her, and she felt his gaze undressing her as she shivered in that bathrobe.

'Well, that's sweet, Bevvy, you'll do for me.'

And there it was. Bevvy. Being called Bev was so fucking annoying, and now this. The blood mixed in with the water in her palm, her voice trembling as she spoke.

'What?'

'Here you go, Bevvy.'

He pushed a digital device in front of her. His fingers were yellowed from too many cigarettes, his nails uncut for a long time. He'd inched closer to her and she smelt onions on his breath to go with the dried tomato sticking to his teeth. She tore her gaze from him and to the table at the side of the door. Paul had left one of his tools there again, a thick wrench covered in grease and dirt. It lay on top of a flyer for this Saturday's school reunion and dripped muck every-where. Their parents wouldn't complain; they never did about their favoured child.

Transfer the pain. Transfer the pain.

She closed her eyes, saw herself snatching up the tool, and then swinging it into his skull. His nose was long and angular, and she imagined the wrench smashing it in half. But he was a big man, much taller than her, and she'd have to reach up to hit him. The muscles in her arms from twice-weekly trips to the gym would be enough to break his jaw. There would be no point kicking him in the balls since she wasn't wearing any shoes, and she'd only hurt her feet. She'd swing again and smash his face, and then, when he dropped his shoulders, she'd crack his head open. Then she could drag him inside, get her legs on either side of him, and batter away until her actions transferred all her suffering into him. His van would be outside their front door, their address in his delivery schedule, but it didn't matter. She was going to crush his fucking skull.

Beverly opened her eyes and he was still smirking at her.

Transfer the pain.

No. She couldn't kill him now, not on the doorstep like this, with possible witnesses and all the things on her computer no one should see. It was her safe laptop with several security systems, but she knew if the police or FBI got their hands on it, then someone would crack through the passwords eventually. So, instead of killing him, she signed the device with her finger.

'Will this do?'

Nicotine stained his teeth and the top of his tongue. She smelt stale booze and desperation on him.

'Thanks, Bevvy.'

He turned away, leaving the parcel at her feet. She dragged it inside and closed the door. Beverly sighed and let the air out of her lungs. Her hand trembled as water dripped from her legs and on to the carpet. She used her foot to push the box to the side and headed up the stairs. It was only when she sat on her bed that she stopped shaking. She'd been so close to ruining all her plans.

But it had taught her one valuable lesson. She had to move ahead with those plans soon before the years of frustration got too much for her. And she knew exactly where she'd go next, with the person who was the first to cause her so much misery.

Transfer the pain.

ithin an hour of leaving the station, Astrid was sorted with a car and driving to the Church house. She needed to look at the building and location before speaking to Adam's sister in her self-imposed exile. She'd wanted to ask him why Eve Church had locked herself away from the rest of the world but decided it was inappropriate while he sat inside a cell. And what sort of names were Adam and Eve Church anyway? She checked the family online on her phone while she waited for the paperwork for the motor to clear.

The first thing she found was the reports of the crash which killed their parents. Sally and James Church, hit while making their way home from the Christians Against Sin event they'd organised. Some of the more salacious websites posted photographs of the debris, including one where Sally Church's hand flopped out of the car and on to the dirt. It reminded Astrid of a scene from the end of *Bonnie and Clyde*. But that wasn't the most interesting thing she discovered: the other driver in the collision was a woman named Annie Chapman. It wasn't that which piqued Astrid's curiosity, but the fact Chapman wasn't drunk and was a member of the same congregation as the dead couple: The Church of the Old Testament.

So why was Adam under the mistaken belief a drunk driver killed his parents? Who told him that and why? The police?

She considered those questions while she found the group's website and forced herself to read through their religious teachings, all of which they claimed came straight from the Old Testament. They appeared to focus only on the negative, a hatred for the following: immigrants, the poor, minorities, science, gay people, liberals, progressives, and so-called social justice warriors. She skimmed most of it and settled on the section saying God hated everyone, finding a long list of Bible quotes as evidence. Three of them stood out to her:

*Psalm 106:40 - "Therefore was the wrath of the LORD kindled against his people, insomuch that **he abhorred his own inheritance**."*

A bad workman always blames his tools.

*Proverbs 22:14 - "The mouth of strange women is a deep pit: **he that is abhorred of the LORD shall fall therein**."*

Astrid assumed it was about her, but it was the last of the quotes which interested her the most.

*Proverbs 6:16-19 - "**These six things doth the LORD hate**: yea, seven are an abomination unto him: A proud look, a lying tongue, and hands that shed innocent blood, A heart that deviseth wicked imaginations, feet that be swift in running to mischief, A false witness that speaketh lies, and he that soweth discord among brethren."*

She studied the words intently with parts of it echoing the case around Adam Church: a proud look, a lying tongue, and hands that shed innocent blood; a heart that deviseth wicked imaginations, feet that be swift in running to mischief; a false witness that speaketh lies, and he that soweth discord among brethren.

The words kept ringing inside her head as she drove towards Adam Church's house. They didn't come with an American accent, but an English one which sounded exactly like her parents. It was mainly her father, Lawrence, but her mother chimed in from time to time. She didn't understand why this was since neither of them was particularly religious.

She tried to drown them out as she headed to the house. Following the GPS directions on her phone, she found herself on Hillcrest Drive, driving down Broadway, then Linthorpe Road and the Westway. She slowed down at the intersection of Berwick Street and High Sierra Cross and stopped. The voices in her head vanished as she stepped out of the car. She was twenty minutes from her destination, but she needed to get her thoughts in order before getting there. The wind brushed her cheeks as she stared at the view of the downtown skyline, peering across the tops of the trees to the buildings of Eureka Falls. People milled around below her, most of whom appeared to be wearing different military uniforms.

Perhaps there's been an invasion.

She returned to the car and set off again, turning on the radio to a station featuring brass band music. She scooted through the channels until she found one playing the latest tune from Beyoncé. She hummed along to it as she drove past shops, restaurants, banks, spas and gyms before reaching a more residential area and her destination.

Astrid got out and peered at the house with the crime scene notifications around it. She removed the phone from her pocket and took some photos. If she observed the neighbourhood curtains twitching, it didn't register with her. She scanned the street, seeing a typical residential area with rows of similar houses and, she assumed, similar people living in all of them.

The temptation to see inside the house was great, but she fought it off, assuming the building was still considered a crime scene by the police. She was unsure if Hudson and Hicks resented her or not from the brief time she'd spent with them, but there was no need to antagonise them unnecessarily. Not yet, anyway.

If my boss had sent me out to chauffeur some stranger back to the office, I'd be less than pleased, that's for sure.

She remembered several of her early assignments with the Agency when George had paired her with experienced agents who would treat her as if she was no better than the gum on their shoes. She'd also spent plenty of days babysitting witnesses or suspects when she could have been doing so much more.

Astrid scrubbed away those memories and picked her way down the side of the building to the back. She stretched her neck to stare up to see if there was any way somebody could have prised a window open to climb inside, but saw nothing from where she stood. Even if the killer had entered that way, how did they get the two girls into the basement? Surely the kids would have run if they'd seen someone breaking into the house, and what were the chances of them going in with a stranger?

She pondered the questions as she gazed from the house towards the trees beyond the back and into the hills running parallel with the street. She removed her phone to check for messages, finding none from George, Courtney or Olivia.

Did I text Courtney to tell her I changed my flight home?

She couldn't remember. Not that her sister would care. She'd probably be glad, knowing Astrid wouldn't be around to fuss over Olivia again.

Astrid returned to the front and stood in the street, gazing up and down its length, surprised it was empty so early in the afternoon. She'd return once Adam had his lawyer and told them to give her a key to the place. It was hard to judge how the killer got in and out with the girls until she looked inside.

And that's all on the assumption Adam Church is innocent.

She considered that as she returned to the car and drove away.

Perhaps his sister might provide an insight on that.

6 LIONS IN THE STREET

Beverly went to her laptop and opened the web browser. She needed something to calm her nerves, and murder news always helped. And this was extra special murder news. She found a flood of media reports concerning the discovery of the sisters, but there were no real details and no mention of a suspect in custody. But she knew there was no way they could keep Adam Church's name from the public. She wiped the sleep from her eyes and scanned the webpages with their lurid headlines.

LOCAL MAN ARRESTED OVER GIRLS' MURDER

SLAUGHTER OF THE INNOCENTS

And her personal favourite:

BUTCHERED BABES

She read through the reports, finding no mention of him. How disappointing. It was the same with all the others. She closed them and switched to social media instead, and there was no holding back in that corner of the digital world.

ADAM CHURCH IS A MURDERING BASTARD.

STRING THE FUCKER UP.

BURN DOWN THE HOUSE.

She liked that idea. That would get rid of any evidence she might have left behind. No, she hadn't missed anything. After five years of careful planning, she wasn't going to miss anything. She returned to the screen, moving down the screaming capitals and those who'd added comments to their outrage. She found one from Judy Moore, the horrible busybody from down their street:

I always said that family was strange, especially the girl with the abnormal face and twitchy arms. What happened to her?

There was a long conversation that followed the post, which she decided to ignore.

Did I make any mistakes? Should I have done anything differently?

She reached under the bed and pulled out her special laptop. She flipped open the lid and waited for the first set of security steps to begin. After three years working at the school, everyone, including her family, believed Beverly was only an ordinary teacher of computer studies and technology. Nobody knew she'd been cracking codes and hacking into secure systems since she was fourteen. The screen flickered into life, and she completed the four-step security system she'd installed on the machine.

When the desktop appeared, she selected the secure web browser, went through another set of security protocols, and made her way on to the dark web. Here, she entered her password, opened her account and examined the latest posts and uploads. The heading New Terrorist Actions caught her eyes and she clicked on the link. Beverly had no interest in terrorists and their manifestos, regardless of what cause they followed, because all ideologies, political, religious and everything in between, were anathema to her.

Fancy being so narrow-minded you wanted to kill someone because of the colour of their skin, or their sexuality, or belief system.

It was the methodology that interested her, not ideology.

Twenty-first-century terrorism had changed the scope of killing; she'd admit that. Driving a vehicle into people as a means of murder seemed so obvious now, she couldn't believe someone hadn't done it sooner. Running down a street stabbing people, though, did seem somewhat inefficient to her. Plus, you're always likely to get arrested doing that, and even though she knew that's what most of the perpetrators expected or wanted, she had no intention of getting caught. Her ultimate act of violence would be grand, but it would be nothing as churlish as driving into a crowd.

And this is where her meticulous planning came into play. She understood doing something close to where she lived was not only dangerous, but probably stupid, but, like fundamentalist terrorists, she had no choice in the matter. Everything she was started with Adam, so her transference process had to begin with him.

She smiled as she thought of him before scrolling through the information on the screen and finding nothing worthwhile. She pushed the computer to one side and let her mind drift back to the events of that night. How easy it was to convince the sisters to come with her; after all, who wouldn't trust a woman? Most serial killers, most murderers, are men. In contrast, women can always be trusted, especially if you're a young girl far from home.

There had been a slight pang of guilt for them, but it disappeared when she realised she was saving them from lifetimes of pain and heartache. Any parent who would let young children wander around on their own at night didn't deserve to have kids. At least the girls would be at peace now. And Church would get what he deserved. But what would be her next step? She hadn't decided what her big demonstration would be, but it would be something to go out with a bang before she left and moved to a bigger city.

She returned to her phone as the laptop hummed in front of her. On the cell was a list of job vacancies she'd saved, schools and colleges well away from her hometown, but she was unsure how far she wanted to travel. She tried to focus on the employment adverts, but the criminality displayed on the laptop screen drew her back to it. Heading for the section on methods of mass murder, Beverly clicked on it and entered the chat forum. She rarely posted there, only the occasional prompt to egg people towards what they boasted about doing. She guessed they never would, but she liked to read the comments.

Someone called MajorDick, who she doubted was named after his military position, proclaimed the only way to go was with assault weapons, while others debated which the best ones were. Beverly rolled her eyes as she glossed over the conversation. She had nothing against firearms and had been an expert shot since the age of twelve when her father took her to the range, but she knew guns were only for those who wanted to die on their mission, which wasn't her. She intended to survive and continue for as long as possible, and using firearms wouldn't help. They were too messy and attracted too much attention. When she settled on her grand exhibition, she'd probably take a single handgun with her for emergencies, but that would be it.

Further down the page, a group praised the virtues of explosives. She'd considered it and still hadn't discounted the option, but several things dissuaded her. Firstly, because of similar attacks in the recent past, it was now much more challenging to acquire the right amount of materials without alerting the authorities. It wasn't a risk she was prepared to take. But the real disincentive for using bombs was numerous people had used them recently. There was nothing unique in it, and she wanted her big statement to be exceptional.

Many users in the chat forum spoke about getting something powerful from one of the old Soviet states, a nuclear device or a dirty bomb, but their ridiculousness made her laugh. If the material were so easy to get, then some terrorist organisation would have done it by now. Plus, for Beverly, the whole thing was far too impersonal. How do you follow up using a nuclear device, for Christ's sake?

She shut the laptop and lay on the bed, allowing time to dry the rest of her body. She had to decide today and set some plans in motion, otherwise there had been no point taking another sick day at work. The school was under-staffed and the principal wouldn't put up with it for too long.

Beverly closed her eyes and thought of Principal Claudia Conway, the woman who had been a teacher when Beverly was a pupil. The woman who told her she'd never achieve anything in life and was only there to be some jock's baby-making machine. Conway was bitter and twisted then, a decade ago, and time hadn't improved her. In fact, she'd only gotten worse. Beverly had believed the old crone would fail her at the interview and was shocked when she was offered the job. But there was method in Conway's madness, which she only understood once she'd been working at the school for a few weeks.

First, it was the extra tasks dumped on her, so she never

got away from school before seven o'clock every night. Then there was the work which had to be done at weekends. And all of it followed by constant criticism, usually in front of her colleagues. If she hadn't had her unique plans to pursue and keep her sane, she was convinced she'd have had a nervous breakdown already. And she knew that was what Conway wanted. No, it was more than wanted. She desired it. Beverly saw it in her eyes each time they met. If only there were a way she could kill Conway without bringing too much attention to her and the school.

The thought of the principal forced her eyes open and her body up. She grabbed the laptop and opened the lid. She continued scanning the information on the screen. A group of people were speaking about poisoning the water supply, but it seemed too impractical to her. Others mentioned arson. She liked that idea, but it needed more consideration. Poison again, not in the water, but certain foods. That had potential. There was enough weed killer and rat poison in the basement, all there legitimately, and it had always been a possible choice. Hadn't she read somewhere that poison was a woman's prerogative, or was that just wishful thinking on her part?

A frustrated yelp slipped over her lips and she fell back into the warmth of the sheets. Her eyes blinked shut, and she dreamt about that night again.

SHE SLEPT FOR TWO HOURS. Beverly sat up and stretched her arms and stifled a yawn. She felt more tired than when she'd first got up, and it annoyed her. Or perhaps it was the lingering thought of Conway nagging at the back of her skull.

She moved to the bedroom window, hoping the sight of the police tape surrounding the house across the road would blow away the dust clinging to her brain. She rubbed at her eyes as the woman stepped out of the car and up to the porch. Beverly guessed she must be another journalist looking for a story until she watched her duck under the tape and march to the front.

There was something in the way she moved which told Beverly she wasn't a reporter. The stranger wore a leather jacket and skintight jeans, which it seemed to Beverly would be impossible to move in, let alone walk with the confidence she had. No, it was more than confidence. It was a certainty that most men have, that supreme belief in their authority. Even from a distance, as she peeled from the window to stride to the rear of the property, Beverly knew this stranger was an alpha. Beverly always liked to believe she was one of those, but realised she wasn't. But this woman, who'd disappeared around the back of the house, certainly was.

She didn't know why, but her heart was pounding against her chest. She wore nothing but the bath towel, but heat was spreading through her like lava running down a volcano. She wiped the sweat from her head and tried to control her breathing. Beverly hadn't had an anxiety attack since university, but felt it coming on now.

But why? The woman couldn't be a police officer, or she'd have gone into the house. Her fingers clasped at the towel. She was probably some freak who liked to visit murder scenes, or maybe one of those sickos who wrote to serial killers offering their hand in marriage. The thought made her smile, and the thump of her heart lessened a little. As it did, the stranger in the impossible jeans returned.

Beverly waited for her to go to her car, but instead, she turned and stared into her bedroom window.

Beverly gasped, stepped backwards, and fell onto the bed. The thump in her chest increased a thousandfold, her mouth trembling as the breath refused to enter her lungs. She twisted on the cover, her head creaking from side to side as she searched for the anxiety medication she hadn't used in three years.

Even if I still had it, it would be out of date.

The idea produced an impossible giggle and the pain wiped away the tension in her chest. She jerked up and continued to laugh, a riotous uproar that would have frightened small children. And that thought made her snort laughter, with her hands glued to her sides as the giggles consumed her.

When it was over, she put her head between her knees and sucked air into her lungs. Then she let it out in one long, slow movement.

When she felt in control again, she stood and went to the window. The woman and her car were gone. Beverly stared through the glass for an age and wondered what she'd do next.

7 THE PALACE OF EXILE

According to the GPS on Astrid's mobile, the drive to the home would take twenty minutes. She didn't mind the journey, using it to check out this bit of the town. Rows of trees looking in desperate need of water lined both sides of the street. Peeping through them was an array of shops, cafes, and small businesses. Perhaps it was too early in the afternoon, the clock on the dashboard said it was just after two, but most appeared shut.

She stopped the car at a red light, allowing an old lady pushing a trolley to crawl across the road. As she waited, she looked closer to see most shops weren't shut, but closed for business. A broken economy was putting paid to some of small-town America as the pensioner reached the other side, and Astrid drove through the lights. She glanced at the woman in the mirror and wondered if it was a glimpse into her future.

Who'll look after me when my mobility is shot and my memories are gone? Is that why I'm so keen to form a bond with my niece, so Olivia will care for me when I can't do it anymore?

Her sudden concern about growing old disturbed her. She wondered if it was the sight of the woman at the lights which had triggered it. If she lived that long and stayed healthy, then she was a good fifty years away from such a thing.

The boarded-up shops alongside the road distracted her from future thoughts, so she returned to the problem at hand: hoping Eve Church could help prove her brother's innocence. But considering Eve had voluntarily given up her freedom for the last seven years, Astrid wondered how that would be possible.

Once she got beyond the high street, where the only activity she witnessed was at a coffee shop and the book store next to it, she headed towards the lake on the other side. During her online research, she'd discovered Crystal Lake was once a thriving holiday and tourist spot inside Eureka Falls, but now had gone the way of most everything else. The only things left were the water, empty buildings, and the care home. Government promises of jobs and extra funding had been as real as unicorns and dragons.

It wasn't a task she looked forward to, having to tell a vulnerable woman the police had accused her brother of murdering two children. Still, until Church got his lawyer, there was nothing else she could do. She hadn't expected to get anything useful from outside the murder house, and that's how it had turned out.

She needed a look inside, and she couldn't do that without the lawyer. At least she'd had a glimpse at the neighbourhood and the back of the house, which led straight into thick woods. She'd surmised the girls and their killer had come from that direction and expected the police to find evidence there. But how had they entered without breaking in?

Did Adam Church take them in? Was that the incriminating proof the police had hinted at?

She pondered those questions as she parked the car at the care home. She stepped out towards the front. Would the staff even let her see Church's sister? If not, she'd give them the details, and they could pass the message on.

Astrid entered a building that had seen better days. The dusty carpet clung to her feet as she made her way to the reception, followed by the patriarchal eyes glaring from the ancient portraits hanging on the walls. The woman at the desk was busy whispering into the phone, her shoulders all hunched and nervous as she realised Astrid was standing opposite her. She put the phone down, ran trembling fingers down her uniform and gave Astrid her best forced smile.

'Hello, welcome to the Tranquil Waters Rest Home. My name is Jenny. How can I help you?'

Astrid returned the greeting with a grin of her own. 'Hello, Jenny. I'm here to see Eve Church.'

Jenny's eyes shrank into her cheeks and she suddenly looked ten years older. Astrid guessed that the whispered conversation on the phone had been about Adam Church's current predicament.

'I'm afraid visiting time is not until two o'clock, Ms... Ms...'

Astrid didn't finish the sentence for her, instead leaning on the desk and increasing her smile tenfold. 'In that case, could you pass a message on for me, Jenny?'

She hesitated for a second. 'What would that be?'

'Can you tell Eve her brother has been arrested for murder, and she might not get a visit from him for a while?'

That was it; she'd done what Adam had asked. The responsibility rested on Jenny to inform Eve of her brother's predicament. Her stomach grumbled to let her know she hadn't eaten since last night.

Was there a mini-bar in my hotel room? I never had the chance to check before Hudson and Hicks knocked on the door.

She turned to leave, but Jenny reached out to grab her arm.

'Oh, that's terrible. I thought what I'd heard was a rumour. Did the police put this on the news?'

Astrid wriggled from her grasp. 'Not yet, but they will soon enough, so if you could inform his sister?'

Jenny strode from behind the desk, taking Astrid's hand in what seemed, to her, to be a wholly unprofessional gesture.

'This is terrible.'

'It is for Adam Church.'

With Jenny's fingers in hers, Astrid felt as if they were about to go on a date. Her mind drifted from her surroundings, from the Church family's problems, from the debt she owed George, and tried to remember the last time she'd gone on one.

Jenny babbled as she pulled her along the corridor towards a set of thick doors at the end. Astrid put weight into her legs and stopped both of them from moving any further.

'What did you say?'

'Adam Church has never visited his sister since she's been here. I think they might have had two or three phone calls in seven years, but that's about it. I don't believe he even writes to her.'

'Well, that's sibling love for you.' Astrid had a brief image of the sister who'd always hated her.

'No, I'm sure he does love her in his way. It's just, well,

this place can be very intimidating for some. But it's Adam who pays the annual fees for residency and buys his sister all she needs.' Jenny lifted a hand to her forehead. 'Who'll pay while he's in prison?'

'Hopefully, it won't come to that.' Astrid scrutinised Jenny and pondered if her concern was for Eve Church's well-being or if her employers might not be getting any more fees from Adam in the future. 'I'm guessing you want me to tell Eve about her brother, then?'

'Please, would you?' Astrid watched Jenny's chest rise and fall against the tightness of her uniform, noticing for the first time how pretty her eyes were.

'Sure.' It wouldn't take long. In and out, then something to eat while waiting for the lawyer to get in touch.

Relief seeped out of Jenny and she grasped Astrid's hands in apparent gratitude.

'I'll take you to her. She'll be in the common room now. Some of the residents do yoga in the morning, but she won't be one of them.' She put her hand on the door. 'But don't call her Eve; she hates that name. Call her Evie.'

Jenny took Astrid into an antiseptic aroma, with a smell of weak orange juice and the tang of fresh sweat. Astrid checked the room as she stood in the doorway. The yoga group was in the far corner, half a dozen in front of an instructor. None of them moved, frozen like statues. She scanned the rest of the place, seeing staff with individual residents.

Her gaze settled on the only person on their own, a woman sitting beneath a large window looking into the gardens. Her head was bowed, buried in a book, headphone wires sticking out from her straight jet-black shoulder-length hair and connected to the phone lying on a table.

Astrid stared at the young woman next to the window. 'Is that Evie Church?'

'It is.'

'Won't she know from the internet what happened to her brother?'

'There's no internet access allowed anywhere in the building unless you're a member of staff. Come, I'll introduce you.'

Astrid followed her over, wondering how she'd tell the poor woman her brother was a suspected child killer.

8 MENTAL FLOSS

Astrid stepped towards the woman engrossed in her book and music. Jenny placed one hand on the table and tapped out a rhythm with her fingers. Evie Church dug her nails into the tattered pages, flopped the book over, and then peered at them with a face consumed by suspicion.

'What?'

Astrid pointed at the image on the shirt Evie wore, a famous still from a classic movie, as Evie pulled the plugs from her head.

'I once saw *Metropolis* accompanied by a full orchestra performing the original music.'

She dropped her hand to her side and smiled at the pale, thin woman, who seemed a lot younger than her twenty-five years. She recognised the physical similarities between the siblings, the same long delicate nose, the same large haunted eyes that sparked to life on hearing Astrid's words. But whereas Adam Church looked like he ate a hearty three meals a day, his sister appeared only to have a passing relationship with food.

Evie tilted her head forward. 'I adore silent films, but

I've only seen them on the DVDs Adam sends me every month. When I get out of here, I'll move to a city, perhaps San Francisco, and spend my spare time watching classic movies on the big screen.' She bit her lip. 'Well, not all the time. I'll travel as well, go by train so I can read on the journey. I love reading as much as music and old cinema.'

In the space of a few seconds, Evie Church's face had transformed from a look of suspicion to one of delight. She also spoke as if she hadn't had a decent conversation with a like-minded adult in some time.

The receptionist played her part before leaving. 'Evie, this is Astrid.'

Jenny slipped away and Astrid wasn't sorry to see her go. Evie placed her book flat on the table, a copy of *The Outsider* by Albert Camus in its original French.

She offered her hand.

'Do you have a surname, Astrid, or are you like Prince, Madonna, or the Queen of the fair island I detect you're from?'

'It's Astrid Snow. Are you fluent in French?'

Evie placed her fingers on the cover of the book. 'I get by in several languages. According to Mrs Moses, I'm an expert in American.'

Astrid's eyes narrowed a little. 'Mrs Moses?'

She nodded towards a woman talking to two staff members in the far corner of the room.

'Mrs Moses was here when I arrived. She refuses to acknowledge that the language of this country is English. Everything has to be American, nothing else. I think her parents put her in here when her, let's say, unusual beliefs started to get out of hand in the public domain.'

Astrid pointed at the headphones. 'What are you listening to?'

Evie lifted her phone to display the screen, showing an album cover with no writing on it but an image of a pulsar from space. Astrid grinned.

'That's cheerful listening.'

'It always gets my mind into shape. I'll follow it with a selection of Tamla Motown I can sing along to, which will annoy Mrs Moses if nothing else.'

Astrid hadn't looked forward to this meeting, but she liked Evie Church already. Now she had to give her the news about Adam. She took the seat opposite. After their brief conversation, it wouldn't be fair to dump the information on her and leave. She doubted anyone in this facility would offer her any counselling.

'Your brother sent me here with a message for you.'

Evie's eyelids sprang into life. 'Your expression changed from joy to despair in an instant, Astrid Snow. I'm guessing this isn't going to be good news.'

She glanced at the cosmic image on Evie's phone. 'The police have arrested Adam.'

Evie raised one hand to her mouth and immediately took it away. 'Oh, dear. Has his fixation caught up with him?' There appeared to be moisture around her eyes, but it was hard to tell if she was upset or not. The long eyebrow stretching across the top of her nose bristled slightly. 'I always wondered if his obsession was worse than mine.' She didn't appear to have grasped the gravity of the situation.

'This is serious, Evie. The police discovered two murdered girls in his basement.'

Evie didn't bat an eyelid. 'That's our basement.'

'What?'

'When our parents died, they left the family home to both of us. Not that I want to live there again.'

'Are you okay?' Astrid couldn't quite get a handle on how Evie was taking the news.

'I'm fine.' She rolled up the headphones and put them into her pocket. 'Are you just a messenger, Astrid Snow, or are you more than that?'

'Your brother is claiming his innocence and asked me to investigate the crime.'

Evie spat air from her mouth. 'Of course, he's innocent. Adam wouldn't hurt a fly, literally. When we were kids, he was always ushering insects out of the house to safety. My parents hated that. The lower creatures were placed here to be devoured. That was God's plan according to them.' Her laugh turned from disdain into giddiness. 'My father thought he was devout until he met my mother. She believed it was the Creator's divine hand that led her to a man called Church.' She peered deep into Astrid's eyes. 'So you're an investigator, a Private Eye?'

'Something like that.'

Evie got up from the table. 'You're a shamus? I've always wanted to meet a shamus. The game's afoot, then. Perhaps I could be Mary Astor, Veronica Lake, Jane Greer, or Barbara Stanwyck. No, wait, they're femme fatales. As tempting as it sounds, we don't want to be one of those, do we? Femme fatale means killer or deadly woman. That's not you, is it, Astrid? I've always loved a bit of Sam Spade and Philip Marlowe, haven't you?'

She spoke at ninety miles a second. Astrid gave her time to breathe before replying.

'Reality is stranger than fiction. I have to go now.' Hunger gnawed away at Astrid's insides.

'No, no, not yet. I need to get my bits in order, and then I'll join you.'

Evie moved from the table and towards the end of the

room. Astrid watched her go, unable to follow her instincts and turn around and leave. Against her better judgement, she'd felt drawn into Evie Church's sphere of influence. She followed the younger woman out and down the corridor, watching her disappear into another room.

Astrid stepped through the door as Evie was packing a small shoulder bag. 'What are you doing?' Apart from a bed and a TV with a DVD player, only books and discs occupied the room.

'I've tried my best to wean myself off material things, which is why I have a bunch of music files on the phone, but I still prefer real books and movies compared to their equivalents as digital versions. I'll get the staff to pack all this away and send it to me. It will have to be at the family home at first, but I don't think I'll stay there for too long.' Her shoulders trembled as she spoke. 'We'll stop there long enough to prove my brother's innocence.'

Astrid surveyed her through incredulous eyes. 'What do you mean by that?'

Evie threw the bag over her shoulder and stared at her. 'Things will go a lot smoother with me than without me.'

'And why is that?'

Evie reached into the drawer near her bed and removed a small box. She opened it and took out a key.

'Because this gets you into the house where someone killed those kids.'

9 THE CELEBRATION OF THE LIZARD

Ten minutes later, Evie was in the passenger seat as Astrid drove into town. She could have ignored the key and waited for the lawyer to get in touch, but something about the younger Church child left her wanting to spend more time with her. And she might learn more about Adam from his sister.

Evie dragged a dark shade of rouge over her lips as the car entered the high street. Astrid looked to the passenger seat at her new companion.

'What did you mean about you and your brother's obsessions?'

Evie peered at her reflection in the mirror so intently, Astrid wondered if she was in shock from being away from the Tranquil Waters Rest Home.

Is this a good idea, having her tag along with me while her brother sits in a cell accused of a double homicide? I don't even know why she admitted herself to that facility seven years ago.

The red sparkled on Evie's lips as she spoke. 'Do you think all children disappoint their parents?'

Astrid peered at the road as she spoke. 'I suppose some parents deal with their kids better than others.' She tried not to think of her father and mother, who always lurked inside the darkest corners of her mind.

'Well, Adam and I certainly were doozies where Mom and Pop were concerned.' She rubbed at the red on her lips, so it looked like blood stained her fingers. 'I'm not sure which one of us infuriated them more, but I hoped it was me.' She tapped on the window. 'Pull up here. I need to go into that shop.'

Astrid didn't argue, starting to question letting Evie join her and contemplating leaving her here in Eureka Falls.

It's her home town, so how bad could it be? But if she starts to open up about her life and her brother, perhaps it will help me discover what happened to those girls in the Church house.

She found an accessible parking spot in front of the shops.

'Do you want coffee?'

The coffee shop appeared empty, apart from an old couple peering out of the window.

'No. I need to go into the bookshop next door. You can wait here. I shouldn't be long.'

Evie bolted from the car as if the solution to all of life's mysteries were inside that place and nearly fell through the entrance.

She said she loves reading, so perhaps she's just missed being in a bookshop.

Astrid turned off the engine and followed her. She walked towards the shop, admiring the antique lettering on the window until she realised the paint had started to fade over the words Kennedy's Book Emporium.

The wood was cold to the touch as she pushed the door

open. The store was long and narrow, stacked with a mixture of new and second-hand books. Down the middle was a table of *Sale Specials* covered in a thin layer of dust. The place appeared to be as empty as the street outside, with no sign of staff or Evie. She seemed to have disappeared. Was this all a ploy to get out of the residential home and give Astrid the slip? Considering she could have left that place at any time, it seemed unlikely.

This was her chance to return to the car and drive away. But what then? The only other option available to her was waiting for Adam to retain a lawyer, then going through what the police had and checking the house. But if the law were confident of Adam's guilt, it would be difficult to prove his innocence without uncovering new evidence.

Evie's laugh gave her position away. She spotted her down the far end of the shop, flicking through a brightly coloured hardback. She held it up as Astrid approached her.

'I can't believe some of the stuff people publish.' She pointed to the top of the page. 'This guy claims we're all descended from space lizards.' She shook her head as she flicked through the pages.

'Shouldn't we be getting to your house, Evie?' Astrid liked nothing better than browsing through old books, but there were more pressing things on her mind.

Evie dropped the book on to a table. 'Soon. I need to speak to the proprietor first.'

She strode towards the desk at the end and knocked on the faded wood. Astrid inhaled the aroma of dusty novels and yellowed pages as they waited. She glanced through the bulging shelves, scanning through the categories and wondering how many residents of Eureka Falls spent time there when they could download thousands of digital books for free just with the click of a button.

Was that why most of the shops on the high street were closed, because most people shopped online? She pictured a point, perhaps in the next fifty years, when nearly all entertainment would be electronic, and most material possessions would only be sought after by collectors. As much as she enjoyed reading and listening to music on her phone, she knew the world would lose something important once that happened.

Evie knocked again, pulling in her shoulders as a man in his late forties appeared from behind a curtain on the other side of a desk. His face was red with some irritable-looking skin condition, his mop-top early Beatles hair dyed black. His eyes sparked into life when he saw the two of them.

'How can I help you, ladies?' His teeth were brilliantly white, exhibited in a smile straight from a Hollywood special-effects studio.

Evie clapped her hands together. 'It's me, Mr Kennedy, Evie Church. You told me to come and see you when I was ready. You know, about my stories.'

Astrid watched Kennedy's face change from sunshine to stormy in an instant.

'Evie, er... Evie, this is, is, unexpected.' The stutter hadn't been there before.

'Well, Mr Kennedy, circumstances have taken a somewhat dramatic turn in my life which necessitated me leaving the place I've called home for the last seven years. But, it does mean I can see you and discuss what we talked about in our emails.'

Astrid observed the two of them, learning more about this unusual woman by the second. Evie's fingers tapped against the air as if she was playing along to music only she heard. He wiped the sweat from his forehead even though it was cool in the shop.

He glanced at Astrid.

'Perhaps we should talk about this in private, Evie.'

'Fiddlesticks, Mr Kennedy. Astrid is my new best friend in the world. I've no secrets from her.'

He flicked his startled eyes from Astrid to Evie. 'Well, Evie, I'm afraid I have some bad news.'

He paused and stared at her. Astrid wondered if the news was as terrible as learning the police, and probably many of the public, suspected your brother of murdering two children. Still, she'd taken that well so far. Perhaps it was because she was convinced of his innocence. Not that innocence would always save you from a prison cell, as Astrid knew only too well.

'What bad news, Mr Kennedy?'

His smile returned. 'Please, Evie, call me Jack.'

Astrid held back her laughter. Jack Kennedy, indeed.

Evie's eyes blinked rapidly. 'What bad news, Jack?'

'The publisher I sent your stories to, well, they said they weren't what they were looking for. I hate to say this, but they said they were too immature, and perhaps you should think about writing for children.' He waited while she took in his words. 'Writing for children can be quite lucrative.'

Astrid watched Evie as the younger woman's hands shook and her eyes shrank into her skull. She turned around without saying another word and stormed out of the shop.

'I'm sorry,' Jack Kennedy said. 'I did try my best for her.'

Astrid thanked him and left the bookshop. She found Evie outside, banging her fist against a tree. Her skin was torn, and blood stuck to the bark. Astrid put her hand on her arm and stopped the physical damage. When she peered into Evie's eyes, she knew the emotional harm would be harder to quell.

'Do you want to tell me what this is about?'

Evie trembled as her face welled up with tears and pain. She ran her fingers across her cheeks.

'It's stupid. Adam's locked up, and I'm upset about some silly stories.'

Astrid led her to an empty bench where they sat together. 'What stories?'

Evie scratched underneath her eye. 'I've always wanted to write, but my parents forbade it. Unless it was to praise God, which it wasn't, everything I put on to paper was blasphemy. And I was already blasphemous enough without adding to it.'

'Is this blasphemy something to do with the obsessions you mentioned?'

A smirk crept over Evie's face. 'Yes, but that's nothing to do with my writing.' She wiped her eyes. 'But, then again, I suppose it is. Without my so-called obsession, my parents' word, I wouldn't have admitted myself into that place, and without the isolation, I wouldn't have started writing properly.'

'What did you write?'

Life returned to Evie's face, and Astrid guessed it was because someone was taking a genuine interest in her for once.

'It was only short stories at first, a whole load of things I'd had inside my head since I was a kid; stuff I thought was rubbish when I read it back. But then some staff at the home read them and said they were great and I should get an agent or publisher to look at them. I didn't know what to do until I emailed a few to Mr Kennedy, Jack, at the bookshop. I didn't think he'd reply, but he did and said he liked them and I should send some more. Eventually, he mentioned he'd get a publisher he knew to read them. That was about a month ago, and I'd heard nothing since. Until now.' There were no more tears, but Astrid recognised the pain in Evie's face. 'I know, it's silly, really.'

Astrid reached out and took her hand. 'No, it's not. And one opinion doesn't mean much of anything.' She squeezed her fingers. She'd never been great at giving comfort to others, but decided she'd gotten better at it over the last year.

Evie stopped shaking and smiled at her. 'You're right. Now let's go to my house and see what my brother has been up to.' They stood together and, to Astrid's surprise, Evie hugged her. 'Then I'll tell you all about the terrible obsessions of the Church children.'

They headed back to the car and Astrid started the engine. As she pulled away from the kerb, she wondered where her hunger had gone.

Five minutes before Astrid and Evie entered the bookshop, Beverly had parked across the road opposite her parents' coffee shop. She hadn't been able to sit still at home, not once that woman had stared at her through the bedroom window. It was only a coincidence, her looking up like that, but it had shaken Beverly so much, she couldn't bear to stay in the house. So, even though she was off work supposedly sick, she crawled into her car and drove to town. Perhaps it would be best to go to school for the afternoon at least. Then maybe old crone Conway wouldn't be on her back all the time.

She was still considering her options as she stared at the coffee shop, wondering how long it would be before her parents went bankrupt. She'd read the accounts, even though they'd hidden them from her. Imagine trying to hide documents on their computer when she was an IT expert. Not that they understood that. She was only a lowly teacher to her family, in a school full of dimly lit kids. But she'd seen the debts and the paperwork for a second mortgage on the house to keep the business afloat.

Beverly peered at the bookshop, surprised it was still open as well and wasn't closed like most of the other shops, not only on this street, but throughout Eureka Falls. She liked Jack, but he hadn't done himself any favours in the current economic climate by inviting along for book signings authors whose work could be described as existing on the extreme periphery of the political spectrum. The protestors weren't numerous, but were enough to scare away most of his regular customers.

At one point, she'd considered doing everyone a favour and planting explosives at his shop to destroy both places, preferably with her parents and brother inside the coffee shop. It was tempting, but she couldn't come up with a way to do it where the positives outweighed the negatives, no matter how she schemed.

Gathering the materials would be tricky. She could use the dark web, but that presented its own problems. Some participants on there were clearly government agents trying to entrap people. Others were criminals playing a game of temptation and blackmail. She knew that, unless you were on a suicide mission, getting such dangerous items from the internet was a process of time and trust. And she didn't have the time.

The other problem with blowing up both shops was catching her family while not harming anyone else, especially Jack. He'd always been nice to her when she was younger, and she felt she owed him something. Not that those feelings had stopped her placing a Trojan file on his computer when he asked her to sort out what he thought was a virus, but was only a collection of annoying popups. She enjoyed the irony of fixing his machine by infecting it.

She was contemplating those issues when someone stormed out of the bookshop. From where she sat, Beverly had to do a double-take, not believing what she saw. She rubbed her eyes, and then blinked at the woman shaking her fist outside the Kennedy Book Emporium. There was no doubt about it. That was Evie Church. Evie Church, who'd shut herself away inside the place most of the town called Shady Acres the day after her eighteenth birthday.

This must be to do with Adam.

Beverly's voice trembled in her head. The rest of her shook even more when she saw the next person come out of the bookshop, take hold of Evie's hand and lead her to the bench.

It can't be.

She sank into the seat, her face peeping above the edge of the window like a periscope. But it was the same woman who'd stared into her bedroom earlier. Her fingers shivered against the door, her heart racing faster than any motor vehicle could. Her first instinct was to drive away, but she was fascinated to see what the two women were doing.

But what if my parents recognise my car and come out to speak to me?

Beverly's mind was a swirl of different options, a voice in her head humming a song she'd heard before.

Should I stay or should I go?

She had no choice. Anxiety had frozen her brain; her breathing slow and laboured as the sweat swam down her face. She was about to sink into the floor when they made the choice for her. The two women stood, Evie Church hugging the older woman before they got into their car and drove away.

Beverly sat there for an age, trying to retain a sense of normality. It was this delay that allowed her to see Jack Kennedy leave his business a minute later. He turned the shop sign to closed and locked the door. She was transfixed by his face, his eyes on stalks and lips trembling as if he'd seen a ghost. She watched him scurry away, and then relaxed as her beating heart returned to normal. Perhaps she should activate the Trojan horse on his computer.

She breathed out slowly and started her car. All she could think about was Conway. She had to kill her before doing anything else. And now she had an idea of how to do it.

—————

FEAR HAD CREPT up to Jack Kennedy and thrust its fingers deep into his ribs. He nearly fainted when he realised she was in his shop. Her, Evie Church, who he thought would be in Shady Acres for the rest of her life. And there she was, as bold as brass, asking him about the collection of short stories she'd sent him. Did she believe the guff he'd spouted? It didn't matter if she did now; Evie would eventually remember the novel she'd emailed him and come back and ask about it.

He'd never been so happy as when she'd stormed out and her friend followed her. He waited what seemed like an eternity before closing the shop and heading home. He scampered out and wondered what he was going to do about the problem of Evie Church.

11 AN AMERICAN PRAYER

Astrid's phone buzzed inside her jacket as she drove. She ignored it while Evie peered at her.

'How come my brother picked you to help him? Has he been making trips to England while I've been convalescing?'

Astrid turned the car right and towards the Church home. 'I don't know where he's been, but I'm friends with your uncle.'

Evie pursed her lips. 'Uncle George?'

'That's the bloke.'

'Neither of us has met Uncle George. Our mother would never speak about her brother. I think he might have had his own obsession, which bothered her.'

'Was she English?'

'No, not really. Her father, my grandfather, worked on military bases around the world. She was the older, but when George was born in England, my grandparents' marriage was already crumbling. I'm not sure what happened, but my grandmother stayed there with George, while my grandfather came back to America with my mother.' Evie's eyes appeared full of what might have been. 'Adam and I only managed to pick up bits of the family history over the years because our mother would rarely talk about it. I wasn't even aware Adam had been in contact with Uncle George.'

'It was a surprise to me as well.' She parked outside the house and turned to Evie. 'I can tell you all about George later, but I think it's time for you to explain you and your brother's obsessions.'

Evie scratched at her head where her eyebrows should have been. 'Have you read that terrible novel *Fifty Shades of Grey*?'

The question was so unexpected, Astrid burst out laughing. 'Unfortunately, I have. Is your brother also a secret writer?'

'No, not that I know. But his tastes run along the same lines as Mr Grey.'

A mischievous look scampered across Astrid's face. 'Is he interested in sadomasochistic sex?'

'He's more than interested, Ms Snow. It was, or is, an obsession that drove every part of his life. Unsurprisingly, my parents were somewhat unaccepting of this lifestyle choice of his. I do believe if he weren't earning so much money, they would have done the same with him as they did with me and convinced him to enter a similar facility.' Evie placed one hand on her cheek and appeared to contemplate what she'd said. 'It wouldn't have looked right for both the Church siblings to be in the same place for wayward and wanton souls.'

'What's your brother's job?'

Evie shrugged. 'I'm not a hundred per cent sure, but it's something to do with Wall Street, only he does all his work from home.'

Astrid considered her next question carefully. 'Is it important for me to understand why your parents were so upset with you and why you voluntarily entered that care facility?'

'There should be no secrets amongst friends, Astrid.'

Evie placed her fingers to her forehead and pushed the hair from the right side of her face. Part of the skin on her skull appeared to have been burnt. She lifted the other part of her hair to show a similar mark on the opposite side of her head. Astrid recognised what they were.

'You've had electroconvulsive therapy?'

The hair covered the evidence as Evie let go of it. 'More than once, but not for a while. I convinced the doctors it wasn't working.'

Astrid grimaced at the thought of what Evie had gone through. She'd seen the procedure used to extract information from prisoners, but they must have used it as a medical process for Evie.

'Treatment for what?'

'My mother said the Devil possessed me while my father told me I was an abomination.'

Evie took one hand and placed her fingers in the palm of the other, pushing a nail into the centre until a small spot of blood trickled out. Astrid kept an eye on the young woman as she drove.

'I went to the website of the organisation they ran, the Church of the Old Testament. I saw enough there to scare adults, never mind children.'

Evie let out a nervous laugh. 'Yes, it was never cold in our house, even during the worst winters. Do you know why?'

'No?'

Her snort of laughter made her cheeks wobble. 'Because it was always full of fire and brimstone.'

She shook so hard, her hair fell to the side in one place, and Astrid saw again the scars where the electricity had burnt through the skin and into her skull in search of her brain.

'Do you want to talk about this, Evie?'

Evie pushed her hands together and rubbed the blood across both palms. Her breathing was slow, and it felt to Astrid as if she was recanting some mantra inside her head.

'Most of my time at the Tranquil Waters Rest Home has been beneficial to me, but the majority of the medical professionals there lack the empathy needed to understand what their patients are going through here.' She tapped the side of her head. 'Electroconvulsive therapy was my mother's suggestion. It's strange really that you're here because of Uncle George because I think my mother always wished he would have undergone that treatment to prevent, as she told Adam and me, the family shame of her deviant brother. Still, when the burning electricity couldn't cure me, another doctor came up with the bright idea that some unknown childhood trauma likely caused my problem.' Evie paused to smile at Astrid. 'She stated that without treatment, adverse childhood experiences could cause long-term health issues for the brain and body, shortening lives and reducing their quality. She claimed one of the most effective remedies was talking to somebody kind, who would listen to you, such as a therapist or someone who loves you and can remain stable and dependable, regardless of what you need to say.'

'And that's what you got in the home?'

Evie laughed again, more quietly this time and in a way that made her look a lot younger than she was.

'No. The management there transferred that lady doctor the following day, and I've been waiting to speak to someone ever since, and that was three years ago.'

Astrid parked outside their destination and turned off the engine. 'Then you can talk to me.'

A single tear slid on to Evie's cheek. 'That's far too kind of you. You've barely known me for a few hours, and I don't want to burden you with my problems.'

Astrid reached across and took her hand, relieved to see the bleeding had stopped. 'Your uncle George is the only friend I have in the world, and he's helped me more times than I'll ever repay. If I can do something for his nephew and his niece, then I will.'

Evie's smile grew wider and she squeezed Astrid's fingers in hers. 'Because of our parents' strict religious beliefs, Adam and I had to behave how they wanted us to, following the teachings of the Old Testament as they and their followers did. It wasn't easy for either of us; we toed the family line for most of the time, but once we hit puberty, it became more challenging, especially when we both realised we weren't like the other kids at school. Because Adam's older, they discovered his so-called deviant behaviour first, but I think it was me who really upset them.'

Astrid let go of Evie's hand, noticing some of her blood on her fingers. 'Your parents discovered you prefer girls to boys.'

Evie puffed out her cheeks as if she was playing a big trombone. 'It's not that I don't like boys – well, men now – because I do; it's just that women are much more fun, you know. And deep down, that's where my heart lies. I'd known from an early age, maybe eight or nine, but when my father caught me kissing a girl on my sixteenth birthday, all hell broke loose. The family priest described me as evil.

Various school counsellors and psychiatrists seemed convinced I suffered from severe depression. But, after the last seven years, do you know what I believe, Astrid?'

'No.'

Evie pushed open the door and stepped out of the car. 'I think I'm just a little bit different than most people and we should all celebrate our differences. Don't you?'

Astrid got out, gazing straight into Evie's wide eyes. 'Amen to that.'

Evie grinned like a schoolkid and removed the key from her pocket.

'Then let's go and prove my brother's innocence.'

12 WOMAN IS A DEVIL

Beverly had stopped shaking by the time she walked into school. She gave the security guard a nod and watched him fondle his gun. Was fondle the correct term? She thought it was since there was something sensual about the way he did it. Her firearm was in her handbag, along with the licence to carry it. Luckily, she also lived in one of the forty-two states where pistol suppressors were legal. She pushed her palm into the side of the bag, feeling the angular touch of the metal, running her fingers over its length through the leather. The bullets were loose inside, rattling against her phone and makeup mirror. To her ears, the sound they made was loud enough to attract everyone's attention, but none of the adults or kids afforded her a cursory glance.

At least Conway's too cheap to upgrade the security with metal detectors.

The receptionist, Sarah, stared at her as she entered the building. She pushed some papers to the side and leant over the desk. Even though there was nobody nearby, Beverly assumed it was to keep their conversation private from the office looming behind them.

Conway's castle.

'Your lessons are covered for the week. There's no need for you to be here, especially with what's happened.'

Beverly fell into step, her words barely a whisper. 'What happened?'

'There's a rumour going around school the police found the Glick girls. Opposite your place, at the Church house. Didn't you see anything?'

She shook her head. 'I've been stuck in bed with a fever.'

Sarah pulled back and raised her voice. 'You should go home and get some rest.'

Beverly smiled, admiring her colleague's sixth sense for knowing when their not so glorious leader was about to make an appearance. The smile vanished as Conway came out of her office.

'I thought I heard your sparkling tone, Bev. You're just the person I want to see.' Conway returned to the office without another command. Sarah frowned as Beverly entered the lion's den. 'Close the door behind you, Bev.'

She cringed inside, her eyes shifting around the room to avoid this woman she detested. As hard as she tried, she couldn't prevent the memory rushing back of her first meeting with her fifteen years ago. She wasn't the principal then, but plain Mrs Conway, the history teacher. Her husband had lost his life in his country's service in a foreign war, so not only the school, but the whole town delivered sympathy to her daily.

For the crime of turning up wearing the wrong socks, Conway had forced Beverly to face the wall at the back of the class, standing her there all morning. The eyes of the school burned into her as her legs trembled. It was an introduction to a new way of life, and it would only get worse.

In the intervening years, Conway hadn't changed much, either in personality or appearance. She was an imposing height, at least six foot two in her bare feet, with shoulders so broad many people thought she was ex-military. But she wasn't. As she was keen to tell everyone she met, she continued a long line of school teachers, going back to the early settlers in the area.

'It was my ancestors who helped clear the rabble from this land,' she was fond of reminding Beverly at every opportunity, never detailing who she meant by that.

Beverly stared at the letter opener on the desk, the light shining through the window and bouncing off the blade. In her mind, she picked it up, moved slowly behind Conway, and dragged it across her throat. Even though it wasn't real, she felt warm blood trickling down her fingers.

'Are you listening, Shaw?'

Conway's voice cut through her, its sharpness dragging her back to reality. 'I'm sorry, Principal Conway. What did you say?' She pressed her fingernails deep into her palm.

'Your performance review is coming up soon, Shaw. The Education Board has made it more onerous for teachers in your position. There's no more room for chaff where children are concerned. Do you understand this?'

She didn't care anymore. The temptation to grab the letter opener made her skin tingle.

'I'll make up for the time I've had off. Just tell me what to do.'

Conway glared at her. 'I'm glad you said that, Bev. I want you to do me a big favour.'

'Anything.' She could feel the blade in her fingers. They weren't shaking anymore. The taste of blood was in her mouth. That wasn't imaginary. She'd bitten into her top lip. 'What do you need me to do?'

Conway placed her hand on the computer screen and twisted it so Beverly saw the front. 'We've got a problem with the school's database, and I don't trust Sarah with it. That's why I need you.'

She walked from the desk and put her arm around Beverly's shoulders.

Beverly wanted to shrink into the floor, her mind fighting through emotions of disgust and murderous hate.

'Of course, Principal. Whatever you want.'

Conway let go of her and pointed at the screen. 'There are some discrepancies in the records and I want you to search through everything and double-check the details. You need to finish it before next Monday.'

'OK.' That gave her enough time with the weekend. 'I'll work at home and make sure it's completed on time.'

Conway shook her head. 'The data is sensitive, so can't leave this building. Plus, it's both staff and student records. You'll have to do it from here, no matter how long it takes.'

The top half of Beverly's body sank into itself. The letter opener screamed at her. But she shut out the screaming and focused on making *A Plan For Conway*. It was sooner than she'd expected, but it had to be done. As soon as she made the decision, she relaxed.

'No problem. Which computer do you want me to work from?'

'You can use your office, Bev. I'll give you the password for the records.'

Conway moved to the other side of the desk and opened a drawer. Beverly wanted to tell her there was no need since she could bypass the school's feeble security system with ease. Instead, she watched her pull out a card with the PIN on it and hand it to her.

'Be careful with that, Bev.' Conway spoke to her like a stern mother chastising a child. Beverly nodded, her mind already in motion as she turned to leave. Conway's words didn't cut through her this time. 'Remember, there are more than a thousand records which need inspecting by Friday.' The glint in her eye sent a shiver down Beverly's spine. 'And then you'll be able to go to your get-together on Saturday.'

Beverly closed the door behind her. She had no intention of attending the reunion with all those people she hated, and she wouldn't be checking the records or doing what Conway said. There was only one record which she had to look at. Then it would all be down to the plan.

13 HYACINTH HOUSE

The kitchen was spotlessly clean. To Astrid's eyes and the rumble in her stomach, it appeared as if nothing had been prepared or eaten there for a long time. Evie opened the fridge and peered inside.

'There's half a bottle of milk and some unappetising looking cheese; little for your growing hunger, my friend.'

'How do you know I'm hungry?'

Evie grinned at her. 'Electroshock therapy may fry the brain, but it also heightens human hearing. The rumbling in your guts has been like exploding rockets in my mind ever since we left my former home.'

Astrid shook her head. 'We'll get something to eat later, but before we go further into the house, do you want to explain about the key in your hand?'

Evie picked up an apple and bit into it. Her eyes narrowed and her lips trembled. She went to the sink and spat the food into it before returning her gaze to Astrid.

'What's to tell? Adam gave it to me after our parents died. He knew if I ever returned, it wouldn't be through the front door where the neighbours might see me. And the security code to the house has never changed.'

'And you've kept this key in your room all this time?'

'I have.'

'And nobody else could access it without your knowledge?'

Evie pondered the question. 'You think someone could have taken it or copied it behind my back, and then used it to bring those girls here.' She scratched at her chin. 'I suppose it's possible, but it would have had to be a copy. There wouldn't have been enough time to get it back to my room. None of it seems probable.'

'Don't say that to anyone. The fact it's a possibility is something your brother's lawyer can use.'

Evie nodded. 'Okay.' She slipped the key into her pocket. 'I know he's innocent, but what makes you so sure, Astrid Snow?'

Astrid glanced around the kitchen. 'I've sat opposite many killers, and most protest their innocence, even when there's overwhelming evidence to contradict their claims. I guess I've learnt how to tell when they're lying or not. And I believe your brother is telling the truth.'

Do I? Or am I only doing this for George?

Evie put her hand on the door leading out of the kitchen. 'When this is over, I look forward to hearing your stories of your life before this. And all about Uncle George.'

She pulled the handle and led them into the corridor. Even in the dark, Astrid saw the faded wallpaper peeling from the wall where it met the ceiling.

'It doesn't appear as if your brother spent much time looking after this house.'

Evie shivered as she went. 'Both of us hate this place. I'd be surprised if he lived much here at all.'

'Where's the basement?'

'Just through here.' Evie led them down the passageway and to an entrance at the far right. She had her hand on the door when Astrid stopped her from going any further.

'You don't have to do this. You can leave it to me.'

Evie flexed her shoulders. 'There's nothing down there now. I'll be okay.' She turned the handle and stepped inside. She puffed out her cheeks and looked at Astrid. 'Will there be a chalk outline where they found the bodies?' Her voice trembled as she spoke.

Astrid put a hand on hers. 'The police haven't done that for years. They use photography and video to record the crime scene. They'll have taken everything they need from the basement. We won't be disturbing anything, but let me go first.'

Evie didn't object and moved to one side. 'The light is on your left.'

Astrid flicked the switch. The bulb flickered into life, and she saw the well-worn steps leading down. She wasn't sure if what she'd told Evie was right, didn't know if the police were through with their investigation in the house. She'd seen plenty of investigators who would have taken the bodies in the basement and Adam Church's DNA on them as watertight proof of guilt. But Evie's key would put a spanner in the works of the prosecution case if handled by a half-decent defence attorney. But none of that would tell her, or anyone else, who killed those two poor girls.

She held on to a handrail as she moved down, tiny bits of it sticking to her fingers. The further she went, the more it smelt of death. Evie coughed, but they continued. There were about thirty steps in all, and Astrid stopped halfway down.

'Is there something wrong?' Evie's breathing was heavy behind her.

'No. I just want to get an overview of the basement before we hit the bottom.'

She scanned every part, gazing over the discarded sofa at the far end, the stacks of dusty magazines in the middle of the room, and the bits of metal and plastic scattered over the workbenches. Old records, mainly albums with a few singles, littered another bench.

Evie's voice trembled. 'Do you know where they found the girls?'

'I don't, but seeing the recent movement in the dust, I'd say it was over there.'

Evie followed the trail across the floor and Astrid's outstretched finger to the sofa. 'Oh.'

Astrid smiled. 'Just watch where you step, and you'll be okay.' She continued to the end, peering over the concrete and finding nothing of interest.

Evie joined her at the bottom. 'How did the killer get the girls here without them struggling or running away?'

Astrid had already considered that and several other questions. 'More important than that, why did they leave the bodies here? Why not somewhere else? And how did they enter and exit with everything locked?'

'Do you think they had my key?'

'No, I don't, but it's a possibility. You said it yourself: someone couldn't have used it, and then got it back in time so you wouldn't notice it missing.'

'They could have duplicated it.'

'True, but when and how long ago did that happen? If it was a copy, it rules out any spontaneous random killing; it's something planned meticulously. Which leads to the next obvious question.'

'Why here and why my brother?'

Astrid nodded and walked to the sofa. She focused on the furniture, letting her mind, no matter how painful it was, picture how the girls ended up in their last resting place.

Evie stood next to her and repeated her questions. 'So why here and why my brother?'

'I don't know yet.' And that was still bugging her. 'We need to answer a few other questions first.'

'Like how did the killer get the girls here without any fuss or noise?'

'Precisely. What do you think?'

Evie scratched at the freckles on her arm, her nose twitching like a rabbit. 'The killer might have drugged them.'

'They could have, but it would show up in the toxicology report from the autopsy. And if you're right, it would lead to another important question.'

'How was it administered?'

'Perhaps the killer put it into their food or drink. But if that happened upstairs or outside, they would have had to carry them into the basement, down those rickety steps, and probably in the dark.'

Evie continued to rub at her arm. 'No, I don't like the drug theory. There are too many things that could have gone wrong, and I get the impression our killer is someone who doesn't leave anything to chance. No, it has to be something else.'

'I agree with you. Forcing the sisters here at gunpoint would have been so much easier, don't you think?'

'Absolutely. And almost every adult around here owns at least one firearm.' She stared at Astrid through wide eyes. 'Do we know how the girls disappeared?'

'Only what was in the news. About four hours before the bodies were discovered, witnesses saw them entering the woods out the back.'

Evie moved towards the sofa, looking as if she'd sit on it until she apparently remembered who had been on it last.

'But that seems very random. How would the killer know the girls would be there?'

'Do you want to know what my educated guess is?'

'Of course.'

'At some point in the next couple of days, we'll find out, either from Adam's lawyer, the police, or the media, that those girls played in those woods all the time, but their parents didn't know, because if they did, they probably would have stopped them.'

'But that means someone did know and they're either our killer, or they know who did it.'

'Elementary, Evie. And finding out who knew will lead us to the culprit, but there's still one thing bothering me.'

'And what's that?'

'I know about being framed for murder and, in my case, the killings only happened to lead to something else. I have a hunch our killer wasn't only targeting your brother; it hasn't ended here.'

Evie lifted her hand to her chest and the tremble returned to her voice. 'You believe they might come after me?'

Astrid walked over to the records and wiped the dust from the top one. A gospel choir stared at her from the cover.

'I think, from this point on, you need to stick with me.'

14 HELLO, I LOVE YOU

It was a twenty-minute walk from Jack Kennedy's bookshop to his house. He'd taken it at least twice a day for the last five years, but this was the first time he'd wanted to sprint all the way. Once he'd locked the store, he'd started with a brisk stride. Usually, he'd take the time to admire the trees and flowers on the way, maybe say hello to Tom and Mary Shaw in their coffee shop. Yet that afternoon, his heart raced around his ribcage while a thousand messages echoed through his skull. And every one of them told him to RUN.

But he didn't. He waved at old Mrs Parsons on the other side of the street, patted the Wilsons' dog when it approached him, and even nodded at Charlie Parker as he idled down the road in his police car.

By the time he reached home and fumbled for the key, it was as if every blood vessel in his veins was about to explode. He stumbled inside, intent on reaching the toilet before nature overtook him. And then he threw up all over a first edition hardback of *The Shining* before he'd gotten two feet inside. His legs gave way and he dropped to the floor as the rest of his breakfast reappeared. What was once scrambled eggs and beans vomited out of his mouth and down his chin. He pressed both palms into the carpet and stared at the new direction his life had turned.

He pushed up, praying the last of it was out of his system. When nothing else came after a minute, he wiped the residue from his chin using his arm. Fog drifted across his sight as everything swirled across his gaze. A thousand pins sent a jolt of electricity through his skull. He rolled on to the floor and stared at the ceiling. There was no roof there, only Evie Church's inquisitive face asking about her writing.

Jack turned to the side. The room continued to spin around him. Perhaps it could swirl into a vortex and transport him back in time twelve months. No, that wasn't going to happen. There was only one thing which would wipe away his current pain. He knew there must still be some in the house. But he couldn't remember where he'd hidden it. Or maybe he did throw it out. No, he wasn't that strong. Not then and not now.

His arms ached as he pushed up from the carpet. The spew settling on the Stephen King book glistened at him. One foot slumped after another as he trudged upstairs. He ran his fingers across the wall, hoping the chill would unfreeze the fog consuming his brain. He turned right at the top, staggered past the toilet, then his bedroom, and entered the small room at the end.

Books and magazines were piled everywhere, including the floor and the bed. He found the only free spot on the bed and slumped into it. A bunch of dusty periodicals slid into him. The air was stale and, for a horrible fleeting moment, he thought he'd throw up again. He stuck two fingers against his throat and took a sharp breath. His heart was returning to normal and the bile sank back into his gut.

He grabbed a magazine, remembering now what they were: a bunch of pulps he'd bought from an old widow a few years back. He'd intended to sell them for a massive profit on eBay until he got caught up with that ridiculous book signing, the protests, and the regular customers lost over it.

Just the memory of it made him queasy again. He looked at the cover of the pulp to distract him. It was the first appearance of Robert E Howard's Conan the Barbarian in *Weird Tales*. It was in pristine condition, with barely a mark on it. He placed it carefully to the side and checked the others. There were dozens of copies of *Weird Tales* and *Amazing Stories*, all in excellent condition. It was a decent collection and would probably bring in more money than the bookshop had done in a long time. Well, at least since the incident. Maybe he should forget everything else, forget about Evie Church, and concentrate on this.

He sucked in stale air and got up from the bed. He couldn't think like that. He had one ambition, had only ever possessed one aim in life, and he wasn't going to throw it away because some loon had returned from the nuthouse. Her turning up at the shop was unexpected, he wouldn't deny it, and her appearance had scared the shit out of him, but all he had to do was forget about her and rediscover his confidence. And there was always one thing which would fill him with enthusiasm, and he wouldn't find it in magazines.

He got on his hands and knees and thrust his hand under the bed. His fingers found more dust, and something with many legs scuttled over his skin. He ignored the reflex to pull away and kept on searching. He moved closer to the bed and reached in further. He was sure he'd put the last one there. He couldn't face leaving the house again to get more. He was about to give up when his fingertips discovered the chill of the glass. A wide grin washed off the last of the vomit clinging to his mouth as he grasped the bottle and pulled it to his chest.

FOUR HOURS LATER, more than half of it was gone, the first drops of alcohol to pass his lips in five years. All the fear and anguish had vanished, replaced with staggering arrogance. He couldn't remember why he'd given up drinking, couldn't recollect the girlfriend who ended up in the hospital getting her stomach pumped, and didn't recall driving the car and hitting the old woman. Only most of his savings and unscrupulous lawyers had kept him out of jail then.

He'd remember all of this later when the hangover kicked in, but for now, he was a born-again Jack Kennedy living a new life. And it was all dependent upon the document staring at him from the computer screen. He took another drink and read it aloud for the umpteenth time.

Hi Jack

Pendant Publishing would like to congratulate you on the upcoming publication of your intoxicating novel "A Dark Heart in the Garden of Delights", a coming of age story illuminating the harsh realities of family life in modern America.

Only it wasn't his work, or his creativity, or his writing. Twenty years of his writing had produced nothing but a dozen disastrous novels and over a thousand rejections. He'd just about given up when Evie Church sent him one of her short stories, wanting to get feedback from someone in the publishing world.

He laughed and snorted booze from his nose.

What a waste.

Fancy believing that he, a soon to be failed bookshop owner, was someone in the publishing world. But he had nothing else to do, so he read the story and the others she sent. *They're good,* he told her. *You show plenty of promise,* he added. It was a long time since anything had intrigued Jack, but this did.

She did. Evie Church. The girl who'd committed herself to Shady Acres. He knew little about her apart from that, but once he decided on his plan, he found out everything he could about her and her family. He hated the internet for what it had done to traditional booksellers, but it sometimes had its uses, and he discovered some interesting nuggets about them.

Her parents were part of a fundamentalist congregation always banging on about Sin and the Old Testament. They'd joined their maker courtesy of a drunk driver. Reading about it made his teeth ache. Then he quickly moved on to the son, Adam. There was little online about him, just a piece he found about some financial firm he left to go to one of the bigger institutions on Wall Street.

He'd recalled the time he'd spent researching Evie and her family as he cleaned himself up and the drinking started. He placed his fingers on to the computer screen and read the email over and over, his flesh trying to transport the words into his skin and bone. He knew what he had to do, but not how to do it. He pulled his hand away and contemplated this problem. He reached for the TV remote and turned the set on. It flickered into life, displaying the local news channel, where something strange and unexpected presented itself to him. He'd muted the volume, so he increased it as he stumbled forward. The words rang inside his ears as his mind adjusted to the confusion. He focused on the rolling ticker tape headline scrolling across the bottom of the screen.

BODIES OF GIRLS FOUND IN CHURCH HOUSE BASEMENT

The sound sprang to life on the TV.

'The police are releasing no more details at the moment, but there will be a press briefing later tonight.'

The reporter was standing in the street, lights flashing around them, as police cars lined up outside a row of houses.

He rubbed at his eyes. The police have found the Glick sisters, but were they talking about the basement of a church building? It didn't look like it as the TV flicked over to an advert about health insurance. He moved towards the computer, glanced at the email again, then opened a web browser. Jack typed in missing Glick girls in the search engine and hit Enter on the keyboard. Hundreds of results bounced on to the screen. He clicked on the first one and scoured the details more than once. This had all happened while he'd locked himself away in the bookshop; the scenes outside the house were from yesterday. After the third read-through, he grabbed the bottle of bourbon and sank into the sofa.

Jesus, Mary and Joseph.

He wasn't a religious man, but he took this as a sign from someone looking out for him. The reports said a suspect had been arrested for the murders of Kay and Martha Glick, but didn't name them. It had to be Adam Church, and that's why Evie was back in the community.

He raised the bottle to his lips, the glass resting between

them. He'd got a second chance and now was not the time to waste it. He walked into the kitchen and dumped the rest of the booze over the dirty plates before dropping the empty into the bin. It was a second chance not to be squandered.

But how could he exploit this to his benefit?

15 THE SOFT PARADE

When the discovery of the Glick girls' bodies hit the media, Astrid knew she had to get Evie out of her family home. Reporters, cameras, and a whole slew of morbid gatherers would turn up sooner rather than later.

She booked her into another room in the hotel where she was staying. It was two floors above hers, but it was the best she could get on such short notice. Once Evie dumped her bag there, they retreated to the diner opposite. Astrid hadn't eaten all day, and her guts were threatening to rip open her stomach if she didn't soon. She also fancied something strong to drink, but wisely put that on hold until after the food; drinking on an empty belly was never a good idea. There was no TV in the place, so they were unaware of what was happening in the rest of Eureka Falls.

After a quick browse of the limited menu and some small talk at the table, which didn't include murder, care homes, or dysfunctional families, their food arrived. Astrid tucked into a large steak, fries, salad and onion rings. Evie struggled to eat her burger without making a mess. Mustard and tomato sauce dribbled over her fingers as she stared at the giant double-decker of meat.

'You could cut it in half to make it easier.' Astrid offered her a knife.

'The town would disown me as a local if I did that. I once witnessed an outsider devour a pizza with a knife and fork, and everyone in the restaurant spent the rest of the night laughing at him.' She returned the burger to the plate and tried to flatten it with her hand. 'Most people here think I'm strange as it is without me giving them any more reasons.'

Astrid was glad to see her smiling. Their short time in the house, in the basement, had left Evie looking depressed, and Astrid thought the disappointment at what the book-shop owner had told her must still have been playing on her mind.

She glanced around the diner, seeing more people there than she'd seen in the town at any other point since she got there. Perhaps Eureka Falls' economics weren't so bad after all if so many could afford to eat out. Nobody gave them a second thought, with no prying eyes at the stranger and the young woman out from a care home because the police had accused her brother of a terrible crime. Was it because no one recognised who she was or that Adam still hadn't offi-cially been named as a suspect?

Astrid finished her meal and ordered two bottles of beer to go. The wine called to her from behind the counter as she paid the bill, but she thought it best to keep a clear head for tomorrow. She didn't know what her next move would be, but hoped Adam's lawyer would let her look at the evidence the police had gathered.

'Is one of those for me?' Evie chewed on a fry as she stood with Astrid.

'When was the last time you had alcohol?'

Evie stuck her tongue into the side of her mouth and rolled it around in a way which made Astrid grimace. 'I've never had booze. Remember, I was eighteen when I voluntarily retreated from the civilised world, and the legal drinking age in the US is twenty-one.' She shook her head and picked at her teeth. 'We're such a backward country compared to you Brits. And, of course, there was no alcohol allowed inside Shady Acres.'

Astrid removed her wallet again and called the waitress back. 'Two more bottles, please.' Then she turned to Evie. 'Shady Acres?'

'That's what all the good people of Eureka Falls call the Tranquil Waters Rest Home. They think we, the residents, don't know, but half the staff there use the same term anyway.' She grabbed the booze from the bar. 'I don't care either way.'

'Okay, but since you're not used to that,' Astrid pointed at a bottle, 'you better take it easy tonight.'

Evie grinned. 'Yes, Mom.'

They drank in Evie's room, but it didn't last long, with the younger woman drifting off to sleep without finishing the first bottle. They'd been spending the time talking about their shared love for reading and old movies when Astrid noticed the glaze in Evie's eyes. She wasn't surprised, feeling the day's events catching up to her as well.

Astrid left her on the bed, fully clothed, and pulled the cover over Evie. She took the spare bottle of beer with her and drank in her room while flicking through the TV. The news stations had no new information on the murders, and there was no mention of Adam's name. She was happy with that, knowing the longer he was kept out of it, the better it would be for both her and Evie. But she also realised it couldn't last long.

———

AFTER A RESTLESS NIGHT of little sleep, Astrid was up at eight o'clock. She wondered how much rest Evie had got as she turned on the TV to bad news. The police had released a statement at midnight naming Adam as a suspect in custody for the murders of the Glick girls. Did they do it then because they thought it would attract less attention at that time? If so, it didn't work. Both the traditional and internet media had gone into overdrive with the news. She scanned through most of it as she wiped the fuzz from her eyes.

She let Evie sleep and trawled through the information. It didn't take long to discover the internet was aware of Adam's so-called alternative lifestyle as it appeared on several websites. Ex-partners had crawled out of the wood-work, all ready to post their stories. She knew it wouldn't look good to an unforgiving and baying public, and probably even less to a jury, but it was a stretch to think his sexual interests with adults would connect him to what happened to those girls. She hoped Evie hadn't seen any of the rumours about her brother online.

She decided to give Evie another thirty minutes of rest before going to her room. She rechecked her phone, expecting a message from Adam's lawyer. There wasn't one, and that was worrying, an indicator something wasn't quite right.

Astrid was flicking a bit of dust from the screen when noises outside the hotel distracted her. She went to the window, but a high ledge obscured what was happening below. The sounds grew louder, a cacophony of raised voices which unnerved her. She sent a text to Evie, and then got her jacket.

I'm coming up to you. I'll be there in one minute.

She grabbed the key to her room and locked it behind her. She took the stairs two at a time, searching for those sounds outside, but finding nothing but the echo of her footsteps. She entered the fourth floor and strode to Evie's room.

The corridor smelt of stale food and dirty carpet as she knocked on the door. 'Come on, Evie. We have to go.'

There was no response. Was she still asleep? Yesterday had been emotionally draining for her. She was raising her fist to knock again when the phone vibrated in her pocket. She removed it and stared at the message.

I'm outside. HELP.

16 LOVE HER MADLY

Astrid was moving before she'd finished reading the last word. The mobile clung to her fingers as she leapt down the corridor, past the lift, and through the exit to the stairs. She took the steps two at once, her shoulder and legs bouncing off the walls. By the time she got to the bottom, the phone was back inside her jacket and the sounds from earlier had become sharper: a crowd was shouting outside the hotel.

She sprinted by the reception and burst outside. A mob surrounded the front of the building. Some of them wore badges identifying them as the media, with arms outstretched and microphones pointed forwards. Television cameras were slumped over shoulders while lights flashed into action as dozens of photographs caught what she couldn't see on the other side of the hive.

Then the shouting started again.

Is your brother a murderer?

Did you help him do it?

Did you help him kill the Glick girls?

Why were you locked up?

A screaming, baying public drowned out those questions.

Child killer!

Murdering bitch!

You'll get yours, bitch!

Hang 'em both!

String 'em up!

Astrid reached the edge of the crowd, standing on the tips of her toes to see Evie quivering in the centre of the storm. Her eyes were ruby red, her lips moist and trembling. Astrid had to get her out of there, but there was a swarm of people between them. The screaming and shouting continued as she stared into the faces of the angry horde. She'd witnessed the likes of this before and knew it wouldn't be long before someone snapped and did something everyone would regret forever.

Astrid grabbed at those closest to her, pulling them back to create a path through. Disgruntled voices shouted at her while fists swung in her direction. She dodged most of them, but one or two connected with her shoulder or hip. Electric shocks coursed through her as she got closer to Evie.

And then she saw the gun.

The barrel came out of the throng behind Evie, crawling in slow motion for her head. Astrid's path was overgrown with bodies blocking her way. Someone stumbled and a television camera flew towards her. She lifted her arm, and the metal bounced off her bones with a crack. The crowd shoved her sideways, so she lost sight of the gun, waiting for the bullet to explode into Evie's face.

She tried to shout a warning, but wild, swaying arms kept falling into her. It was all she could do to stop from crashing to the ground. Astrid pushed out with all her strength, moving the human obstacles back until she saw

Evie again. The pistol had disappeared. Then the air exploded with gunfire. People screamed and moved as one. Some dropped to the ground with their hands over their heads; the rest split on every side, streaming away as fast as they could. The screams were ones of panic and distress, mingled in with the crying and sobbing.

Evie was nowhere. Astrid twisted her neck, looking for the woman she'd sworn to protect. Amongst the shouting and the terror, she saw the back of Evie's head vanish into the alley by the side of the hotel. She leapt forward, jumping over cowering bodies and broken cameras. She reached the passage in three strides, her gaze adjusting to the sight in front of her. A girl had a gun pressed against Evie's stomach. Astrid froze to the spot a few feet away and stared into manic eyes.

'You don't want to be a murderer.'

The teenager turned to her, the weapon still pushed against Evie. 'She needs to pay for the sins of her family.'

Astrid held out her hands, showing she wasn't armed. 'How old are you, seventeen or eighteen? Your life will be over if you shoot her. And for what? She hasn't done anything wrong.'

The pistol shook in her hand as she spoke. 'You don't know what her family did, none of you does.'

Her hands were still outstretched and open as Astrid moved forward. 'Whatever you have to say will be lost with the murder of the innocent woman next to you. Give me the gun, and you can leave. I don't know who you are, and I won't tell anyone what happened here.' She took another step, near enough to smell the lavender of her perfume, close enough to recognise the pain in her eyes. 'It's not too late for you.'

The girl clutched the fingers of her free hand deep into

her palm. Astrid calculated what the damage would be if she lunged for the gun. Would one bullet in the gut kill Evie? She'd need immediate medical help to stop her bleeding to death, and that's only if the squashed metal didn't hit any of her internal organs.

She was weighing up the options as the girl dropped the weapon to the ground and ran into the shadows at the other end of the alley. Astrid kicked the gun into a gutter and grabbed hold of Evie before she fell. Sirens wailed behind them, conveniently late. Evie held on to her for dear life.

'I thought I was a goner for sure.'

Astrid's body stiffened, uncomfortable with such a show of affection. She eased Evie off her gently.

'Do you know that girl?'

She shivered as she spoke. 'I've never seen her before.'

Astrid turned to the footsteps approaching behind them.

'Maybe she's a relative of the dead girls.' Two uniformed police officers ran in their direction. 'I guess we're going to get a lift to see your brother.'

17 THE SPY

Two hours before the events outside the hotel, Beverly sat in her car near the school. She'd been the last to leave the evening before at eight o'clock, even spending fifteen minutes setting the alarm as Conway told her to, and now she was the first there at six-thirty. It had been a productive night in formulating her plan. The staff database turned out to be more interesting than she'd expected. The entry for Conway, detailing her address and financial situation, was highly informative.

She stepped out of the car and left the grounds. Her destination was a couple of minutes away. The early morning breeze brushed against her cheek and into her hair. She shouldn't have been surprised to discover Conway lived close to the school she viewed as her personal fiefdom. With this information, Beverly realised she could finish Conway once and for all.

Beverly strode out of the gates and turned right. There was a narrow path leading down the front of the building, which then took a sharp left. When she reached the end, she saw four large houses surrounded by rows of trees.

Once she'd seen the address in the database, she'd gone home to do research on her secure computer. The houses were originally built and owned by four brothers at the start of the twentieth century. Each house had stayed within the family for a hundred years until a set of disastrous financial decisions had led to their enforced sale over five years. Conway's husband had bought one not long after leaving the military, and then the property fell to his widow when he died a decade later.

Beverly found the house and walked between the large billowing trees which hid the front from the rest of the street. It was perfect for what she had in mind. She strolled up the steps and rang the bell. It was six forty-five in the morning.

Birdsong littered the air as the door opened. Conway stared right through Beverly, and the Principal's clean white shirt shimmered as the wind whistled across the front step.

'Are you lost, Shaw?'

Beverly ignored the sarcasm. 'I'm sorry to appear at your house like this, Principal. I found something important in the staff database, which I thought you should know as soon as possible.'

Conway's eyes narrowed, her gaze continuing to cut right through Beverly. 'Come in, then.'

As her arm trembled, Beverly stepped inside and marvelled at the luxury around her. A vast staircase from an old Hollywood movie loomed ahead, while doors on either side of her must have led, she assumed, to the main rooms and kitchen on the ground floor. She also guessed there'd be a bathroom with a toilet there. The thought of it made her legs ache, and she wondered if she'd need to take a leak soon. She shouldn't have had those two cups of coffee before leaving.

'Go into the first room on your right,' Conway instructed her. Beverly did as she was told, catching a glimpse of an extravagant chandelier in the entrance as she pushed the door open and stepped inside.

Against her better judgement, she gasped. The place was big enough for a basketball court, the floor covered with a thick Persian carpet. A large fireplace took up space against the far wall, while rows of dark wood shelving clung to the room's edges. Bunches of antiques, porcelain figurines, and other curios filled the shelves. She seemed to be standing inside an expensive junk shop.

To her right was a bright velvet sofa, on which sat the two whitest cats she'd ever seen. Their fur was thick, like balls of wool. Both animals glared at her.

'So, Bev, what's so important you had to come to my house this early in the morning?' Conway marched past her and stroked each of the moggies in turn under their snow-white chins. They continued to peer at Beverly as they purred.

She was desperate to sit down, her legs ready to spill all over the floor. She placed the fingers of her hand into her wrist and pushed down. Even though she'd done her research, the size of the house had thrown her plans out of whack. She didn't know if she could go through with it now.

'Shaw, are you listening to me?' It wasn't a shout, but she'd raised her voice enough to shock Beverly back into reality. She lifted her hand to her face and pushed a flopped hair out of the way.

'I'm sorry, Principal Conway.' She gathered her thoughts and remembered the speech she'd spent hours preparing. 'When I went through the staff database, I noticed some of the personal information appeared to have been duplicated.'

Conway picked up one of the cats and scrutinised Beverly. 'All the files on the school's system are backed up and copied each night for security purposes.'

Yes, I know. I'm not an idiot. I've forgotten more about computer security than you'll ever know.

'What I discovered was different.' In reality, she'd found nothing. This was all a ploy to get into the house. 'It appears some data has been copied to an external drive and transferred off the system.'

Conway's eyes took on the appearance of black holes. She gripped on to the cat so hard, it squirmed from her hands and dropped to the carpet with a squeal.

'I thought that was impossible with the security we have in place?'

Beverly presented her best look of disbelief. 'Nothing is foolproof where computers are concerned.'

'Do you know which data has been copied?'

Well, none of it, but this is the lie I'll tell you.

'It's the financial details the school uses to pay salaries into staff bank accounts.'

Conway's expression never changed, her face resembling a blank wall in the desert.

'Only one person has access to the database apart from me.'

'I see.' Beverly didn't care since it wasn't true.

'And you found this out last night?'

'Yes.'

'What time did you leave work?'

'About seven.' She coughed and scratched at her throat as if she needed a drink.

Conway stared at her. 'Have you told anyone else?'

'No.' And she never would. She coughed again.

'You must double-check everything today. I'm out of

school at a conference. I won't be back until after eleven tonight. I want you to call me then and give me a report.'

'Yes, Principal.' She coughed louder this time.

'Do you need water, Shaw?' Conway reached for her jacket and car keys as she spoke.

'Yes, please.'

'The kitchen is across the way. Get a drink, and then meet me at the front door. We'll leave together.'

Beverly nodded and left. She was out of the room and running across the corridor in an instant. She burst into the kitchen and ignored everything but the backdoor. She hoped it wasn't like a modern house with numerous locks and bolts and a state of the art security system. She sprinted towards it, thankful it was only a door with a single lock and key. She removed the key and slipped it into her pocket.

'Are you finished, Shaw?' Conway's voice was close by. Beverly moved to the sink and turned on the tap. There was a glass on the side. She picked it up and thrust it under the flowing water as Conway entered the kitchen. 'Come on. We haven't got all day.'

She switched off the tap and drank the water in one go, realising she'd turned on the hot tap by mistake. The liquid burnt her throat as she followed Conway out. Her mouth throbbed and she wanted to throw up as the two of them exited the house, her face turning red.

Conway looked at her suspiciously. The key felt like an exploding rocket inside her pocket.

'Did you walk to here from school?' Beverly nodded, afraid to speak in case hot water erupted from her mouth. Conway took one final look at her before heading to the car. 'Ever since you stepped into the playground as an eleven-year-old, I've known you were weird, Shaw.'

With a hand on her trembling throat, Beverly watched Conway walk away in the knowledge the next time they met, it would be their last.

18   BREAK ON THROUGH

Half an hour before the panic outside the hotel, Jack Kennedy stood inside the Shaw coffee shop and waited for his first cup of the day. He eyed up the blueberry muffins on the counter, his stomach saying yes while his head said no. He was the only customer there, and he wondered if their business was already dead on its feet. For some unknown reason, *The End* by The Doors was playing over the shop's sound system. He was pondering how many blueberry muffins Jim Morrison could put away in one go as Mary Shaw returned with his drink.

She must have recognised the strange look on his face.

'I'm sorry,' she said without really appearing as if she was. 'Tom thinks he can play what he wants when we have no customers.'

What does that make me, then? Am I invisible?

He hoped he was to Evie Church. But then he had a plan for her, and he was quick to get to it. He paid for the coffee and two muffins. He'd keep one for lunch later on. And if it was good enough for the Lizard King, it was certainly good enough for Jack Kennedy. *Break on Through* erupted above his head as he left and travelled the short distance next door to his failing empire.

I don't think The Doors is appropriate music for attracting customers. Perhaps I should tell them.

But he didn't.

He left the sign displaying CLOSED as he shut the door. There was something he needed to do before the day's official business began. The coffee cup warmed his hands, the blueberry muffins smelling fresher than they appeared. He guessed they had been defrosted not long before the Shaws opened up.

His feet crunched over a stack of envelopes as he strode inside. He sighed as he put the food and drink on top of a copy of *The God Delusion* and scrunched down to pick up the mail. He was sure none of it would feature good news. He scanned the front of each envelope, not bothering to read his name.

Jack Kennedy. Whose parents were self-obsessed enough to call their only son that? He'd received so much stick at school because of it that even the teachers would laugh a little when they said his name.

He stuffed the envelopes under his arm and grabbed the coffee and sweet things again. He'd need some caffeine before discovering how much of the mail was reminders for unpaid bills. He strode around the front desk, dodging a pile of non-fiction books about gender equality, and settled into his seat. He got his laptop and turned it on. He'd watched the news before leaving that morning, feeling disappointed there'd been no new revelations regarding Adam Church and the Glick girls.

The coffee snapped at his lips as the computer sparked into life. He had to be proactive before Evie returned to him. Amongst his cocktail of panic, confusion, and joy last night, his first reaction had been to remove all the correspondence he'd had with her. He'd organised them into one folder in his email app, and his finger had hovered over the delete button for some time before he'd decided on the best course of action.

He was no computer expert, but he was sure people with more knowledge than him would be able to recover anything he deleted. He knew enough to understand any messages he received were not stored on his machine, but somewhere in the ether. The only evidence he had regarding the book she'd sent, the one to be published under his name, was the original email with the attachment. He'd never replied to it or acknowledged he'd got it. That was the point when he realised he'd steal her work and claim it as his.

Jack had no control over the evidence she'd messaged him. If it came down to that, he wouldn't deny the conversations they'd had. There was only one email he had to refute. So, he deleted the copy in his account. The tricky bit would be getting into hers and removing the original message. As he'd lain on the floor drinking yesterday, that was the only thought possessing him. He'd been struggling to find an answer when the news broke about the arrest of Adam Church.

That was the game-changer.

That was when Jack Kennedy decided he wouldn't just be a thief and a plagiariser; he'd also be something much worse.

I'm going to be a killer.

In for a penny, in for a pound, that's what his father would say as he beat seven shades of shit out of his son.

He'd spent all night coming up with a plan and felt pleased with it. But he had to start now before he changed his mind and chickened out. He drank half the coffee and nibbled at one of the muffins. Blueberries dribbled out of his mouth and on to the keyboard as he opened the web browser and his email account.

Jack ignored the junk mail offering him cheap Viagra pills and the chance to get a million dollars from a Nigerian Prince and went to the folder containing Evie's messages. He scanned the list twice before deleting the one with the attachment. Then he started a new message.

Dear Evie,

It was a surprise to see you at the shop yesterday. I thought you were still receiving residential support at the Tranquil Waters Rest Home, but it was good to meet you.

You should continue with your writing because, as I said before, you show great promise as a writer, and I believe when you find your authentic voice, you'll flourish in the challenging world of publishing.

One final note, Evie. I was sorry to hear the news about your brother. I hope everything works out for you.

Yours sincerely,

Jack.

He read it three times before hitting send. He wasn't a hundred per cent sure what she'd do next, but was confident of a reply. Then he needed to arrange an opportunity to see her alone. If the circumstances were appropriate, he'd put the final part of his plan into action.

He settled into his chair and finished the muffin. He'd open the shop in a few minutes, but he wanted to check the morning news one last time before that. He nearly fell out of his seat when he did. One of the TV broadcasters had recorded the chaos outside the hotel a short while ago. He watched the clip from the start, witnessed the people shouting abuse at Evie, and then sat gobsmacked as some-body fired a gun and bedlam ensued.

The news report underneath the video made him smile. Evie had survived an attempt on her life. He couldn't believe it. Someone somewhere was shining down on him. He left the computer and went and changed the shop sign to OPEN. The sun shone through the window and illuminated his grin.

His initial plan was to kill her and make it look like suicide. Because who wouldn't believe a woman with mental health problems, one who'd recently fled a facility that had looked after her for seven years, might be desperate to take her life once she discovered her brother was a child murderer?

But this morning's news made things even better. People wanted to murder her. Random folks repulsed by her brother's behaviour wished to kill her. So, who would believe he was the culprit once she turned up dead? Would the police bother with her emails? He didn't think they would.

Jack stepped out the door and let the sunshine wash over him. Then he went back and ate the second blueberry muffin.

19 BEEN DOWN SO LONG

Astrid sat behind a desk in the police station. Evie was in another room somewhere, and Astrid hoped she'd stick to the story they'd agreed on as the cops rushed towards them in that alley. She saw Detective Hicks looking at her. She got up from the chair and went to him. His face was a blank canvas.

'Does trouble find you so easily back in Britain?'

'I saved Evie's life. Where were the police when she was being harassed outside that hotel?' Astrid let the irritation seep out of her.

'We were too busy dealing with the fallout of her brother's actions.'

'Do you have proof he's guilty?'

'Why should I tell you anything?'

'Because when I prove his innocence, I promise not to make you look like a fool in the media.'

You could cut the tension between them with a flick of a finger. She wondered what it would take for him to lose his cool. When Evie came through the door, she ignored him.

'They've said I can see Adam. I need you to come with me, Astrid.'

'I'm afraid it's family only, Ms Church.' Hicks didn't appear to be afraid at all to Astrid.

'When I left the Tranquil Waters Rest Home, I appointed Ms Snow as my guardian. She has the legal right to go with me wherever I want.'

She doubted the legality of Evie's words, but Hicks's face told her he wasn't sure if it was true or not. And he didn't look that bothered.

'Okay. But there'll be a uniformed officer with you at all times.'

Evie rolled her eyes and grabbed Astrid's hand. 'Whatever, Mr Policeman.'

A policewoman took them to see Adam. Astrid wondered why they hadn't moved him to another facility and what had happened to his lawyer. She got the answer to the second question when they stepped into the room.

'You have to leave,' Adam told the officer. 'This meeting is covered by the attorney-client privilege.' The cop left without any complaint.

Astrid gave him a curious look. 'You're representing yourself?'

He grinned. 'Sure. I don't trust anyone else.'

He switched his gaze from her to Evie, his grin evaporating as he stared at his younger sister. After seven years, the two of them gazed at each other as if for the first time. Astrid couldn't imagine what was going through their heads. Her relationship with her sister was complicated and conflicted, with issues between them that wouldn't be resolved no matter what.

Evie broke the silence. 'You need to tell us everything, Adam, if we're to prove your innocence.'

He studied her before sitting at the table. 'I didn't do it.'

'I know,' Evie replied.

'Why did you leave your home?' Genuine sadness coursed through his words.

'I wanted to help Astrid help you.'

He stared at Astrid. 'I'm sorry for getting you involved in this, for getting you both involved.'

'You've got Uncle George to thank for that.' And how convenient he hadn't texted her since she got there. 'Why aren't you using a professional lawyer?'

'Which of them would believe I'm innocent with what the police have?' The weight of defeat appeared to push him to the ground. Evie snatched at his fingers, shock evident on both their faces. Astrid guessed it was the first physical contact they'd had with each other in a long time. 'Plus, I can see the prosecution's case and the evidence against me.' He smiled at her. 'And then I get to pass it on to you.'

'So, tell me what happened that night.'

He pulled his hands from Evie. 'I got back late, just after midnight. There were things I had to put in the basement. When I went downstairs, I found the girls on the sofa.'

There were no emotions in his face or his words, only that simple, matter-of-fact description of discovering death where you live. She recognised it as detachment, understood it as the brain's way of attempting to stay sane, of trying not to collapse under the reality of the horror it witnessed. She had one corner of her mind overflowing with such detachment. She needed to coax the details from him carefully, or that delicate balance may tip into insanity.

'Where had you been that night?'

She observed him staring at her as if it was a question

he'd avoided before. Lying to her would be no help to any of them. If he'd lied to the police, it would have been the first nail in his coffin. One of his shoulders dropped lower than the other, and he scratched at his chin.

'I was at a party out of town.' A nervous tic flicked across his face.

Astrid peered at him. 'You must be more forthcoming if we're going to help you.' She watched as Evie tapped her fingers on the top of the table in a slow, monotonous rhythm. Was there a danger of resurrecting unwanted family history here? 'You need to tell us what you said to the police.'

His nails dug into his flesh and drew a slight trickle of blood. 'I can't talk about this while Evie is here.' He switched his attention from Astrid to his sister. 'It'd be easier if you stepped outside.'

A sharp dagger of familiarity hit Astrid in the chest, memories of all those moments when Courtney rejected her. Evie's face was impassive, but the tapping of her fingers increased, her skin and bones bouncing off the wood. She raised her fist and slammed it on to the table.

'I know all about your so-called secret life, Adam. I've known for years. Did you think Mother and Father wouldn't tell me all about it? They enjoyed blaming me for your deviant behaviour.' Steam came out of her ears while her cheeks turned a fine pink. Then she calmed down just as quickly. 'That was their word, not mine. I was happy if you were happy.'

Silence chilled the air after her outburst. Astrid was right next to her, but it felt as if she wasn't there at that moment. She was content not to interfere, but didn't feel awkward being there. This was something the siblings had to resolve before they could prove his innocence.

He reached a hand out for his sister, and she took it.

'I'm sorry, Evie. Is this why you went into the home?'

She let out a nervous laugh. 'Shady Acres? No, that was nothing to do with you, Brother. That's a story for another day. Now, will you tell us what happened that night?'

He sighed and let go of her. He sank into the chair as if the weight of his life was drifting out of him. 'There's a weekly meet up of... of...' he struggled to say the words in front of his sister, so Astrid said them for him.

'Sexual fetishists.'

He nodded. 'For want of a better term. I was returning from one of those meetings.'

Astrid's mind had ticked over into investigation mode. 'How are these meetings arranged?'

He allowed himself a tiny smile. 'How most things are nowadays, through the internet. We have some, to put it politely, older people who swear the internet is the greatest thing ever invented. You should hear how they moan about how difficult it used to be in the old days.'

His face returned to its previous embarrassed appearance as if he'd remembered one of the women he was speaking to was his younger sister.

'Did you tell the police this?' Astrid said.

He nodded. 'I did, but it won't make any difference. Nobody ever gives their real names at the meetings, and the internet contacts change all the time.'

'How long did it take you to return home?' If they could at least place him on the road, with traffic cameras or witnesses, it might put a spanner in the prosecution case.

'It was about two hours.' He must have guessed where she wanted to go with the question. 'But it was via a desolate road, and I don't remember seeing any other vehicles.'

'Have the police told you the time of death for the Glick sisters?' Evie said.

His eyes narrowed as he spoke. 'They said the girls were killed about an hour before I called it in. I'd been home maybe fifteen or twenty minutes.'

'The killer was comfortable in your house.' Astrid tried to build a profile in her head. 'They also knew you'd be out and had access to your property.'

Evie turned to her. 'How is all that possible?'

'We'll come back to that. First, we need to establish what relationship Adam had with the girls.'

It was his turn to slap his hand onto the table. 'I've never had anything to do with them.'

His eyes were about to burst from his head. Evie found his fingers again to calm him down.

'But you had seen them before that night?' Astrid said.

Sadness replaced the anger in his face. 'Yes, I'd see them playing in the woods which back on to my property. I'd smile and wave and they'd do the same. But that's the closest I ever came to them. I never even knew their names until the police told me.' His chest sank into the rest of his body as Astrid watched the burden push him into the chair. 'They say I enticed them into the basement and then killed them when they refused to do what I wanted.'

None of them mentioned what that might be, but Astrid understood from scouring the internet that the less responsible media outlets were already publishing the most salacious theories. It wouldn't be long before some of his S&M associates came crawling out of the woodwork with tales about the depravities of Adam Church. Then some people would connect the dots between his secret life and what happened to the Glick girls.

'Who has access to your house, Adam?'

He appeared happy to talk about something else. 'There's only me with keys and the security code.'

'You don't have a cleaner or a friend with those?'

He shook his head. 'No.'

Astrid watched Evie reach into her pocket, guessing she was about to pull out her key. Had he forgotten about that? She stopped Evie with a hand on her arm. 'Do you have any enemies, Adam? Anyone who hates you so much, they'd do this?'

He ran his fingers across his chin. 'Well, I wouldn't think so.'

'Nobody from the fetish world or your work?'

He appeared to consider the question for a second. 'You do get some strange personalities at the parties, some extreme people who like to hurt others, but I've never met anyone who went too far, and I can't believe anybody at the meetings would commit murder. As far as my job is concerned, I deal with millions of dollars a day, and sometimes investors lose money they can't afford, so I'm sure I've pissed off plenty of people over the years. But to do something like this, no, I can't see it.'

Astrid had her doubts. She'd known people kill for far less.

There was a knock on the door, which told her time was up. She saw the fear freeze Evie into her chair and had to lift her out of it. Adam's voice shook as he spoke to his sister.

'Are you feeling better? Will you go back into the home?'

His words broke her from her reverie. 'Yes and no, Brother.' Determination steeled her words. 'We'll get you out of this, Adam, I promise.'

A uniformed officer and Detective Hicks entered. Astrid turned to Adam.

'One last thing.' His gaze met hers. 'What's your preference, sadism or masochism?'

All eyes were on him now, including the police's. He didn't hesitate with the answer.

'I take after my father. I'm a sadist.'

Detective Hicks smiled at Astrid as he closed the door behind them.

20 SOUL KITCHEN

Beverly watched Conway drive away, her fingers resting on the ribs which threatened to burst from her. It was a risk going there, but it had proved worth it. She sat on the steps and gazed into the palm of her hand. Plus, as she'd always known, you can't kill indiscriminately in a supposedly civilised society without taking risks. Where would the fun be in that?

Leaves floated off the trees shielding her from the rest of the street. She let her hands slip on to the key inside her pocket. Her original plan had worked: she'd acquired a way back into the house, but Conway's unexpected day out had presented her with a glorious set of opportunities.

She checked the clock on her phone. It was ten minutes to eight. Most of the staff would be arriving at the school now. Other teachers were covering her lessons for the rest of the week, Conway had seen to that. And she was sure nobody would attempt to bother her in her office. They were all too busy stressing over their excessive workloads to worry about anyone else. Which meant she had plenty of free time to go exploring.

Beverly removed the key and stood. The trees around her provided the perfect camouflage for returning to the house unseen. She stepped into the grass, the damp green of a dewy morning squelching under her feet. An aroma of peach blossom infected her senses. She took a deep breath and made her way to the side of the building. There were fewer trees and bushes at the back, but there was enough cover, she hoped, to reach the door unobserved.

She slipped the key into the lock, the cold metal tingling against her skin, and twisted it once. Only it didn't turn. It was stuck in one spot. She tried it again and got the same response.

'Fuck, fuck, fuck.'

Beverly whispered the words, but stomped her foot into the ground. She turned from the key and peered at her hand, holding on to her chest as she took deep, slow breaths. It had been much easier than this at the Church place. But then, she'd had plenty of time to plan and prepare for that. This was an instantaneous reckless spur-of-the-moment action.

Her knees buckled and she sat down. Getting the key was great, but it was a waste of time if it didn't work.

She got to her feet. It was better to find out now than tonight when she'd have walked there in the dark. She turned to the door and stared at the key again. Maybe it was one of those that needed a jiggle before it worked. There was a similar lock at the coffee shop. Perhaps the same person had fitted both.

Beverly rubbed her hands and blew warm air on to them. She grabbed the key once more, twiddling her fingers and twisting the metal. Then she turned it and got the same result. Tiny hammers drummed inside her skull, and all the disappointments of her life crashed through the shadows of her mind.

She removed her hand and blew on it again. If it didn't work this time, she'd abandon the plan and leave. Her trembling skin touched metal and gripped it tight. She put all of her strength into it, imagining the cold material was the neck of Martha Glick, smiling as she recalled twisting Martha's flesh as her younger sister looked on, horrified. It was only enough to leave her unconscious, but death would come soon after. Then she grabbed Kay before she could do anything. Not that screaming would have made any difference. Beverly knew the basement was soundproof.

The girl's tortured face was in her mind, the memory of her gloved fingers squeezing tighter and tighter as the key twisted and turned in the lock. The door opened and she stepped inside. She smelt the meat from the Bolognese Conway had prepared for her evening meal. It was in the fridge, but the recent aroma continued to linger in the kitchen. Funny how she hadn't noticed it earlier when she stole the key.

My mind is playing tricks on me.

Beverly searched for the cats, but couldn't see them anywhere. Her parents had never allowed her to have pets, no matter how much she begged them. Conway's cats were eminently strokable, wherever they were, but she had to ensure she avoided them. She didn't want any of their DNA on her as evidence, and vice versa.

She went to the fridge and opened it. The Bolognese nestled on the middle shelf between expensive-looking cheese and a pasta salad. A clear slice of cling film covered the meat. It would be easy enough to return with a sufficient amount of poison to end Conway once and for all. She considered it briefly before dismissing it out of hand. She wanted to watch her suffer and die, and tainted food wasn't going to give her that satisfaction. Beverly closed the fridge and stepped into the corridor linking the rooms together.

She returned to the living room where she'd spoken to Conway earlier. She expected the cats to pounce as she trod inside, but they must have been off somewhere else, enjoying their time away from their owner's harsh gaze.

Her eyes darted around everywhere, searching for anything helpful. It wasn't long before she found what she wanted. She strode towards the sizeable ornate desk behind the sofa. Resting on it was a laptop. She picked it up and settled on the couch. She was sure she'd come back to the house later, before Conway returned, and wait for her. The walk from her parents' place would only take an hour, and there'd be enough shadows to obscure her features until the trees outside covered her in a warm umbrella of concealment.

Then she'd sit in the living room and shoot Conway as soon as she entered. The gun suppressor would dampen any potential noise, although she didn't expect the isolation around the house and the street to be shattered by firing a weapon. She expected the first bullet to hit Conway in the shoulder. She'd reach for the wound and stumble back, probably into the wall or the door.

Beverly's second shot would destroy Conway's knee. She'd crash to the floor in agony, screaming in pain. Then, Beverly would move closer to her, ensuring she wore the plastic covers over her shoes, and kick Conway so she sprawled on to her back. Then she'd shoot her in the gut. She saw it all in her mind, precisely as she'd played it out beforehand with the Glick girls. Preparation was every-thing, making sure to eliminate all the possible unknown and complicating factors.

As she considered that, she once again wondered where the cats were. It seemed unlikely, but it wasn't beyond the realms of possibility they might do something to complicate matters. She didn't want them running around mewling while Conway spent the last remaining minutes of her existence listening to Beverly torment her. She needed to find where those animals were before she left and returned to school.

Before that, she started the laptop. It fizzed into life and she wondered how security conscious Conway was. She had no alarms for this expensive house, so surely she wouldn't bother with a password on her computer?

Beverly grinned when the screen appeared and it didn't ask for a login. She checked the time in the bottom corner. She gave herself twenty minutes, and then another ten for searching upstairs. The first thing she did was check Conway's emails. She knew most people never signed out of their accounts when using a computer at home, and she wasn't disappointed.

She skimmed through the newest ones, messages from retailers and food outlets, turning her nose up at Conway's apparent obsession with the latest food fads. A few from the school governors caught her eye; why was Conway getting those in her private account and not the school one? But they were irrelevant when she opened and read them. Experience had taught her the things people tried to hide the most were inside the Deleted folder. And she wasn't wrong this time.

Apart from the usual junk, she found more than two dozen messages from the same person, stretching over three months earlier in the year. The first ones included language and photo attachments to make her blush. The later messages were full of bitterness and bile that, if said out loud, would hurt your ears. It was a tale of a secret romance broken down into an apparently irreconcilable hostility. At least on his part. And his part was younger than Conway's. Beverly had long ago become unshockable to the secrets people kept; after all, she had a few of her own, but this was a complete surprise. She had to read the name of the sender more than once to confirm it was him.

She relaxed on the sofa, wondering how best to use this new information. She'd come to the house not only to finalise her murderous plan, but to discover something equally important. Killing Conway was only going to be satisfactory if, like with Adam Church and the poor Glick girls, she had the right fall guy to become the scapegoat. And now she did.

Beverly created a new message and added the appropriate address for the recipient. Then she flexed her fingers and typed.

I'm sorry. I was wrong. I've missed you. I think we should get back together.

Then she hit the Send button. She doubted he'd be at his Inbox this early, so she didn't expect an immediate reply. Beverly removed a USB pen from her pocket and attached it to the laptop. She opened the drive and found the app she needed. It took less than a minute to install the Trojan on to the machine. When it finished, she removed the drive and put it into her trousers. Once she got home and activated it, the Trojan would give her access to all of Conway's files and accounts without her knowing.

She shut down the laptop and closed it. There was no need to go through the whole thing now she had the virus installed; she could peruse it at her leisure. But did the discovery of the secret lover mean a change in the timescale to her plan? She placed the machine back where she'd found it and went upstairs. There was still no sign of the cats.

Beverly discovered some interesting toys and publications in the bedroom, but there was nothing there to alter her strategy. She returned downstairs and stepped into the kitchen. The key was in the lock when the felines reappeared, staring at her from across the room. Had they been there all along?

She dismissed any more thought about pale cats and left the house, locking the door behind her. The moggies were up on the window ledge, peering at her as she headed back to school. Would she have the time to reel in her fish and finish off Conway tonight?

The key was warm in her hands as she saw the first step in her ultimate goal coming to fruition.

21 SHAMAN'S BLUES

It was a productive morning for Jack. Half a dozen customers spent close to four hundred dollars on books which cost him a fraction of that. He'd never seen any of the people before. The town wasn't a big draw for tourists at any time of the year, so it was unexpected. On the east side of Eureka Falls, there was the site of a minor battle in the Civil War, and the area's most famous citizen was a singer from the 1960s who'd had one hit single while wearing a hat on fire.

Adam Church, you've made us infamous.

He scanned the latest news about the Glick murders. According to local social media websites, people from nearby towns and villages had been coming over since last night, while the attempted murder of Evie had added to the mob.

And you delayed the wolves hanging around my heels, my Evie.

His eyes drifted from the screen towards the bills on the desk. He was only capable of reading two of them before his stomach resembled the worst ride on Coney Island, and he was reluctant, especially after yesterday, to throw up when he had new customers in the shop.

The first letter he opened was one of a handful he'd brought from home. He found it easier scanning bad news in the bookshop, and it was the bank reminding him he'd missed three mortgage payments on the house. There was a polite reminder in the middle paragraph to arrange a meeting to see the bank manager if he was having difficulty with his finances. He rolled his eyes as he read it; that option had long passed. There was also a statement at the bottom, this time in a larger text to ram home the point that another missed payment would lead to an automatic process for repossession proceedings. That next payment was due in two weeks.

Beneath the bank's letter were three others from the credit card companies to which he owed thousands of dollars. He didn't bother opening them. The only other one he read was from the bookshop's landlord; this was even worse than the one from the bank. It was less money he owed, but he also had less time to pay this debt: a week before he'd have to close the shop. Then, with the house repossession on the horizon, there would be nowhere to put the stock. He couldn't afford storage, and if he sold them, the total value of the books and magazines wouldn't cover a fraction of his debt.

And he still had six months of alimony to pay his ex-wife. He'd forgotten everything about their three years together apart from the last thing she said to him.

'When did marriage become My Rage?'

He pushed the memory of her from his head and returned to the internet as social media chatter about the

Church siblings distracted him from his money worries. There was a lot of anger directed at Adam and Evie. He thought it was harsh on her. As far as he knew, until very recently, she hadn't left Shady Acres since stepping inside the place seven years ago, but it had proved potentially beneficial to him. Evie's novel, queried in his name, had gotten him a well-respected New York literary agent, and she'd told Jack she was convinced 'his' book would make him famous and wealthy.

He'd initially told himself the theft of her work was only about the money and preventing his life from collapsing into the same one which overtook his father. If the house and the business were taken from him, he'd be homeless and jobless with few opportunities on the horizon for a nearly fifty-year-old former alcoholic ex-bookseller. And how long would it take before he returned to the booze? Yesterday proved how easy it was for him to return to the bad ways.

So, yes, the money from the sale of the novel would stop his life from crumbling into dust and despair. Still, he had to admit, if only to himself, after having spent more than thirty years failing as a published writer, now that it was in his grasp, even if the book wasn't his, it was equally as important as the financial rewards.

He raised an invisible glass to the empty shop and the woman who, unwittingly and unknowingly, was about to save his miserable life.

'Here's to you, Evie Church.'

But how was he going to deal with her? In those moments between handling customers, Jack had considered several internet searches which might be helpful, from "how to get away with murder" to "how to commit the perfect murder". But even he knew those would leave a trail across his computer, which the police would easily access. Only last week, he'd read about a man in the next town over who'd murdered his wife and then disposed of her in an acid bath. And what had the police discovered when they took his computer away but numerous searches for "the best way to dispose of a human body using acid"?

Jack realised desperation was starting to consume him, but he wasn't that stupid. Plus, he had the next best thing to a worldwide web of limitless data: a bookshop heaving with true crime books. He browsed several of them over the morning, his mind drifting between serial killers' motivations and the processes leading to the police or the FBI catching those same killers. The information was illuminating in sort, but none of it helped him. Eventually, it led him to a different idea altogether.

I don't have to kill her. I only need to get rid of those messages she sent me.

And that meant getting into her email account, and it might not be as difficult as he'd first thought. He'd dismissed the idea initially when his bloodlust overtook his common sense. It would be too challenging to find her computer, then access it and, it seemed likely, break any passwords and security.

But the more he considered it, the more he understood he wouldn't need to do any of that. In the modern age, most people, including himself, accessed their emails through their phones as much as their computers. If she was like him, she probably didn't log out of any of her internet accounts on her cell. So, in theory, all he had to do was get hold of her phone.

He'd pondered the difficulty of that on the way to work, but the news of what had happened to Evie outside that hotel presented him with an excellent opportunity to get her and the phone within touching distance. All he had to do was put his plan into action.

First, it was lunchtime, and he'd had nothing to eat all morning but those two muffins. With the shop empty and his stomach growling, he strode to the front, changed the OPEN sign to CLOSED, then locked the door behind him. He returned to the Shaws' coffee shop and enjoyed one of their excellent savoury bagels and a piece of the homemade apple pie which was Mary Shaw's speciality.

After ordering his food and a drink, he picked a seat near the window. The coffee shop had a similar increase in customer traffic to that which his bookshop had experienced that morning. It would appear that death and murder were great as consumerist aphrodisiacs. He smiled as he nibbled at his excellent bacon and cheese bagel. In the distance, he noticed Mary staring at him, and he transferred his smile to her. She blushed and turned away.

Over the years, he'd overheard the Shaws engage in verbal marital disputes too heavy for the gap which separated both businesses. His conversations with them had been professional, polite, and pleasant, with his thoughts about Mrs Shaw rarely drifting into behaviour of a sexual nature. There was one time he'd caught the daughter, Beverly, staring at him when she was a teenager, which had unnerved him, but he'd soon forgotten about it.

He knew the girl had suffered at school, had listened to the parents more than once arguing about what they should do about their unpopular child, and took pity on her when she'd left her educational tormentors behind. She was something of a computer whizz kid, and he'd paid her more than it was worth when she'd sorted out his computer problem. She worked at the school now, and he wondered if her salary was enough to help her parents with their financial issues.

He finished the bagel and took the rest of the coffee and the apple pie back to the book store. He'd finish his lunch there and plan for meeting Evie Church again.

Then she wouldn't be a problem anymore.

22 STRANGE DAYS

Jack went into the shop and towards his desk at the rear. Somebody told him when he first opened the business, he should have the desk at the front to stop people from facing the temptation to steal from him, but he preferred being away from the front. If someone walked in with a gun, which was always possible, then it would be easy to nip out the back; and he kept the few valuable books he had left there.

He settled into his seat and finished the coffee. He wondered if the place would be as busy in the afternoon - not that it would ever be as full as he needed it to be - as he refreshed the news on the computer. The latest chatter claimed Evie was still at the station where the police held her brother. The online anger was growing, and Jack was happy at that. He'd decided what to do and was reaching for a new browser tab to access his email when his phone rang.

It vibrated in his hand as he removed it from his pocket. The happiness generated by Evie's continuing problems had evaporated as soon as he heard the ringtone of *Don't Fear the Reaper*. He couldn't remember the last time he'd gotten a call which hadn't been bad news. He looked at the number, and his heart lifted a little when he saw it was from his agent. He'd met the woman only once, in New York two weeks ago, and she'd scared the shit out of him. She was taller and bigger than Jack, but it wasn't her physical presence which bothered him; she was more aggressive than a killer shark. He knew a writer needed a literary agent who could stand up to the big publishing companies and their editors to succeed in the publishing world. Still, he also understood if she ever found out what a fraud he was, she'd eat him up and spit him out in one go.

She'd glared at the restaurant staff during the meeting, glowered at the other customers, and peered so deep inside him, he thought she'd see the small boy cowering behind his heart with the words "thief" and "liar" tattooed on to his head. At the end of the meeting, she'd shaken his hand and told him to get ready to be rich and famous. His legs wobbled like jelly when he walked away. They'd had a couple of email conversations since, one of which was to sign his contract with her, and he'd had to keep patient and not blurt out how frantic he was for an advance or any early payment for the novel.

For the book which isn't mine.

And now she was ringing him. He knew it wouldn't be good. Bits of the bagel gurgled at the bottom of his gut, swimming through a glut of sugar and coffee. He had a desperate need to go to the toilet, but he ignored it. He couldn't talk to her while he was there.

He accepted it would be terrible news as he took the call.

'Hello,' he whispered.

Her voice reverberated through his ears like a boom box on a street corner.

'I've got bad news for you, Jack.'

His tongue shrivelled in half, curling up inside his mouth and threatening to choke him. The bell rang over the door and someone entered the shop. He looked up, but couldn't see anything through the moisture clouding his eyes.

'What?'

The word stumbled out through his chattering teeth. There was silence down the other end, and he imagined his agent chewing on one of the twenty cigarettes she smoked every day.

'Not all of the big publishing houses have agreed to take part in the auction for your book. I can't tell you the name of the only hold-out, but they're arguing for worldwide rights. I told them to go away and have a lie down; only I wasn't that polite.' Her laugh was like a steam train chugging down the line and rolling into his head.

'What do you mean about an auction?' A spectral hand prodded a cold knife into the deepest parts of his brain. 'You said there was bad news. I'm confused.'

He hadn't meant to say the last two words out loud, but the pain in his head had left him with little control over his actions. It felt as if he was going to piss himself at any second. Footsteps echoed in the shop, but when he glanced up, he still couldn't see anyone.

She howled down the phone. 'Poor Jackie boy. Haven't you read the email I sent you this morning?' She didn't wait for a reply. 'I've been touting your masterpiece with the big publishers all week. An auction is when those interested - and they all are, believe me, even the hold-out - place secret bids for the right to purchase your book. I'm still ironing out the terms and conditions, such as what else they'll get apart from the hardback and American paperback rights, but I think the auction should be ready to go ahead this weekend. You'll need to get yourself here if you want to be in the room when they open the sealed bids.'

The constant thumping of his heart matched the pounding inside his head. There was going to be an auction for his book. And it was his. Fuck Evie Church. He'd do whatever was necessary to stop her messing up his life. He controlled his breathing and crossed his legs, uncaring about the noise in the shop. Whoever it was could take whatever they wanted since none of that mattered now.

'How much... how much do you think the book is worth?'

And how soon can I get some of the money?

The silence was golden, her laugh having evaporated somewhere in the ether. 'Well, Jackie boy, there are no guarantees, but with a novel this good, I'd expect nothing less than a couple of big ones.'

His heart sank and his legs wobbled. He wondered how long it would be before he passed out.

'Two thousand?' Disappointment washed out of him in waves. 'I thought it would be worth a bit more than that.'

Her cacophonous cackle threatened to snap the phone in half. 'Oh, Jackie boy; you may be a great writer, but you know jack shit about the value of what you have. It's probably a stretch to think we can get two million, but if you sign a three-book deal with one of them, and you will, that's the least I'd expect.'

'Two million?'

He staggered behind the desk and stumbled into the chair. The sound of a hardback thumping on to the floor barely troubled the dust floating around inside his skull.

Now, down the line, her voice was as angel's tears to his ears. 'There'll be much more than that once we factor in ancillaries like eBooks, audiobooks, film and TV rights, and other stuff. You're going to be a wealthy man, Jack. You better start getting used to it. And get working on the next book or two.'

She ended the connection before he could reply. He placed both hands on his chest in an attempt to stop his frazzled heart from jumping through his ribcage. A smile danced across his face.

I don't have to worry about writing more books; I've got ten of them sitting in my rejected folder on the computer.

'Do you have a first edition of *Dune*?'

He heard the voice before he saw its owner. Jack peered straight ahead into space. It was only as he looked down that he knew who'd spoken to him. A man in his forties, unshaven with grey flecked hair unused to a comb or a brush, gazed at him. He was Napoleonic in size, with a grin as wide as a coffee table.

'I'm sorry, I don't have that.'

He didn't need this now, his mind buzzing with the conversation he'd had with his agent, her words on a repeated loop, two million words which wouldn't disappear.

'Could you order it for me?'

'Go away.' It was only a few days before the auction. He had to sort out the problem with Evie Church before that.

'I'll pay good money for it.'

'Fuck off!'

Two years of frustration flew out of him like lava from a volcano. His cheeks burned, and he could only imagine what he looked like. The customer turned and sprinted from the shop. Jack followed him, locked the door, and put the CLOSED sign up. He didn't think he'd use the OPEN one ever again.

He pressed his cheeks against the window, his eyes

following the startled shopper as he ran across the road. Jack returned to the back and his computer. He opened his email account and checked his messages. There was the one his agent had mentioned with confirmation about the book auction. He read that at least six times. He scanned the spam mail and settled on a message from someone he'd never expected to hear from again. The text was short and to the point.

I'm sorry. I was wrong. I've missed you. I think we should get back together.

The shocks kept on coming that day. First, the possibility of earning two million dollars, and now the woman who'd broken his heart was back in touch. How could things get any better for him?

23 UNHAPPY GIRL

Astrid stood in the corridor with Evie opposite her. Detective Hicks stared at them both. Astrid watched as Evie's eyes grew large enough to obscure the barren part where her eyelashes should have been.

She lurched to her feet.

'You need to get my brother a proper lawyer.'

Hicks picked at his teeth, his focus drifting between them and back again. 'I don't need to do anything. Your brother's a grown man and can make his own decisions.'

Astrid held on to Evie to prevent her flailing at the policeman. Her arm was around Evie's shoulder, but her gaze bored into Hicks.

'You know he'll have no chance in court unless he gets professional help. You or someone better than you should convince him to stop messing about.'

He grinned and shook his head, nodding at the uniformed officer next to them.

'With the evidence we have, he has zero chance in court anyway.'

Evie fumed in Astrid's arms and it was a struggle to

keep her from exploding. Astrid needed to get her out of there as soon as possible. 'All you've got is his DNA, which would be there anyway considering it's his home.'

Detective Hicks started to turn from them, letting the officer know it was time to see them out.

'The killer didn't break into the house. Somebody with a key and the security code let those girls in, and then murdered them. If you can find someone with another key, and a motive, then get back to me.'

He walked away as Evie wriggled out of Astrid's grasp and stared at her. She guessed they were both thinking about the key in Evie's pocket. They followed the policeman out of the building and straight into the glare of TV cameras. Lights flashed around them while an eruption of noise shattered the air.

Astrid dragged Evie back into the station, glaring at the cop who'd led them outside. She pointed at Evie.

'She needs police protection.'

He shrugged. 'We don't have the resources for that.'

Astrid restrained herself. 'We can't return to that hotel.'

He shrugged again. 'It's not my problem.'

Evie stared at her phone while Astrid considered what to do next.

'It's okay; I know somewhere we can go.' Evie turned to the cop. 'Can you let us out of here through another exit, preferably one the media and the public can't access?'

He appeared to be about to shrug once more when Astrid stepped towards him. Her glare would have given him no doubt they weren't moving until he helped them.

'Sure,' he said. 'Follow me.' He took them through the station and into a lift. Then it was down two flights and out into the car park underneath the building. He pointed to an exit on the far side. 'That's your best bet.'

Then he left them there. The place was cold and littered with shadows. For once, Astrid was perplexed regarding what their next move would be, so she turned to Evie.

'You have somewhere we can go?'

'I got an email from a friend. I asked if we can stay with him for a little bit.'

'And?'

'He hasn't replied yet.'

It was Astrid's turn to shrug. 'It will have to do for now. I hope it's not far.'

She set off for the exit, Evie walking next to her. Astrid shielded her eyes from the sun as she reached the other side. She bade Evie wait while she checked outside, peering around the corner to see nothing but a road and an industrial estate opposite.

'You stop here while I get the rental car.'

'My friend's house is about a thirty-minute walk from here. We should be okay. I've been away for seven years, so I doubt anyone will recognise me. I don't know how everyone turned up at the hotel.'

Astrid stepped on to the pavement. 'Someone there probably tipped off the media, and then it ended up on the internet. Then chaos followed.' They strode together from the station, Astrid's gaze switching everywhere to make sure they were safe. 'What I don't understand is why you were outside in the first place.' She tried to keep the frustration from her voice.

Cars hissed by as they picked up a brisk pace.

'I wanted some fresh air. Apart from the occasional wasted afternoon in the garden, I haven't spent much time outside in the last seven years. I'm sorry I didn't tell you what I was doing.'

Some bloke shouted at them from his car. Astrid didn't worry, realising it wasn't someone who recognised them, only a lout shouting at two women in the street.

'It doesn't matter now. We need to concentrate on getting you to this safe place and then letting me get on with proving your brother's innocence.'

Of which I've been doing a sterling job so far.

Evie stopped and grabbed Astrid's arm. 'He won't change his mind about representing himself; he's super stubborn.'

'That doesn't matter if I can't find out who killed those girls.'

They peered at each other for a brief second before moving again.

'I agree,' Evie said.

'So where are we going?'

'Do you remember yesterday when I dragged you into that bookshop?'

A lot had happened since then, but Astrid did remember. 'Of course; is that where we're headed?'

'Not to the bookshop. I've been corresponding with the owner for about a year. I've asked him if we can stay at his house.'

Astrid tried to get her bearings as they walked, using the police station's location and where they were in relation to the main street with that bookshop halfway down it.

'We're going the wrong way.'

She stopped Evie and stared across the road towards the dilapidated looking industrial estate. Evie put a hand to her cheek.

'Oh. I think seven years away has confused my sense of direction.'

Astrid took out her phone. 'I'll get a taxi to take us to the hotel and drop you off around the corner. Hopefully, most of the crowd will have left by now. I'll get your bag and my rental car. Then I'll take you to the bookshop owner's place.'

'What will you do then?'

'I'm going to check out those woods at the back of your family's house. Whoever killed those girls must have met them there, or at least known they'd be there.'

She dialled the taxi number as she spoke. They'd walked about half a mile from the station, and she hoped it would be a good enough description for the driver to find them.

'I want to go with you.'

'It's too dangerous, Evie. I'll do my job better, and you'll help your brother if you stay inside and out of the public eye.'

The phone connected to the other end and she spoke to the taxi company. She gave the directions as well as she could; then they waited.

The wind howled around them as cars and trucks sped by and the stink of asthmatic exhausts filled the air. They moved from the edge of the road, Astrid searching for somewhere comfortable for both of them to sit, but having to settle for an emaciated grass verge littered with discarded food wrappers and old newspapers.

Evie gazed across the road. 'The steelworks closed down not long before I went into self-imposed exile. A lot of jobs vanished with it, and not only at the plant. There was a huge amount of businesses and people relying on the extended supply chain. I don't think the town's economy has recovered since.'

Astrid pulled at her nose in an attempt to squeeze out the aroma of motorised vehicles with not much luck. The ground under her hands was dirty and cold.

'Some people always do well out of economic chaos.'

'You mean like my brother?'

'I have no idea what he does for a living.'

'Do you think it might be somebody he met through work who's done this to him?'

'He's made an enemy somewhere. People don't go to this amount of trouble if it isn't personal. Do you know anybody who hates Adam this much?'

'Someone who hates him so much, they'd murder two innocent girls? No, I can't think of anyone like that.'

There was a mixture of anger and frustration in her voice. Astrid decided to change the conversation.

'Did you bring any medication with you from the home?'

'You mean for my mood changes?'

'I mean for anything you feel you might need.'

Evie stood as a taxi approached them. 'Exercise is the best medication. Now let's get back to the hotel.'

They got into the car and Astrid gave the driver directions. It was a fifteen-minute journey, the two of them getting out around the corner from the hotel. The driver didn't appear to recognise Evie, and Astrid settled for that.

They stood outside an apparently deserted garage.

'I'll be in and out as quick as possible. What do you want from your room?'

'There's a bag on the bed with my spare clothes, plus my toiletries in the bathroom. That's all I need. Are you going to keep your room there?'

Astrid considered it. 'I will for now, in case I have to stay somewhere away from you.'

Evie grinned at her. 'Are you getting sick of me already?'

She ignored the jab. 'The more I question people about

the whereabouts of the girls before they died, the likelier it will be I'll annoy several of them. It might be best to keep you distant from that and me.'

Evie gave her the room key.

Astrid wasn't happy with it, but she left Evie on her own. She walked as fast as she could without drawing attention to herself and headed to the hotel. There was no crowd outside this time, only a few stragglers hanging around. She stepped into the building, and the reception was empty as she ran upstairs, past her floor and to Evie's room.

She put the key in the door and opened it. The bag was in front of her. Astrid grabbed it and went to the bathroom, snatching Evie's things and stuffing them into the bag. She left as quickly as she'd entered, rushing down without bothering to go to her room. She'd return later when she was satisfied Evie was safe with the bookseller.

Her car was across the road. She threw the bag into the boot and drove to where she'd left Evie.

But Evie was gone.

24 THE CHANGELING

Beverly spent the rest of the morning holed up inside her office. The hustle and bustle of the school went by outside, and she didn't notice, never thought about who was in charge while Conway was absent; didn't care who would be in control when she was gone for good.

She browsed websites for the latest developments regarding the Glick murders and Adam Church. The natives were somewhat restless and it made her smile, although she didn't know what to make of Evie Church's dramatic return to town. She read the reports of the incident outside the hotel, watched the video several times, and perused all the social media chatter about the event and the Church family, and was still in a quandary as to how the sister's reappearance could benefit her.

Beverly scanned through the photos posted on the web of Evie. There were a few blurry ones from the morning before everything went to shit. Apart from that, the latest one was from seven years ago, a snapshot from before the girl had volunteered to take up the help from those friendly people at Shady Acres. And now there was lots of talk as to why she did that, with reams of analysis on the state of her mental health from those who didn't know her, who'd never met her, and who were no experts in the field. It hadn't taken long before many put two and two together and came up with five.

Beverly logged the current popular themes: Evie went into residential care because her brother was abusing her, or she knew he was harming others, or they were both psychopaths sharing the same genetic disorder. Some internet posters even decided it was likely to be a combination of all three theories.

She was unsure of what to think. She was the same age as Evie, had gone to the same school, was in the same year group, and they were near neighbours, but their paths rarely crossed once they went to high school. They were both outcasts, but for entirely different reasons. Mother and Father Church's fundamentalist religious beliefs meant they stuck to their own little community, and this followed for the kids.

And then there were the reasons why Beverly was a pariah at school. Things she didn't want to think about now. She continued to stare at the old photos of Evie and pondered how she fitted into Beverly's evolving plans for Conway and the rest of the town. Maybe Conway would be the last of it before she'd leave for fresh pastures.

She opened a different web browser and typed in a new search option: "Murder Capitals of the US." If someone asked later, she'd say it was research on where not to move for her next job. It was, in fact, for the opposite reason she wanted the information. The nervous joy she experienced from her plans for Conway, plus the satisfaction she got from framing Church for the Glick girls, not to mention the pleasure she still had from the touch of her fingers squeezing the life from them, had led to the inescapable truth she had to deliver death regularly to feel alive. If she was going to kill and keep on killing, she needed to do it somewhere she could blend in; Eureka Falls was far too small for her future projects.

Beverly clicked on the Wikipedia link for a list of cities by murder rate and scrolled down it. The information was five years out of date, but it would do. The first American city mentioned was St Louis, with more than two hundred recorded murders a year. It was nothing compared to Cape Town's impressive two and a half thousand, but she had no intention of moving to South Africa. Baltimore, New Orleans, and Detroit made up the four US cities on the list of fifty across the world.

She closed the link and clicked on another for more recent statistics, the *Top Thirty Murder Capitals of America Report*. It was a diverse data sample with different parameters and made for exciting reading. She'd always assumed Chicago was the murder capital of the US, having frequently heard that from the media and various politicians, but, according to the data on the screen, Chicago's murder rate was nowhere near the nation's worst. On a per-capita basis, murders per one hundred thousand residents, the city regularly experienced fewer killings than places whose murder rates got far less national attention, like Kansas City, Missouri, or Cleveland.

Her brain sucked in the information as she scanned half a dozen different reports, considered the analysis from academics, researchers, and law enforcement organisations, all of which came to the same conclusion: the murder rate in the US was declining.

Well, we can't have that.

She closed all the browsers and shut the computer. The

digital clock on the wall crawled over to midday, and her guts growled in anticipation. Because of her excitement this morning, she hadn't eaten any breakfast or brought anything with her for lunch. The thought of getting something from the canteen made her stomach shrivel.

Beverly got up from the desk and looked around the office. There was no point in staying there all day. She had to leave to eat and was impatient to use the Trojan to access Conway's computer, and she couldn't do that in school.

She locked the office and went to the reception. Kids were already hurrying across the building to get to the terrible food provided for them. Or maybe they'd become so desensitised to what was good to eat they truly believed cardboard pizza, soggy fries, and meat which most other countries wouldn't touch with a bargepole because of health and safety issues were the height of gourmet cooking.

Beverly laughed as she approached the desk. Most of these kids wouldn't be able to spell the word gourmet, never mind understand what it meant.

'Are you popping out for lunch, Ms Shaw?'

Jo Collier, barely out of school herself, was on reception, and Beverly found her formality somewhat irritating. She put a hand over her mouth and rolled her eyes.

'I'm not feeling too good, Jo. I'm going home for the rest of the day. I expect I'll be okay for tomorrow.'

She wouldn't want to miss how the school would react once the news of Conway's death hit. She already imagined what her sorrowful face would look like. An adult she didn't recognise pushed through the front door. She assumed it was a parent or guardian as they burst into tears. Jo gave Beverly a pained look.

'Don't worry, Ms Shaw; I'll deal with Mrs Hartman. You take care of yourself, and I'll see you tomorrow.'

Beverly nodded and slipped out of the building. In less than a minute, she was heading home. She stopped at a drive-through on the way and ordered the largest burger and fries possible. She was desperate to get into Conway's computer but knew it would be impossible to concentrate if she didn't satisfy the other urge rushing through her.

She ate across the road from her parents' coffee shop. Beverly wasn't sure how she felt about them. For most people, she either had indifference, which was the majority, or pure hatred, which was a significant minority. But for Mother and Father, it was somewhere in between, and she didn't know how to define it. She didn't love them. She'd never loved anybody, but she also thought of them with the occasional smile on her face, and she was never sure why.

It's probably because I have them to thank for this life.

It had taken her a long time to be grateful for her existence, and that only happened when she understood how to be happy. She was aware, from experience, that many people struggled with contentment in life and how lucky she'd been to have her epiphany. If not, she'd probably have fallen into the traps most got stuck in with the search for happiness, the delusion that excess is the panacea for what ails them. It didn't matter what the excess was: booze, sugar, sex, drugs, exercise, power, shopping, rock and roll, whatever; none of it was the answer.

Control of desire, that was the answer for her. Once she realised her passion was for revenge, it became a simple process of numbers. She could either ignore it, be consumed by it, or control it. Ignoring the desire was impossible; only a few were capable of that, maybe monks or hermits. Most were obsessed by their passions or other people's, and it was an easy trap to fall into. It would bring pleasure, but, she understood, ultimately, there would be nothing inside you but an emptiness which could never be filled. It would be a vacuum that would eat at you until the day you died. It would be a toss-up as to which would go first, the mind or the body.

So Beverly dedicated every waking hour to identifying her desire and controlling it. It wasn't long before she understood that meant deleting it from her body, like letting gas out of an overfilled balloon. If she didn't, like the rapidly expanding balloon, she knew she'd explode.

Inflicting pain was the way to do it. She finished the burger, her stomach bloated with processed cheese and bits of dead cow, and peered out of the car at the shadows of her parents struggling to make ends meet behind the window over the road. She often wondered if they believed they were living the American Dream. She was convinced she was.

A newspaper blew across the street, its headline shouting out GLICK GIRLS' KILLER ARRESTED. She smiled at its inaccuracies. The sisters weren't her first kills, but they were the ones who'd finally quenched her desire. Quenched, but not eradicated, not that she'd expected them to, which is why Conway had to go tonight.

Beverly turned on the engine and drove away, the ghostly silhouettes of her parents fading in the background.

Astrid's reflexes kicked into gear without her leaving the car. She scanned everything nearby, seeing the homeless woman pushing a trolley piled with bags, the over-turned pram and the guy on a mountain bike, until the stray dog caught her attention. Only it wasn't a stray, but running towards its owner, a large man who was dragging Evie next to him. As he bundled her into the back of the vehicle, Astrid was already driving towards them. At her speed, she'd catch them before they pulled away. But did she want to?

Maybe this abductor has something to do with the Glick murders?

Which meant Evie was in danger. Yet if others were involved, then it also meant Astrid could follow this car to them. It was a risk, but was it one worth taking? She relaxed and eased the pressure on her foot, letting the car slow to stay a safe distance behind them.

What if there's someone else in the car and they're hurting Evie now?

Not if they've got a dog with them. It was an irrational

rationalisation, but she didn't fight against it. She followed them across the river and away from the residential areas, past a long barren field where horses searched for something to eat and into what appeared to be an abandoned industrial park. It had taken no more than fifteen minutes as they stopped near a large factory. Astrid parked outside the gates, hoping she was well out of sight.

Two men and the mutt got out and the bloke she'd seen earlier dragged Evie into the open. The men talked to each other while the dog barked, and Evie squirmed in the arm of the big guy. Then he let her go and she spoke to him.

Why doesn't she run?

Astrid watched them chatter away as if they were old friends, surprised to see Evie scrunch over to pat the dog on the nose. Astrid scratched her head as they entered the factory. Her confusion lasted no more than twenty seconds before she got out of the car and followed them into the industrial park and up to the factory gate. The hound stopped barking as Astrid stepped inside.

There was a long corridor ahead of her, with offices on each side. They were either empty or contained a single upturned chair or desolate table as if the former occupants had recently left.

The sound of voices dragged her to the end of the corridor and a wide entrance. She hung back in the shadows and peered inside, seeing Evie hugging the dog and surrounded by six people. Two were the blokes from the car, another man and two women she didn't recognise, but one she did: the girl from outside the hotel who'd pulled the gun on Evie.

She was ready to rush forward when they bent their knees to Evie. Astrid restrained the gulp in her throat and steadied her hand against the wall. The cold concrete flaked onto her fingers, and bits of it dribbled across her leg. She shook it off as she strode towards the strange scene ahead of her.

'What's going on, Evie?'

All of them jumped with a mixture of shock and suspicion aimed at her. The mutt stepped forward and growled, until Evie pulled it back.

'Down, Chief. She's a friend.'

Astrid kept one eye on the hound and the other on the group. 'Do you know these people?'

Evie's eyebrows narrowed as she controlled the dog. 'I recall Chief from my time in the church.' She glanced at the men and women around her. 'I was too young to remember most of them, and Josie was younger than me.' She stared at the girl who'd threatened her life. 'She's still younger than me, but that's why I didn't recognise her at the hotel.'

The questions stacked up in Astrid's head. 'Josie tried to kill you.'

Evie continued to peer at the petrified young woman. 'I don't think she meant me any harm. She's just scared.'

'Scared of what?'

Evie moved forward and put one hand on Astrid's arm. 'She's scared of the same things we all are: of loneliness, of not being loved, of rejection, of ridicule. And that's just the start. They had an environment which protected them, but it's gone now, and they're confused.'

Astrid analysed each of them, recognising what Evie was speaking about and understanding what this was.

'Are these what's left of your parents' congregation?'

She nodded. 'After the accident, after they died, there was no one strong enough to hold it together. Most drifted off to other churches, some abandoned their beliefs, and this is what remains.'

'Six people and a dog?' Astrid didn't know whether to laugh or cry. She watched Josie retreat into the shadows. 'Did she come to the hotel to ask you to lead the church?'

Evie leant into her so the others wouldn't hear her words. 'Can you imagine such a thing? I'd laugh, but I don't want to upset them.'

Astrid addressed the biggest bloke. 'Did you go to her brother first?'

His face was grim enough to give young kids nightmares. 'There were more of us then. He laughed in our faces and slammed the door on us. But now we know why.' The group mumbled between themselves.

'Adam didn't kill the Glick girls.' There was a fire in Evie's eyes Astrid hadn't seen before. 'And I'm not leading your church. My parents funded the website for a decade, so you've got plenty of time to attract more members without me.'

She turned her back on them and stormed away. Astrid lingered there for a second, wondering if one of the adults was the drunk driver who'd killed Evie's parents. Then she put the thought from her mind and followed her outside. She found her next to the car, smoking a cigarette. Astrid coughed as if she'd caught her doing something illegal.

'Where did you get that?'

Evie took two drags before throwing it down. 'It's been in my pocket with the matches for seven years.' She held the box up. 'They still work, but it tastes terrible after all this time.'

Astrid kicked the butt into the gutter. 'They're all terrible, no matter how old they are.'

Just like people.

Jack was struggling to process Conway's message when another unlikely email arrived. He read it three times, each time his heart skipping more beats than he thought possible.

Evie Church wanted to stay with him.

Only for a short while, she'd typed.

The wind rattled the door at the front of the shop. He held up his hand, and his skin shimmered as if it was translucent. The thump of his chest appeared to echo through his veins, the blood sparkling like a disco ball. He clasped his hands together and squeezed as hard as he could. He placed his fingers on the keyboard, waiting for them to stop shaking so he could type his reply. His eyes burnt into the screen, his mind turning over the words to use. He had to keep it simple.

You can stay as long as you want, Evie.

There was no need for elaboration, no mention of their previous correspondence, no talk of her writing, no comments on her brother, no lamentation for the Glick girls, no questions about why she wanted to stop with him or what happened at the hotel that morning. He added the address and his phone number, and then sent it.

He slipped back into the chair, trying to relax, but finding every muscle straining against an unseen pressure emanating from his head.

What about the woman she was with in the bookshop yesterday?

In all his nervous excitement, he'd forgotten about her. Evie hadn't mentioned her, didn't ask if two of them could stay with him, so he dismissed it as inconsequential. Perhaps she was from the residential home, a nurse or a carer. He started to panic again. What if the woman knew about Evie's writing and the book she'd sent him?

He was considering these questions as he received another message.

Thank you so much, Jack. Astrid is taking me to the hotel for my stuff, and then we'll come straight over. Is that okay?

Astrid was her name, and they were both coming to his house. What could he say? Should he ask if he needed to make up two beds? What if this Astrid wasn't a staff member from Shady Acres but Evie's lover? She was a bit older, but nothing to raise eyebrows at. Would it be clumsy if he asked? Or maybe offensive. Even worse, how would he get hold of Evie's phone to delete his message to her if the other woman was present?

The room span around him, hundreds of book covers stabbing at his eyes. A young girl drawing a question mark on the moon turned to him and wiggled her finger in his direction. A silhouetted hand stretched out a dark rose to him, which evaporated as he went to grab it. A cat in a hat shuffled towards him, its belly growing larger by the second before its stomach exploded and a murder of crows flew straight for his face. Jack raised his hands to swat them away, then realised it was all a product of his overexcited imagination. His fingers trembled so he slapped them on to the desk and let the pain flow through him. His skin darkened as his thoughts stopped fluctuating and gathered into some form of sanity.

He typed his reply.

That's fine, Evie. Give me twenty minutes to get home from the bookshop.

He was about to hit send when he thought of something else.

Have you and your friend had anything to eat?

Yes, that was informal enough to garner more information regarding the position of this Astrid. He didn't want to have to kill two people, but would if left with no choice. Her reply was instantaneous.

Don't worry; we'll get food on the way. See you in about an hour.

And thanks again!

She'd added a smiley face at the end of the text. He gazed at it, hoping it would make him feel good, but it didn't. Things appeared to be working out in his favour, but years of bad luck made him hesitant. He puffed out his cheeks and pulled in his chest. He left the bookshop and wondered if he'd ever go back to it.

He glanced into Shaws' coffee shop as he strode down the street. He was pleased to see they had several people inside, murder tourists he guessed, and they were making a roaring trade for once. Once he'd got everything sorted with the book and dealt with Evie and her friend, he'd send an anonymous message to the council recommending the regular sacrifice of children to improve the financial security and longevity of the town. They could call it the Wicker Man Law.

As he went, he hardly recognised himself in the reflections in the shop windows, the smile consuming the whole of his face. Perhaps that Wicker Man Law could be the basis of a short story. He felt the creativity flowing through him, his feet appearing to lift off the ground. In his mind, there was no consideration the novel was anybody else's but his. Evie would lie about it, but that was because she was mentally unwell. There was no hesitation in his thoughts, no deliberation of what was the right thing to do.

The journey home disappeared in a flash, so much so he shaved at least five minutes off his usual time. There were no vehicles and no people. Bits of trash and paper tumbled around the street as if thrown from one side to the other by an invisible giant. The trees groaned as he marched past them, with leaves drifting to the ground through the breeze. The rain came as he strode up the steps, and the water lashed against his skin as he put the key in the lock and stumbled inside.

Nature dripped off him and on to the carpet as he pulled the curtains back to peer out of the window; there was no sign of them yet. He picked up books and magazines and dropped them on the first empty shelf he found. The kitchen sink was piled with dirty dishes and cutlery. He turned on the water and covered them with lemon-fresh washing-up liquid as he cleaned them and left them to dry.

He ran upstairs to tidy the spare bedroom and ensure the bathroom was clean. He wiped toothpaste from the basin and dumped half a pint of bleach down the toilet. He sprayed everywhere with an alpine air freshener. Once he'd done that, he threw hot water on his face and peered at the stranger staring back at him from the mirror. He couldn't remember the last time he'd wanted to make a good impression on anybody.

Jack sat on the edge of the bath and put his head in his hands. Should he think of a plan to get Evie's phone from her or play it by ear when they arrived? He was considering an answer and coming up with nothing when the doorbell rang.

He nearly twisted his ankle as he sprang to his feet. He took the stairs two at a time, his elbows bouncing off the walls and sending stabs of static agony through his arms. He had to stop himself from falling into the door as he reached the bottom. The mirror on the wall reflected the craziness in his eyes, and he was considering ignoring the bell when someone banged on the door.

'Jack, it's me, Evie.'

He sucked in his chest, took in a massive gulp of air, and opened up. She threw herself at him, her hair damp from the rain, hugging him around the waist so hard, he thought he'd faint. She let go before it became embarrassing for both of them. The woman with her, Astrid, glanced outside and shut the door. She stared at Jack.

'I don't think anyone followed us.' She smiled at him. 'Evie needs to stay here until the frenzy calms down in the town. Is that okay with you, Mr Kennedy?'

'Of course, it is, Ms...?'

She held out her hand. 'My name is Astrid Snow. Thank you for your hospitality, Mr Kennedy.'

He shook her hand. 'Call me Jack.' Her fingers were wet.

She let go of him and all three of them stood there in the narrow corridor listening to the rain splattering against the house. Evie dropped her bag onto the floor.

'Can I get dry and change my clothes?'

'Absolutely,' he said. 'The bathroom is at the top of the stairs, and I've made the spare bedroom up for you next to it.' He turned to Astrid. 'I can make a bed for you on the sofa in the living room, Ms Snow.'

She smiled at him and shook her head. 'There's no need for that, Jack; I'll be using the hotel. And call me Astrid.'

'No flirting between you two,' Evie said as she grabbed her bag and ran upstairs.

He looked at Astrid and felt the heat swell through his face.

'Ignore her attempts at humour,' Astrid said and didn't wait for an invite to move into the living room. He laughed nervously and followed her inside. She walked to the window and peered out of it. He hadn't realised how tall she was until he watched her standing there. There was an assertiveness about her which unnerved him. And that accent froze his bones every time she spoke.

'Are you British?' He didn't know what else to say. She continued to peer outside.

'I'm English.'

He moved further into the living room, suddenly feeling like a stranger in his own home.

'Is this something to do with her brother?'

She turned towards him. 'Did you see what happened outside the hotel this morning?'

Her words cut into his stability, his legs threatening to snap underneath him. He put his hand on the arm of the sofa and dropped into the seat. His voice was the opposite of hers, quivering as he spoke.

'Yes, that was terrible. The news said someone tried to kill Evie because of what her brother did to those poor girls.'

Astrid moved towards him, standing alongside a set of shelves reaching the ceiling and covered in dusty books.

'Adam is innocent until the law proves otherwise.'

'Of course, I'm sorry.' His hand trembled against his leg. 'I'm just worried about her.'

She fixed her eyes on Jack, unmoving and making him even more uncomfortable. 'How did you two meet?'

He grabbed the edge of the sofa, his nails digging into the material. 'She contacted me through the bookshop website. We struck up an online friendship, but I hadn't met her until yesterday.'

'She told me she sent you some of her writing to get your opinion.'

Fuck, fuck, fuck.

His fingers cut into the sofa's cheap fabric, feet squirming against the carpet and kicking up dust which invaded his nostrils. He lifted his arm to prevent a sneeze, catching his teeth against his flesh to stop his hand from shaking.

'Yes, yes, she did.'

Don't mention what she sent; she might not know of the novel.

Astrid grabbed a book from the shelf, a tattered copy of *Do Androids Dream of Electric Sheep?* She flicked through the pages, with one eye on him. A mournful synthesiser droned through his brain.

'And what was your professional opinion?'

The noise increased inside his skull. Was the professional bit her having a jab at him?

'I tried to give her the best feedback I could. Her work exhibits plenty of potential.'

He waited for another question, aware she was interrogating him. Before she could speak, Evie bounded into the room. She'd changed into a clean shirt and new pair of jeans. She flopped on to the sofa near him.

'I'll have to buy more clothes when this is all over.'

He didn't know what to say. The whole situation confused him to the point he wanted a drink again. He knew he'd be fine if it were just him and Evie, but this British woman increased his unease by the second. He was pondering how to get rid of her when she did it for him.

'Okay, Evie, I want you to stay here; don't go out and don't speak to anyone. I'm sure Jack will keep you entertained until I return.' She headed towards the exit.

'What will you do while I'm here?' Evie said.

'I'm going to interview some witnesses,' Astrid said as she left.

Stability returned to Jack's body and brain as he turned to Evie. She had her phone in her hand. 'What's your Wi-Fi password, Jack?'

He smiled and blew an invisible kiss to Lady Luck. 'Give me your cell, Evie; it'll be easier that way.'

27 DEAD CATS, DEAD RATS

Astrid parked a few yards from the Church house. At first glance, the street appeared empty, but there was no telling how many morbid onlookers might be hanging around the bushes for a sight of the sister of the alleged child murderer. She got her phone and brought up the research she'd saved earlier. Outside, a slight drizzle peppered the car. She didn't mind the rain. It would probably keep the tourists away.

Elm Street was nearby, and the irony of the name wasn't lost on her. She ignored it and rechecked the details. There were two dozen houses there, twelve on either side, from number one at the top to twenty-four at the bottom, the Church house. She brought up the list of occupiers she'd found in the land registry. The Glick family wasn't on it. Their house was on the street parallel to Elm.

Astrid zipped up her jacket and stepped into the rain. The droplets caressed her skin and settled her thoughts. She walked down Elm Street to the end. Once there, she turned right and into Maple Street. The Glick house was halfway down, but she didn't go to it, her gaze following the route from the house and then towards the trees. She switched back on to Elm, but there was no access to the woods at that end. The only way in was down the path separating the Church house and number twenty-two next door.

She rechecked the details on her phone. Number twenty-two belonged to Mr and Mrs Range. She gave Maple Street a last look, and then headed up to that track. The rain increased from a trickle to more of a drum beat. She trudged through expanding puddles and reached the Church house after a few minutes. A dark cat ran across her route, dodging her as she splashed between the houses. When she neared the rear of the Church property and the dirt track into the trees began, she gazed at the basement where somebody had murdered the sisters.

The wind swept her hair across her face as she strode uphill towards the woods. She pushed the damp from her eyes. If the weather had been this bad on that day, she was sure the girls would have stayed at home. But who knew they regularly played in the trees looming ahead of her?

She stopped halfway up, turning around to observe the landscape. The back of the Church house reared up in front of her, its dark shadow casting a chill over everything. She glanced over the other homes. Either the killer had stumbled across the girls up there, or they knew they'd be in the woods that night.

Astrid reached into her mind, searching through the maps stored there, maps she'd used over the years as answers to difficult situations. It was a process she'd started as a kid to escape from the realities of her life. Those early maps always led her to a Disney Castle of joy and hope. Now, new ones formed in her head as she continued to the edge of the trees. She'd walked at a steady pace, probably quicker than the girls did that night, but they could have run. And the descent was likely faster than getting into the woods.

The walk was between three and four minutes. Why didn't somebody see them as they came down? Was it too dark? Unless someone stood along the path she'd taken, it was only from the houses on that side anyone would have seen the girls or what happened to them. Unless they hid inside the woods and peered down, but that was another issue. The police would have interviewed all the residents, so perhaps they did have some eyewitness reports. Hudson or Hicks, she couldn't remember which, had hinted at having more incriminating evidence against Adam, so perhaps that was it: witnesses from one or more of Adam's neighbours. She'd have to knock on all the doors when she got back down.

She picked up her pace and found shelter from the elements under the trees. She closed her eyes and remembered what it was like to be full of youth and innocence, imagined the Glick girls playing on this spot: Kay and Martha. Martha was the older, ten to her sister's nine years. Even as young kids, they'd have known their parents wouldn't want them in the woods on their own. They must have realised how dangerous it could be, especially once it got dark. And they definitely would have listened to warnings about talking to strangers.

She couldn't see any way the girls would leave the woods, go down the hill, enter the house, and then the basement with a stranger. They would have screamed blue murder. And if they had, some residents would have heard, and the police would be swamped with witnesses. It left her with only one conclusion. The murderer was someone the girls felt safe with.

Astrid peered through the trees, through the elements,

and down at the houses. It had to be somebody who lived on that street, who had access to the Church house.

'Somebody with access to Evie's key?'

She listened to the words drifting between the wind and the rain. She'd spoken them out loud to judge how likely that was. And it didn't seem likely at all. They would have to be a staff member at the home to have an opportunity to get that key, use it, then return it, and all without Evie noticing. It would take a lot of lucky breaks for that to happen.

No. Astrid was convinced it was an Elm Street resident who killed the Glick girls.

But murder wasn't the motivation. The killer hated Adam Church.

So why would someone hate him that much to do all of this? He must have made enemies somewhere, either at his work or through the S&M meetings. She needed to speak to Evie again, to delve deeper into their secrets. And then quiz Adam.

Whoever killed the Glick girls did it to get back at the Church family.

28 TAKE IT AS IT COMES

In his book *The Soul's Code*, James Hillman, Pulitzer nominee, Jungian psychologist, and best-selling author, states that individuals hold the potential for their unique possibilities inside themselves already, much as an acorn holds the pattern for an oak tree. It had taken Beverly a long time to realise this, but her road to Damascus had only happened three years ago, and nothing had been the same since.

It was an accident that brought about her revelation, a trip far from Eureka Falls and its constraints. Conway had forced her to go on teacher training sessions for her subject speciality, information systems and computer technology. So, she'd found herself alone in New York, bored out of her mind and scared of her shadow every time she stepped out of the hotel room.

Then some of the other participants of the three-day course convinced her to go for a drink in a bar near to the hotel. Beverly wasn't a prude, she'd drunk alcohol before, but the idea of having to converse with other people made her nauseous. But then fate intervened. Someone had left

Hillman's book in the hotel, and she devoured it over the first two nights she stayed in and ordered room service. So by the time she got the invite on the third night, she thought, *What's the worst that could happen?*

And then the worst did happen, or at least it nearly did. She drank far too much, and none of the others noticed when she stumbled into the dark backstreet between the bar and the hotel and spilt her guts. She could still smell it now, sitting at home in her bedroom preparing to use the Trojan she'd placed on Conway's laptop. The air smelt of the city, of gasoline and street food, of smoke and rotten vegetables, as her stomach threatened to crack in half in that gloom-filled alley.

The noise in her head was so much, she didn't hear the footsteps behind her, but she felt the hand grab her long hair and pull her back. And she experienced the sharp stab of pain as her attacker tossed her into the far wall, as her shoulder hit the concrete and she stumbled to the ground. He said something to her, obscenities and threats she couldn't quite make out with the freight train steaming through her skull.

But she heard his laugh and the sound of him unzipping his trousers. He grabbed her again as her hand reached into the dirt and touched the broken bottle. And Beverly found something else as she clutched on to the glass, discovering the bravery to thrust the cracked edge deep into his throat.

She stepped back as he crashed to the ground, clutching at the spot where the blood flowed from him. She waited for someone to come running into the alley to help him, but they didn't, and she didn't either. Beverly stood there and watched him die a slow, agonising demise. And that's when her revelation came.

She'd enjoyed what she'd done. There was no guilt or

shame, only the greatest joy she'd ever felt. There'd always been darkness inside her, and she knew this had always been thoughts of murder and death, but she'd confined them to fantasies which would never come true.

But they had in that small alley in a big city.

Once he'd stopped squirming, she cleaned her finger-prints from the bottle and dumped it down a drain. Then she wiped the vomit from her chin and returned to the hotel. She got little sleep that night, her mind full of the mantra which changed her life for the better.

Transfer the pain.

NOW HERE SHE was three years later, clicking on the connection between her computer and Conway's, all thanks to the virus she'd left there. She hadn't known it at the time in that alley, but transferring the pain meant more than inflicting violence on others, it meant making certain people pay for what they'd done to her. There were many of them in her thoughts, frequently in her mind, but Conway was always near the top of the list. But after tonight, she'd be able to scrub her name from the paper.

The laptop hummed as she accessed Conway's desktop and proceeded to scan through her files. She searched for recently used documents and discovered two databases, opening the one named *School Staff*. It contained over two hundred entries, and it took her an hour to flick through most of them. The file headings were numerous, but the four main ones were: Taught, Pastoral, Management and Leadership. As she scanned through them, it dawned on her that it was a record of those Conway had worked with or taught during her years at the school.

Why keep all this data?

She soon answered the question when she read the information in more detail. Conway's unofficial school database contained her observations of others, and none of them were complimentary. Beverly scrolled down the list and stopped at the entry for Mr Brooks, the previous principal before Conway.

His incompetence knows no levels it can't sink to. He's failed this school for ten years, and I don't know of one pupil who has a good word to say about him. Most of the kids and the staff laugh at him behind his back. He arrived at school today smelling like a brewery. He wore a suit which appeared to have shrunk in the wash, the sleeves a quarter way up his arms, the jacket tight around his chest, the pants on his legs so high, you could see he had no socks on. Everything was the wrong size for him: his clothes, this world, and his personality.

Yet that was kind compared to some of the other entries. She found the latest data point from two days ago concerning a fifteen-year-old pupil, Joe Jackson. Beverly knew him as a troubled child with a problematic family background, and Conway was scathing in her observations.

The boy has a world-class case of acne, with his face resembling a pizza gone wrong. The other kids tease him mercilessly, but he deserves it for being so stupid. He's an inspiration for idiots everywhere. He's proof that evolution can go in reverse. I foresee a future career for Joe cleaning toilets or selling himself for crack cocaine in a dark street somewhere far from Eureka Falls.

She browsed through more of the records, discovering amongst the insults for the pupils that Conway would predict how she thought their lives would progress.

The last time I saw a face like hers, it was on a slab in the morgue. She's guaranteed to have four kids before she gets out of her teens.

The boy makes me believe in reincarnation. Nobody can be as stupid as that in one lifetime. He'll be flipping burgers for the rest of his life.

Beverly pushed the laptop from her legs and on to the bed. Did she care why Conway kept such a warped collection of records? No. But did she need to see if there was an entry for her in the database?

She reached into her memories and resurrected the one of her thrusting the broken bottle into the thug. This time, she imagined his blood gushing on to her hand, flowing over her in a torrent until she could no longer see her skin. Sitting on the bed, her imagination turning the chill in her chest to warmth covering her arm, she used the heat growing across her and grabbed the computer, pulling it towards her. She found her data entry in an instant.

Bev Shaw. A complete waste of space. All the other kids hate her, especially the girls. She smells like old potatoes and always comes to school wearing clothes her parents must have got from charity or dumpsters. She's as bright as a black hole and twice as dense. I can't see any boyfriends on the horizon, so even marriage won't save her from a future of drudge and misery. The lowest level of shop work might be her only saving grace. She'd be better off committing a crime and spending a long time in prison.

There was more to it, but she didn't read it because she'd picked up the laptop and thrown it on to the floor. The heat surged through her, transforming her blood into molten lava flowing into her skull. She was a kettle ready to boil over as she grabbed at the bed cover.

Fuck, fuck, fuck.

No, that wouldn't help.

Transfer the pain. Transfer the pain. Transfer the pain.

Yes, she had to transfer her pain, to move it into every part of Conway. But she needed the computer for that, and she'd just dumped it on to the carpet.

Fuck, fuck, fuck.

She jumped down, snatched the laptop into her chest, and cradled it like a child. The screen seemed fine and no strange noises were coming from it. She sucked in air to still her beating heart and returned to the bed. Conway's comments on her filled the monitor, so she closed the database. Then she opened the second one titled S&M. These records had nothing to do with the school and were peppered with links to photos and videos.

Why, Mrs Conway, what have you been up to?

She only needed to look through a few images and watch two clips to understand Conway's hobby outside of work. Beverly was no prude, but she nearly gagged on some of the things she saw.

Conway must have concealed a tiny camera on her to get the videos. It seemed a remarkable achievement considering most in the clips were as naked as when they were born. Beverly was about to close the clip when she saw something which stopped her hand, recognised somebody that made her gasp. In the background, beyond those squirming on the floor, a man stood there while someone off-screen whipped his chest and blood dripped from his flesh.

Adam. Adam Church.

She couldn't contain her joy as she copied the file on to her computer. She'd kill Conway tonight, there was no doubt to that. Then she'd release the video online, and with the police focused on that and the town in a frenzy, she was sure not many people would care about the school principal dying from an apparent suicide. There'd be no gunshots and no mess since she'd changed her mind on that. She had the pills ready to administer, only needing to return to the house and wait for Conway to appear.

When the video finished its download, she checked Conway's emails, happy to find a reply to the message she'd sent to Kennedy earlier. It was vomit-inducing in its content, but she didn't care what it said. She sent another email to him from the account.

Come to the house at midnight tonight. Don't drive here. Make sure no one sees you. I'll leave the back door unlocked. I can't wait to see you.

Her heart jumped when he replied within thirty seconds.

I can't wait either, my mistress.

Beverly grinned as she closed the screen. There'd be no need for the pills. Torturing Conway was on the agenda again.

And now she had someone to frame for the murder.

29 CRAWLING KING SNAKE

Jack needed to get Evie out of the house before Astrid returned. But how? They sat opposite each other in the kitchen, with her drinking the coffee he'd made while he sipped on a glass of water and wished it was stronger.

Don't worry. I'll have something later to celebrate.

How would he tempt her out and retrieve her cell? He didn't have time earlier, when he put his number into her contacts, to access her email and delete the message she'd sent him containing the copy of the book.

Evie smiled at him. 'I need to read some new books, proper ones I can hold in my hands. I mean, I like reading eBooks on the phone or the computer, but nothing beats feeling the paper in your fingers and staring at a real cover. Do you know what I mean, Jack?'

Her enthusiasm made him feel giddy. 'Absolutely, Evie, absolutely.'

'Great.' She finished her drink and stood. 'Can I turn on your TV? I want to see if there's anything new about Adam or the murders.'

'Sure. It's in the living room.'

She grinned at him and left the kitchen. He watched her go as he formulated a different plan. He followed her as she switched on the set and an advert for breakfast cereal sprang into life. It featured a song he recognised, but couldn't remember the band as cartoon elves and dragons jumped around on the screen as they ate something containing a year's worth of sugar.

Evie grimaced. 'This is terrible, really, really terrible.'

He sat opposite her. 'You don't like that breakfast cereal?'

She twisted her cheeks. 'No, it's not that. I've never eaten that crap. It always annoys me when bands or singers sell their music to advertising companies for shit like this.'

'I guess they have to make money some way.'

Evie shook her head. 'Songs carry emotional information, and some transport us back to a poignant event in our lives. I understand why a corporation would want to hitch a ride on the spell these songs cast and encourage us to buy soft drinks, underwear or breakfast cereals while we're in the trance. But artists who take money for ads poison and pervert their art. It reduces them to the level of a jingle, a word that describes the sound of change in your pocket, which is what the music becomes. Remember, when you sell your art for commercials, you're selling your audience as well.'

'I suppose so.' He didn't really care.

She turned to him. 'I mean, imagine you write a book or a set of books, and then someone comes along and wants to turn them into a TV show or a movie. No matter how faithful they say they'll be to your material, it won't be the same because it won't be what you wrote.'

'But it would allow you to spread your work, your creations, to a wider audience. That must be good, surely?'

'For your bank balance, yeah, that's about it. If I wanted to write for television or the movies, I'd produce scripts, wouldn't I, not novels.'

She doesn't deserve to have her name on this book. Just listen to the nonsense coming from her mouth.

'It would be nice to have the choice, though, don't you think?'

Evie slumped into the chair and her eyes sank into her cheeks. 'I guess I'll never find out now.'

Now. This was his chance. 'Would you like to see the comments the publisher made about your book?'

She sprang from the seat. 'Have you got them?'

'Yes, but not here. I printed them at the bookshop. I could take you there to read them if you like.'

He waited for her to say 'Why can't you print them here?' or 'Why can't I read them straight from the email?', but she didn't say either of those things or find any other reason to stay in the house.

She grabbed her jacket and grinned at him. 'What are we waiting for?'

DARKNESS ENGULFED the road when Jack opened the bookshop. He flicked on the light and considered what to do next. All the way there in the car, she'd gone on and on about how if agents or publishers didn't want her book, she'd publish *A Dark Heart in the Garden of Delights* independently. She followed him inside and he locked the door. The last thing he needed was someone to stumble in as he was killing her.

And he had to kill her. Just deleting the emails wouldn't work.

But how am I going to do it and make it look like an accident?

She gazed at him as he led her to the back of the shop, stepping over a leaflet for the upcoming school reunion.

'I'm not sure about the title, though. What do you think, Jack?'

He opened the fridge he kept behind the desk. 'Do you want a drink, Evie?'

Her shoulders shivered as she removed a hardback copy of Lee Child's *Killing Floor* from a shelf creaking under the weight of books stacked there.

'Do you have a beer? Now I've got my freedom again, I'm desperate to catch up for lost time.'

He nodded. 'There are a few bottles of Belgian lager a customer sent me from abroad at the back of the fridge. It might be a bit strong for you, though.' They'd been there since he'd hit the wagon three years ago.

She waved the Reacher novel at him. 'Nonsense, Jack. Pour it into a glass while I peruse your stock.'

Evie returned the hardback to where she'd found it and wandered through the shop, stretching out her arms and running her hands over every book she could. He got the bottles of beer and put them onto the desk near his computer. As she flicked through various volumes, Jack grabbed glasses from the shelf above his head, and then emptied the alcohol into them. Then he removed the phial of pills he'd brought from home, drugs which were illegal to buy in the US, but were easy to purchase on his trip to Eastern Europe two years ago. He'd bought them for his insomnia and never used them, until now.

He made sure Evie was engrossed in a book, crushed the pill between his fingers and dropped the Rohypnol into her beer. It fizzled, and then vanished into the liquid to be completely invisible when she returned carrying a paperback copy of *Milkman* by Anna Burns.

'I've been dying to read this for ages. How much is it?'

The joy in her eyes made his heart tremble as he handed her the drink.

'Have it for nothing, Evie. It's the least I can do.'

If she hadn't been holding on to the glass, he thought she might have thrown her arms around his neck.

'Thank you, Jack. You've done so much for me. How can I ever repay you?'

His lips crawled together into a crooked smile as she downed half the beer.

I don't know how long it takes to kick in. And then what do I do with the body?

He could dump her in the woods or somewhere remote, but that would mean getting her there without anyone seeing him, and someone would find her eventually. And the police would know he was the last person to see her alive. It would be the same if he buried her somewhere, plus that Astrid woman was bound to ask too many questions. No, he needed another solution. And quick.

'There's no need to thank me, Evie. It's been my pleasure.' He sipped at his beer. 'I only wish I could have helped you more with the publishers. And you shouldn't change the name of the novel; it's perfect.'

Her hand trembled and she nearly dropped the book. She swayed to one side, and he caught her before she fell. Jack took the paperback and drink from her and placed them onto the shelf behind her. It wouldn't be long now.

'Wow, that's strong stuff.'

'Perhaps you need some rest. It's been a tiring day.'

Her eyes glazed over as she shook her head. 'No, I'll be fine. I want to look through more of your books.' She steadied herself on a pile of encyclopaedias as she glanced across the shop. He still hadn't figured out what to do with her when she gave him the solution. 'You should be careful, though, with all these volumes packed together; it's a right firetrap.'

It was the last thing she said before she collapsed into his arms.

A fire. It's perfect. And I'll collect on the insurance for the stock.

But how to make it look like an accident and explain his absence? He considered the options as he dragged Evie to the rear of the shop and placed her next to a pile of old newspapers. Then he reached into her pocket, took her phone, and found the matches and cigarettes.

Perfect.

He went back and retrieved her glass and knew how it would work. Jack emptied her beer into the sink and washed the glass. Then he got his drink and poured it over the papers. He left both the empty bottles on the desk, but wiped his fingerprints from them. Then he took her matches and cigarettes.

I didn't even know she smoked.

Jack removed one cigarette and replaced the packet in her pocket. He was about to put the ciggy into his mouth to light it until he realised how stupid that would be.

My DNA would be all over it, you idiot.

So, how could he light it? He had the matches and the cigarette. He stared at Evie, prone on the floor, watching her slow breathing and hearing the low moan crawling from her lungs. He had no qualms about what he was about to do, and it didn't surprise him. The thought of two million dollars and a new life would do that to you.

He struck the match against the box and watched it

burst into life. The smell made him giddy as he stuck the cigarette into the flickering spark. Jack held it there until the end of it burnt into a dark shade, and then placed it next to Evie's hand. Then he discarded the still-burning match into the beer-stained magazines. He watched the flame dance across the paper and smiled. There was one last thing for him to do before he left.

He placed the shop and car keys on the desk and imagined what he'd tell the police.

I stepped out for my nightly walk, Detective, and left Evie in the house. She said she needed some rest, and I could see she was upset about her brother and what happened outside the hotel. I guess she took my keys and the car and went to the bookshop.

Why would she do that, Mr Kennedy?

He'd shrug and look baffled.

I don't know, Detective. Perhaps you should speak to the people who were treating Evie at the Tranquil Waters Rest Home. I'm sure they'll have a better understanding of her state of mind than anyone.

He didn't glance back as he left and abandoned his lifetime's work, but he already felt the heat growing behind him. As he got outside and slipped into the dark spot in the alley next door, he looked at his phone and read the email from Conway.

Yes, being at her house would be the perfect alibi. He knew it was earlier than she said, but he didn't care. He was on top of the world, and tonight, for the first time, perhaps he'd be the dominant one.

30 QUEEN OF THE HIGHWAY

Beverly stuck to the shadows all the way to Conway's house. The cold meant she saw nobody during her journey. As she used the stolen key to enter the house, she was in dire need of something to warm her up, but the thought of what she was about to do to the old bat warmed her heart.

She left the light off in the kitchen and grabbed a large knife she'd seen earlier. There would be time to have some fun with Conway before Kennedy arrived. But what would be the best way to frame him for her murder? Once he entered through the back door and found her in the living room, he'd either call the cops or flee. Fleeing would be better because that's a clear sign of guilt, but there was no guarantee he'd do that.

She was pondering what to do as the cats strode up to her.

Conway must be in bed now, so perhaps these moggies could help me get her downstairs. If they make a sound, she might come to see what's happening. Or perhaps it would be easier to stick to the original plan and go upstairs and push the blade under her throat. I could kill her in the bedroom anyway. It doesn't have to happen downstairs.

She was considering her options when she heard a noise from the living room. Was Kennedy already there? She clutched the knife in her hand and left the kitchen. Then it came again: a cough. The cats followed her into the corridor. They gazed at the intruder in their house as Beverly stepped into the living room.

'At last. I thought you'd never get here.'

Anxiety swept through her as she stared at who sat on the sofa. Her arm shook as she lifted the knife and pointed it towards the school principal.

It's okay, don't panic. You wanted her downstairs anyway. She's playing into your hands.

'How come you're back so soon?'

Conway picked up a glass of wine from the table and brought it to her mouth. She smiled and sipped from it at the same time.

'I never left, Bev.' The alcohol glistened on her lips. 'Do you want to know why?'

Beverly regained her confidence and moved forward. 'Go on, then, surprise me.'

The grin consumed Conway's face. 'Oh, you'll be surprised, Bevvy.' She removed the phone from her trouser pocket. 'My late husband, God rest his soul, had hidden cameras placed in every room of the house when he returned from Afghanistan. He never told me what happened to him there, but the constant nightmares and increased paranoia undoubtedly accelerated his early death.'

'Cameras?' Beverly looked up into the corners of the ceiling.

'You can't see them, can you? But they saw you when

you stole my key and came into the kitchen. They also recorded all your actions in my house and triggered an alarm on my phone when you didn't add the code to the security system thirty seconds after you broke in.'

'You knew I placed spyware on to your computer?'

Conway raised the glass to her. 'And to think some of my staff, your colleagues, believe you're stupid.'

A dark mist descended over Beverly. 'It doesn't matter. I'll still gut you now like the pig you are.'

Conway shook her head. 'Perhaps I was too quick to give you credit, Shaw. The cameras are recording as we speak, and they'll upload the video to a server which, if I don't enter the right password in the next twenty-four hours, will automatically post it online.'

'You're lying.'

The principal finished her drink. 'Then do what you came here to do, Bev.'

The name bounced off the insides of her skull, joined by the words she'd memorised from that database.

Bev Shaw. A complete waste of space. All the other kids hate her, especially the girls. She smells like old potatoes and always comes to school wearing clothes her parents must have got from charity or dumpsters. She's as bright as a black hole and twice as dense. I can't see any boyfriends on the horizon, so even marriage won't save her from a future of drudge and misery. The lowest level of shop work might be her only saving grace. She'd be better off committing a crime and spending a long time in prison.

Beverly moved forward with the knife pointing straight for Conway's throat. 'I read what you wrote about me in that database.'

'I know you did, Bev, but I had to leave out some of the things your peers said about you.'

Her fingers trembled. 'My peers?'

'You wouldn't believe how nasty some of those girls could be.' Her grin was unmoving. 'Still, I suppose you do understand how ghastly they were.' She ignored the threat right in front of her. 'You cheer people up just by walking out the door; that's what one of them said about you. I think it was that tall girl with the mole on her cheek.' Conway rubbed at her chin. 'Now, what was her name?'

'Carole Malone. That was her.'

'Ah yes, Malone. It's a shame, really.'

Ignore her. Just get it over with.

'What's a shame?'

'Well, if you kill me tonight and it's all over the internet tomorrow, you won't be going to the school reunion on Saturday where you'd get the chance to see Malone again and all the others who tormented you as a student.'

Beverly controlled her trembling hand and stared into Conway's eyes. 'How do you know who is attending the reunion?'

'Because, my dear girl, it's by ticket only. The invites went out to your year group, and those who are coming had to confirm their attendance, and we sent them a ticket to get in. It's the best way of keeping the riff-raff out. And I also noticed you didn't apply for yours.'

Nervous laughter burst out of Beverly. 'Why would I want to see any of them?'

Conway leant forward so her face was an inch from the blade. 'Did you read everything I said about you in the database?'

You could plunge it straight into her eye now with no trouble.

'No, I didn't.'

'Well, you should have. Would you like to know the last

thing I wrote, what my prediction for your future was?'

'Sure, if that's what you want your final words to be.'

'I see a lot of me in Beverly Shaw. She'll grow up to be a killer.'

The thump in Beverly's heart grew loud enough to resonate inside her head. 'You've killed?'

Conway's eyes narrowed. 'In a manner of speaking. I prefer to observe people in pain instead of getting my hands dirty, but, as I'm sure you know, it's difficult to avoid at times.'

Beverly smirked. 'You've just admitted that on camera. That wasn't very clever, was it?'

'Perhaps not, or maybe I did it to prove you can have something much greater than killing me here tonight. A grand plan we'll both share.'

The din inside Beverly's head grew louder by the second. 'What are you talking about?'

'I learnt from an early age that the only enjoyment I get from life is watching the suffering of others. My mother drank every day, and when my father came home, she'd beat him with anything she could lay her hands on. He was bigger than her, but he was also a mild man who would stand there and take it. I don't think either of them knew I saw what was going on, but it didn't matter. I loved it, hiding in the shadows and watching her inflict extreme pain on to him. I've tried to analyse myself over the years, wondering if seeing those things created the way I feel or if it was inside me from birth. Eventually, I decided it didn't matter and embraced who I am.'

Against her better judgement, Beverly found herself dragged into Conway's psychodrama.

'Is that how you got involved in the S&M scene?'

Conway shrugged. 'I guess so, but that's not enough to

satisfy my cravings; not anymore.'

'What do you mean?'

'Observing the pain of others wasn't sufficient. I have to witness death, to be close to it. The desire has grown stronger as I've aged, and I need one last bang in my life.'

'Is something wrong with you?'

'You could say that. My blood is riddled with cancer, and I have less than a month to live.' She drank more of the wine. 'So you see, Beverly, you could kill me now if you want to, but in the grand scheme of things, it makes little difference to me. If you listen to my proposal, I'll provide you with something much better than killing me.'

Beverly stepped back and sat on the sofa opposite the woman she'd gone there to torture and murder.

'I'm listening.'

IT DIDN'T TAKE LONG for Conway to outline her plan. And it took even less time for Beverly to agree to it. She had reservations, but the way it was laid out to her, well, just the thought of it, gave her palpitations. But there was one thing she had to agree to first.

'What do you want me to do?'

'You must fulfil the promise I saw in you all those years ago, Beverly.'

'What does that mean?'

'I need to watch you kill another human being.'

Beverly was tongue-tied for a second. And then she laughed out loud.

'Do you have anyone in mind?'

Conway glanced at the clock on the wall.

'Jack Kennedy will be here soon. Let's start with him.'

31 ALL HAIL THE AMERICAN NIGHT

If the journey from Elm Street to Kennedy's house hadn't gone through the town's centre, Astrid wouldn't have seen the fire at the bookshop. It also meant she got there before the emergency services, parking the car fifty yards from the shop and sprinting towards the inferno. The heat forced her back, so she stumbled into a bench opposite the boarded-up bakery. The smoke drifted into her lungs as she stood, causing her to bend and cough out her guts as she fumbled for her mobile. She used one hand to push the hair from her eyes while the other dialled Evie's number. She let it ring as she peered into the bright red and yellow eating the darkness surrounding it.

The phone went to voicemail. Astrid fought her way through the smoke to get to the bookshop. The flames reached into the sky with fiery fingers clawing into the coffee shop next door. Luckily there was a gap between them, and there was no wind to spread the destruction further down the street.

Only when she scanned the area did she realise Jack Kennedy's car was parked opposite his shop.

He must have driven here after I left his house.

She ignored her instincts and moved closer to the blaze. If Kennedy was in there, he wasn't getting out. But what if Evie was with him? She gripped her phone, fighting through the smoke until she saw the devastation inside: the fire had consumed the front of the shop as hundreds of books perished in flames. She dialled the number and waited, her heart frozen as the heat threatened to overwhelm her. It went to voicemail again as the sirens screamed in the distance.

Astrid was at a loss for what to do when she heard the coughing behind her. The glass cracked in the window as she searched for the origin of the noise. The phone clung to her fingers, the sound of Evie's voice repeating from the voicemail. She peered through the smoke and the gloom to see feet sticking out from underneath Kennedy's car.

She rushed forward and crouched down, her free hand reaching for Evie and pulling her out and on to the pavement. The fire crackled in the air behind her as she forced Evie up and dragged her across the street. They coughed in stereo as the younger woman twitched into life in her arms. As they stumbled over the kerb, Astrid popped her against a wall.

'Are you okay, Evie?'

She rubbed at her eyes, her lips quivering as she spoke. 'I will be in a second.'

Then she twisted her head away from Astrid and threw up. The sirens grew closer, and Astrid knew they had to be somewhere else before they arrived. She let Evie drag everything from her guts, and then she pulled her up.

'Come on, let's get out of here.'

Evie was unsteady on her feet as she rubbed bits of vomit from her mouth. 'Shouldn't we wait for the police?'

'And say what?'

Evie's eyes burnt as red as the flames across the street. 'Jack drugged me and then started the blaze.'

Astrid ushered her to the car. 'You can tell me all about it on the way to his house.' Evie didn't protest as they drove away thirty seconds before the fire trucks arrived.

'Why not tell the cops what he did?'

'Because I need a word with Kennedy first. Once the police get their hands on Kennedy, there'll be no chance to speak to him.'

Evie glanced at her reflection in the window as they drove. 'Do you want to ask him why he tried to kill me?'

The empty road encouraged her to drive faster. 'That and what he knows about the murders in your basement.'

Evie's voice shook as she spoke. 'You think he's connected to that?'

Astrid shrugged. 'Perhaps. It seems a bit of a coincidence he tried to kill you a few days after the Glick murders.' She turned right, aware they weren't far from Kennedy's house. 'Tell me what happened after I left you two together.'

So Evie did, her voice calm until she got to her and Kennedy in the bookshop.

'He must have put tranquilisers in my beer. After seven years inside Shady Acres, I know how my body feels when I take them. Thankfully, my time under medication in the home means I'm used to higher dosages than what he gave me. It was still strong enough I couldn't control myself, but it didn't knock me out. That's why I saw what he did when I was helpless on the floor.'

'He set the place on fire?'

'Only after he dumped me into a pile of magazines. He took the cigarettes from my pocket and put one in my hand.

Then he lit the paper he'd poured the beer over. I watched him do it all, but couldn't move. Not until he left. Somehow, I dragged myself across the floor and outside as the blaze engulfed the building.'

Astrid parked the car fifty yards from Kennedy's home. 'Why do you think he did it?'

Confusion crept over Evie's face. 'I don't know, but, since you mentioned it, perhaps he knows something about the murders in our house. You said before it had to be someone who had a grudge against my family, so maybe it's him.'

'But you're not sure what that might be?'

She shook her head. 'Yesterday was the first time I'd ever met him. I've only been in contact with him through email for a few months.'

'Because of your writing?'

'Yes, but it can't be about that, surely?'

'Let's go and ask him.'

Astrid led the way, not hesitating as she pushed the unlocked front door open, ready for any attack.

Unless he decides to shoot me. I should have told Evie to stay in the car.

But twice she'd left her alone, and both times she'd been attacked. She wouldn't do it again.

The living room was empty, as was the rest of the ground floor. After she'd checked upstairs, she found Evie stuffing bunches of papers into a bag containing a laptop and the things she'd brought from Shady Acres. Astrid assumed the computer was Kennedy's.

Evie stared at her.

'Anything interesting upstairs?'

Astrid shook her head. 'Nope. What have you got there?'

'His laptop and pages from his desk.' She nodded towards the bureau behind them. 'There might be something useful here.'

'Okay. Let's go before the coppers arrive. Nobody knows he brought us here or his connection to you since you left the care home.'

'We're still not going to the police?'

'Not yet. You need some rest, and my brain needs recharging before we decide on the next move.'

Evie clutched the bag to her chest. 'So where are we going to stay?'

Astrid smiled at her. 'Don't worry. I have just the place for you.'

———

SHE PARKED the car fifty yards from the hotel and looked at Evie.

'Do you have something in your bag to hide your face, like a hat? After what happened last time, I don't want anyone to know you're here.'

Evie dug deep into her bag and pulled out a hooded top. 'Will this do?'

'Perfect,' Astrid said. 'Wait here until I check reception.'

She got out of the car and walked into the hotel. A young man sat there, smiling when he saw her. She didn't return the pleasantry.

'We thought you weren't coming back.' His voice was like a motorbike tearing across a dirt track.

Astrid slapped her room key on to the desk. 'Did they fix the busted flush?'

His thick glasses slid down to the end of his nose, so he prodded them up. 'What busted flush?'

She pushed the keys towards him. 'I told one of your colleagues the toilet in my room wouldn't flush and to get it fixed. Are you saying they haven't done it?'

Her anger was genuine, but not about this phantom dodgy toilet. It was an accumulation of making zero progress in the investigation and worrying about how close Evie had come to dying in that fire.

He pulled out a book and rifled through the last few pages. 'Nobody has mentioned it here, Ms Snow, I promise.' He grabbed her keys. 'I'll go and have a look.'

He stepped around the desk and up the stairs. She leant towards the front door and waved at Evie in the car. She watched her get out, her head covered by the hood, and sprint into the hotel.

'Is everything okay?' Evie said in muffled tones.

'Wait here. When you hear my voice, come up in the elevator.'

She nodded as Astrid went to catch up with the young man. She took the steps two at a time and was there as he opened the door.

'You could have waited downstairs, Ms Snow, while I sort this out.'

She shook her head. 'I'm fine here.'

They entered together and he headed into the bathroom. The noise of a working flush meant he'd be leaving straight away. There was a massive smile on his face as he spoke.

'They must have fixed it without reporting it in the book. I'm sorry about that, but everything should be okay now. Is there anything else you need?' He pushed the glasses up his nose again.

'No, that's great, thanks.' She ushered him out of the

room and watched him walk to the stairs. As he reached the top, she ran towards him.

Confusion spread across his face. 'Was there something else?'

She held out her hand. 'You forgot to return my key.'

He let out a nervous laugh, dug into his pocket, and handed it to her. 'Here you go.'

She took it and he headed downstairs. As he disappeared from her view, the lift opened behind her. As she turned, a hooded Evie stepped out.

'Come on,' Astrid said, 'let's get you safe.'

Evie staggered into the room and flopped on to the bed without removing the hood. She gripped the bag as Astrid locked the door and sat next to her. Evie's breath came in slow, sharp movements. Astrid eased the bag from her and pulled the hood from her head. The poor woman smelt of smoke and looked exhausted. Astrid took her hands and lifted her into a sitting position.

'We need some rest. You take the bed and I'll have the sofa.' She moved the bag onto the floor. 'We'll go through Kennedy's stuff in the morning.'

Evie didn't protest and crawled under the covers fully clothed. Astrid left her like that and went to the chair. She wasn't tired and needed something to occupy her mind. The blank wall attracted her attention, her eyes focusing on the peeling paintwork as she imagined all the actors in this drama as pins she could play with.

And right at the centre were the Church siblings.

32 NEWBORN AWAKENING

Jack's head was full of plans as he slunk towards Conway's house. The sirens were blaring in the distance behind him, but he knew it was too late for them to save either Evie or his business. The loss of the stock gathered over twenty years left a slight twinge in his gut, but it could all be replaced, especially once he received his book advance from the publishers.

Two million dollars. Fuckety fuck me!

He had to still his beating heart and steady his pace. She wanted him there at midnight, and he'd be forty minutes early at this rate.

So what? I'm going to be in charge now.

But was he? Jack stopped at the bridge over the river, ensuring he was on his own, and then peered into his reflection in the water. She'd always been the dominant one and he the submissive, so how could he change that?

He'd remembered the first time he realised who she was, even with that full face mask she wore, noticing how she moved at that party in Texas, convinced she was the school principal from his home town of Eureka Falls. She'd seen him staring at her, and that's when he'd guessed she knew that he knew. Conway had never interacted with him before then, but after that, they became inseparable for three months. Until she informed Jack it was over right at the point when he understood he couldn't live without her.

So he'd skulked away with his tail between his legs, knowing full well he'd hit the bottle sooner rather than later. And that's where he was when he decided to send Evie's novel off as his own. He told himself it wouldn't make any difference to her. She'd probably never leave Shady Acres anyway, plus, he didn't expect agents or publishers to show any interest. They never had for his books, and he'd been writing for more than thirty years, so why should they for the first book from a young girl?

Imagine his surprise when he received that phone call and had to meet an agent who loved the book, who loved *his* book. And it was his book by then. He'd convinced himself of it every time he gazed at the bottles of alcohol in his house or when he dwelt upon his relationship with Conway.

My failed relationship and my failed books.

But they were all in the past, or so he thought until Evie turned up at the bookshop. And then Conway sent him that message.

He left the river behind and picked up the pace.

Yes, my new life begins tonight. There's no more being submissive.

Conway's house was in sight as the sirens faded in the distance. He gripped the key in his pocket, making his way through the shadows and a promise to himself.

If those cats get in the way, I'm going to wring their scrawny necks.

Jack slipped around the back and approached the door.

He didn't make any attempt to stay quiet, knowing she expected him. He was fifteen minutes early, but that didn't matter as it was more time they could spend together.

He entered the house, striding through the kitchen and corridor before stepping into the living room. Conway sat on the sofa, drinking a glass of wine. Disappointment swept through him when he saw she wasn't wearing her bondage gear. But then again, neither was he.

But this is the start of a new dynamic in our relationship, so I suppose it calls for an end to the old ways as well.

He moved into the centre and gazed at her. 'Is there one of those for me?' He pointed at the wine.

Her smile unnerved him. 'You won't need it, Jack.'

It was only as he narrowed his eyes and clenched his hand into a fist that he realised someone was behind him. The scarf was around his neck before he could do anything, pulled tight as he struggled to snatch it away. His attacker dragged him back as his vision blurred. The breath struggled in his lungs as Jack's legs buckled under him. The light was going out as his assailant drew the scarf away and he dropped to the floor. His face hit the carpet as Conway spoke.

'He'll be okay. You've always liked it rough, haven't you, Jack?'

He wheezed and gasped as he rolled on to his back. Standing over him was a young woman with glistening eyes.

Conway invited someone else into our game.

He dug his fingers into the rug and tried to push up, only to be stopped by her foot on his chest.

'Down, boy,' she said. 'So, what do we do with him now?'

'Whatever you want, Beverly.'

Bev Shaw? When the pain vanished from his eyes, he saw her clearly. She grinned at him.

'Whatever I want?'

Conway finished her drink and got out of the chair. 'Let me get something first.'

She left the room as Jack found his voice. His throat croaked and burnt as if electricity surged through it.

'Do your parents know about this, Beverly?'

She glowered at him. 'What?'

Conway returned with a large piece of plastic. She unrolled it opposite him as he stared at her.

'We know you stole Evie Church's novel, Jack, and claimed it as your own.'

The pain in his throat shot through the rest of him. 'Wha... what?'

'Beverly is much cleverer than I ever knew.' She glanced at Shaw. 'And so devious. I guess you didn't realise she put a virus on to your machine when she fixed your computer. She told me she only did it out of force of habit as well.' Her face trembled with laughter. 'She hadn't used it until today, and then she found all your little criminal plans in your emails and files.' She shook her head at him. 'And I thought you were better than that, Jack. I think you deserve all the punishment my new partner is about to give you.'

Shaw kicked him on to the plastic before he could protest.

Then she plunged the kitchen knife into his chest.

33 ROADHOUSE BLUES

Evie was watching the news when Astrid entered the room. She hit the mute button on the remote and scowled at her.

'Where have you been?'

'To get us breakfast.' She dropped bagels and doughnuts on to the table and offered Evie a coffee. 'How are you feeling?'

She took the drink. 'Have you been out all night?'

Astrid pursed her lips. 'No. What makes you say that?'

Steam came out of the cup as Evie sipped it. 'I woke in the middle of the night and looked over, and you weren't in the chair. I fell asleep again, but you were still missing when I got up thirty minutes ago.'

'I needed some fresh air.' Astrid moved towards the bathroom. 'I'll have a quick shower, and then we'll go through what we took from Kennedy's house.' She pointed at the TV. 'Has there been anything on the news about it?'

Evie shook her head. 'Nothing. Just bits on the internet about a blaze at the bookshop. The fire service managed to put it out before it spread to any of the other buildings beyond the coffee shop next door.'

'That's great.' Astrid kicked off her shoes and unbuttoned her shirt. 'Oh, I've got some good news for you as well.'

'What's that?'

Astrid turned on the shower and waited for the water to get hot. 'Your brother must have had a change of heart about the lawyer. I received a text from one, a Joan Harris who claims she's representing him and wants to meet you at the station this afternoon.' She'd closed the door before she heard Evie's reply. Astrid discarded the rest of her clothes and stepped under the water. The heat seared her skin and she pressed her head against the tiles.

Twenty minutes later, she was dressed and drying her hair as Evie looked over the papers they'd taken from Kennedy's house.

'I know why Jack tried to kill me.'

Evie shuffled the papers together and handed them to Astrid, who draped the towel over her shoulder and read from the first page. Water dripped from her and onto the paper.

'Why would he want to kill you over this?'

'Read the title at the top of each page.'

Astrid flicked through the first four pages. '*A Dark Heart in the Garden of Delights* by Jack Kennedy.' She handed the papers back to Evie. 'So he wrote a book.'

Evie laughed. 'He didn't. That's my novel, the one I sent him for feedback after he praised my short stories.'

Astrid continued to dry herself as she sat down. 'Why did you go to the bookshop with him when I told you to stay at the house?'

Evie placed the pages on the table between them. Then

she repeated the story Kennedy had told about the publisher's interest in her novel. 'I know I shouldn't have gone, but I was too excited.'

'That's what he wanted.' Astrid finished drying her head and put the towel on the back of the chair. 'He must have been desperate to get rid of you once you turned up at his shop. I assume he didn't plan this. He probably thought you were never going to leave that place you were in.'

'You don't think there's a connection to what's happened to Adam?'

Astrid reached for the laptop and opened it. 'Anything is possible.'

'Do you think Jack would've returned home?'

'If he did, I'd expect the police to speak to him about the fire. He must know there was no body found in the bookshop.'

The computer sprang to life. The light on the screen was in stark contrast to the gloom spreading over Evie's face.

'Maybe people in this town don't like my family.'

'Do they have any reason?'

Evie shrugged. 'Not that I'm aware of, unless it's to do with my parents' congregation. Why do you ask?'

'Family history could be important for discovering who framed your brother. Was your parents' church popular?'

She pondered the question for a minute. 'They called themselves traditionalists, though I suppose others would see them as fundamentalists. It did cause a few problems sometimes in the community.'

'What type of problems?'

Evie grabbed the papers and straightened them so they lined up on top of each other without a single one out of place. She stared at them, averting her gaze from Astrid as she spoke.

'They took as gospel everything written in the Old Testament; it was the Word of God, and nothing would convince them otherwise.'

Exactly as Astrid had read on the church website. 'And they expected you and your brother to do the same?'

Evie's lips curled up. 'Can you imagine how much of a disappointment we were to them?'

Astrid peered at the computer and the image of the front of Kennedy's bookshop. She tried not to let her memories come scampering out of the shadows, but it was impossible. The desktop vanished, replaced with different sets of books, ones from her childhood home, and the sight of her father towering over her. He had a belt in one hand and a Bible in the other, but he was no Christian. Just when she thought she'd eradicated those scars, they came screaming back to haunt her.

She twisted her head from the screen and looked at Evie.

'At some point, your past will no longer matter.' She put a hand on the stack of papers and smiled at her. 'This must be something special to drive Kennedy to attempted murder.' Evie grinned at her, and Astrid returned to the computer. The ghosts of her past had vanished. She twisted the laptop around so they could both see the screen. 'Let's check his email first.'

They spent twenty minutes going through the inbox, the deleted folder and sent messages. Evie's face grew more expansive with every message they read, especially the last one from the publisher Kennedy had sent the novel to under his name. She lifted her hand to her forehead.

'There's going to be an auction for my book at the weekend.' Her voice was shrill and on the edge of laughter.

Astrid stood and grabbed her jacket from the back of the

door. She reached inside and removed what she'd bought on her trip for breakfast earlier. She handed it to Evie.

'Since Kennedy took your phone, I got you a new one. My number is in the contacts, and it has internet access. You need to log in to your email and message this agent and tell them the truth.'

Every part of Evie's face sank to the floor. 'I can't prove it's mine. The original file is on my other cell.'

She dropped her head into her palms as her body trembled. Astrid placed a hand on her arm.

'Don't worry, Evie. The copy you gave Kennedy will be on this machine somewhere. Even if he deleted it, there's a good chance it will be recoverable on the hard drive. That version of the file will have an earlier date stamp than the one he sent to the agent. All you have to do is inform them to cancel the auction, and you'll send proof of your claims.'

Evie peered at her. 'Fancy me getting upset over this when Adam's accused of murder.'

Astrid returned to the laptop and read out the agent's email address. She left Evie to contact them while she checked the rest of Kennedy's computer. The first thing she did was a search for other versions of Evie's novel. It didn't take long to discover several copies, including the original. She reached into her trouser pocket and removed the USB drive she'd bought with the phone. She connected it to the machine and copied the book while telling Evie the good news.

'Kennedy deleted your original file, but he left it in the Recycle Bin like an idiot. I've restored it and made a copy. How are you getting on with your email?'

Evie's eyes lit up. 'I've sent it now. Couldn't we send an email from Jack's account, pretend to be him, and admit to what he's done?'

'It's not that simple, Evie. We don't know where he is. The computer would timestamp the message, and for all we know, he could be sitting in the police station at this precise moment.'

'So what's next?'

Astrid minimised the web browser. 'We'll spend the morning going through this machine, and then I'll drive you to the station to see the lawyer.'

'And what will you do?'

'I'm going to speak to as many residents of Elm Street as possible.'

She was looking forward to questioning the neighbours, but first, she returned her attention to Jack Kennedy's computer. It didn't take long to find his not so secret folders containing thousands of sadomasochistic photos and videos. They looked through half a dozen before Evie turned away.

'Do you think he knew my brother was into the same thing?'

Astrid closed the laptop. She'd seen enough for now. 'It's possible. Many people like to wear masks at these parties, but others are happy to be themselves.'

'You sound like you're talking from experience.'

Astrid stood and checked the time on her phone. 'I've seen and done a lot of things in my life.'

Evie flopped on to the bed and groaned. 'And all I've done is run away from everything.'

'I wouldn't say that.' Astrid picked up the papers. 'You wrote a novel someone was prepared to kill for and which a bunch of famous publishers are going to bid lots of money on. I'd say you've already accomplished quite a bit in your short life. And I'm sure there's more to come. But now you have to get ready to go and see your brother and his lawyer.'

Evie nodded and went to the bathroom. Ten minutes

later, her face was obscured by the hooded top as they left the hotel and stepped into the car. She kept the hood up all the way to the police station.

'I'll text you when it's over,' Evie said as she got out of the car.

Astrid watched her enter the building before driving towards Elm Street. As the car rumbled down the road, she wondered what Adam's neighbours would tell her.

34 WE COULD BE SO GOOD
TOGETHER

A strange day turned into an even stranger evening for Beverly. It took fifteen minutes to get the blood from her hands, but how she'd got like that lingered in her mind. And now she was walking out of Conway's spare bedroom wearing the clean shirt the older woman had given her. The aroma of eggs and bacon greeted her as she went into the kitchen. She resisted the temptation to peek into the living room to see if Kennedy's body was still there. A shock of memory returned, of the frenzy which overtook her once she started on him, the mania which possessed her the more he screamed, and the joy she discovered on seeing the euphoria in Conway's face. She was exhausted by the end of it. When Conway insisted she stay the night, she didn't object.

'Leave the cleaning to me,' Conway had said as she guided Beverly upstairs. The glint she saw in the principal's eyes then was still there now.

'Are you hungry?'

Beverly sat at the table and took in the smell of scrambled eggs. 'I'm famished.'

She dived into the food. Most of the plate had gone before she noticed the clock on the wall stood at ten-thirty in the morning. 'We're late for work.' She reached for the coffee at her side and drank half of it.

Conway buttered a slice of toast. 'Don't worry about that. We've got more important things to consider. I called and said you were working out of school with me today.'

The cup warmed Beverly's hands. 'Do they think I'm at the conference with you?'

'There was no conference, Beverly. I was somewhere else yesterday. I'll tell you all about it in the garage.'

Conway chewed on the toast as she left the kitchen. Beverly followed her like a little dog. The principal went into the living room. Beverly was two steps behind, holding her breath in the expectation of a waft of dried blood swamping her senses, but all she got was a bouquet of lemon and strawberry. The room was cleaner than yesterday, with no sign of Kennedy or the gruesome chaos Beverly had created.

She stared at Conway. 'Did you get any sleep last night?'

'At my age, you don't get much rest. Would you like to see what I did with our friend Jack after you finished with him?'

Before Beverly could reply, Conway stepped into the corridor, standing in front of a large carpet hanging on the wall. Beverly hadn't noticed the cloth before, but she watched as Conway pulled it to one side to reveal what was behind it.

'That's an inside door to your garage?'

She pushed it open. 'Robert had it installed once he started bringing home souvenirs from his trips abroad.'

'How long was your husband in the military?'

Beverly followed her into the garage. Conway flicked on the light.

'All his adult life, and long enough for him to collect this.'

She held out her hands at the contents: a stack of army uniforms and clothing piled on the far side, three rows of boxes stamped with the words PROPERTY OF THE US ARMY, canisters of unlabelled liquid, a table full of electrical components, half a dozen firearms hanging from the wall, a large number of rectangular blocks covered in brown paper, a broken-down motorbike, and four plastic bags leaning against the back of the garage door.

'Is it legal to have any of this here?'

Conway grinned at her. 'Of course not. Especially what's in those.'

She pointed at the plastic bags. Beverly suddenly realised what had happened to Jack Kennedy's body.

'You cut him up?'

'It had to be done. Luckily I have an excellent electric saw. I hope the noise didn't keep you awake?'

'I heard nothing.' Beverly resisted the temptation to peer into the plastic bags. Instead, she returned to something from earlier. 'So there was no conference yesterday?'

Conway's smile disappeared. 'I had my final appointment with my oncologist.'

Beverly didn't know what to say to this woman she now had mixed feelings about. 'Oh.'

'It's time for me to go out with a bang. And I think you and I can build on the fun we had last night and help each other get what we want.'

She moved to the table, picked up a brown block, and turned it upside down. Stamped on the bottom was a letter and one number: C4.

Beverly gasped. 'You have explosives?'

Conway ran her finger across the top of the block. 'We have explosives, Beverly.'

Beverly lifted one block, imagining the power in her hand. 'What will we use this for?'

Conway put her free arm on Beverly's shoulder. 'Don't you remember what's happening at the school on Saturday?'

Beverly glanced at the plastic bags and wondered which one of them contained Jack's head.

'It's the reunion for my year group.'

'And you're not going.'

'No. I never liked any of them.'

'Isn't it more than that?'

'What do you mean?'

'I remember your time at school, Beverly, and I kept a keen eye on you. Some of those girls, and a few of the boys, were horrible to you. Don't you need your revenge?'

A shiver ran down Beverly's spine as she wriggled out of her grip. She'd wanted a grand farewell before leaving the town, but this was too much.

Wasn't it?

Her eyes returned to the plastic bags, and then back to Conway.

This could be glorious.

'Why do you want to do this?'

Conway walked over to the firearms hanging on the wall. Below them was a photo Beverly hadn't noticed before. Conway picked it up and showed it to her. In it was a younger version of the principal and a handsome man in a uniform.

'I have about a week or so left. This will be my legacy to this town and all the people I've hated and never been able to lay my hands on. And you'll enjoy it immensely.'

'How will it work?'

'The reunion is taking place in the school hall. Underneath it, there's the boiler room. Three or four blocks of C4 pressed between these bags will dispose of poor Jack and take out most of the people above it.'

'And where will you and I be?'

Conway lifted a rucksack from the floor. It had a faded sticker on it advertising the Kennedy bookshop.

'I'll be placing the bags in the boiler room. You'll be upstairs with this.'

'Where did you get that?'

'Jack left it with me ages ago. When I detonate the C4 below the hall, it will scatter his DNA all over the place. When you blow up this one upstairs, bits of the bag will be left behind for the experts to find. They'll spend years trying to work out why a failed bookshop owner killed all those people.'

She placed four blocks of the explosive in the bag and zipped it up before offering it to Beverly. Her hands trembled as she took it.

'I don't have a death wish. How will I set this off and get out safely? I don't want to drop it on the floor and blow myself up.'

She gripped on to the bag, her fingers wanting to toss it to the side while her brain told her to nurture it like a newborn baby.

Conway picked up a block. She smiled at Beverly before throwing the block into the air. Beverly's heart thumped against her ribs, sweat dripping from her head. Her legs quivered as the principal caught the explosive and slammed it on to the table.

'Don't worry; you won't kill yourself by accident.' She grabbed a knife from the side and sliced the brown packet open. Inside was a thick white substance which she broke in half with ease. 'You can mould this like putty. This, in itself, is not dangerous. You can drop it, punch it, even shoot a bullet through it, and it won't go off. Unless the shell has a tracer round, nothing will happen. There are bullets like that stored behind you if you want some.'

Beverly clutched the bag to her chest to hide her throbbing heart. 'No, thanks. So how do we make this stuff explode?'

'It takes a combination of shock, impact, and temperature for that. It needs a detonator inserted into it, and then fired. And there are plenty of those in here.'

Beverly's arms relaxed as she placed the bag on the ground. 'I'm assuming somebody can fire these detonators remotely?'

Conway patted her on the shoulder. 'Of course, they can. It's not like we'll have wires stretching everywhere so everyone will see. All we have to do is make sure we're at a safe distance, coordinate our timings, and then flick a switch. Far stupider people than us do this all the time in the less civilised parts of the world.'

Beverly picked up Kennedy's bag and resisted the temptation to throw it across the garage. 'Don't you think the investigators, the FBI or whoever, will wonder why Jack would do such a thing? I know we need a scapegoat, and we have his bits bagged up, but why him?'

Conway moved behind her and opened a drawer. She removed two detonators and handed one to her.

'Don't worry; it's not set up yet. We'll do that tomorrow. As for dear old Jack, well, the police are already searching for him anyway, so I assume they'll settle into their usual lazy ways and say the bomber died because of his incompetence.'

'Why are they after him?'

'Apparently, his bookshop went up in flames last night, and no one has seen anything of him since. He told me about his business operation and he had thousands in debts he couldn't pay off. It won't be long before someone wonders if the fire was for the insurance. And when that went wrong, he turned full postal and blew up the school. And all those poor people inside it.'

Beverly placed the detonator in the bag. 'You seem to have thought of everything.'

Conway moved across and put her arm around her again. 'None of this would be possible, Beverly, without you. Now let's get you and your carrier of goodies home so you can prepare. We have a big day ahead of us at the weekend.'

She let Conway lead her out of the garage and back into the house, her emotions a swirling cocktail of nerves and excitement. The principal continued to talk to her, but she hardly heard any of it. It was confusing to feel, in equal measure, both love and hate.

She hoped the next few days would blow all her confusion away.

35 LOVE STREET

After dropping Evie off at the police station, Astrid drove through the town centre. She slowed down as she went past Kennedy's shell of a bookshop. The front bit was better than she'd expected, but beyond the logo of a stack of books above the door, she saw where the roof had started to collapse. It was amazing the fire hadn't taken up the rest of the buildings, apart from the coffee shop next door. The owners appeared to have responded well and were offering mobile services a couple of units down in one of the boarded-up properties she'd seen yesterday.

She resisted the urge to visit them for a drink and made the drive to Elm Street. Once there, she parked outside the Church house, expecting to see ghoulish onlookers loitering everywhere, but the street was empty.

Astrid got out of the car, removed her phone and went through the list of residents she'd acquired from the internet. She'd be happy if she found half of the houses occupied, even happier if half again of the residents spoke to her. And she'd be ecstatic if she got something useful out of this. She hadn't seen Adam's lawyer when dropping Evie off, but she knew whoever she was, she had to be better than Adam defending himself.

She started on the Church side of the street. There was no response at the initial three houses, but she met one of the oldest people she'd ever encountered at the fourth. The woman was ageing, but fighting it with every cosmetic wonderment available to her. She'd dyed her hair jet black, the colour of it in stark contrast to the white pancake slapped over her face. It was as if Queen Elizabeth the First stood before her. Her false eyelashes flickered like butterflies as she attempted to force her stretched skin into a smile, her bright red lips quivering as she spoke.

'How can I help you, dear?'

It looked as if the effort of speaking would make her fall over. Astrid put out her arm for support, and the old woman took it. Her gnarled fingers resembled the bark of a tree.

'Do you have a few minutes to talk to me?'

'Of course, dear. Come on in.' She let go of Astrid and shuffled her legs to the side to turn around. Astrid kept a watchful eye to make sure she didn't fall. 'Close the door behind you.'

She did as instructed and stepped into the house. The place smelt as old as the woman appeared, a dusty aroma of damp and decay. It reminded Astrid of her grandparents' home in England. Her parents only took her there once, but she never forgot how it reminded her of a hospital morgue.

The elderly lady used her feeble hands to cling to the wall and move into the living room. The first thing Astrid saw as she entered was a large orange phone which looked as if it hadn't worked since the 1920s. The furniture was sparse and simple, a two-seater sofa and a single chair on either side of an ancient fireplace which was probably colder than the woman's flesh. She slid into the seat as if her legs would never work again.

Astrid took the couch opposite, examining the severed heads of deer, foxes and bears covering the walls.

'Is there a lot of hunting in these parts?' She pictured the woods where the Glick girls had played.

The aged eyes peering at her sparked into life, the cackle of the old woman's laugh making the dust bounce from the carpet.

'Not for many years, dear. Not for animals, anyway.'

'If not for animals, then what?'

Her bones creaked as she leant forward. 'What's your name, dear?'

She smiled at her. 'I'm sorry. I'm Astrid Snow.'

'You sound British, like those old actors from my favourite movies.' Her eyes glazed over, and Astrid imagined she was reliving something from a long time ago. 'Like David Niven, but as a woman.' She laughed again. 'Not that you look like him.'

'Niven was a classic actor,' Astrid said.

The woman's eyes lit up like a bonfire, a radiance shining through the crap caked on her face. 'My name is June, after a character in *Stairway to Heaven*. I wanted to meet a nice British officer in a uniform after watching that. Are you a British officer, Astrid Snow?'

'No, June, I'm not. I'm just trying to help a friend out. That's why I'm going door to door on this street, talking to your neighbours.'

'It's about the Glick girls, isn't it?' Astrid nodded. 'Well, I'll tell you what I told the police. I can hardly hear the TV unless I'm in front of it, and I never go to the door or the windows if I don't have to. This is what happens to you when you get to be ninety-two years old.'

'That's an impressive age.'

June flashed an incomplete set of brownish teeth at her. 'I'm aiming for one hundred. Then I'll pop off to whatever is next. So what else do you want to ask me?'

'Does anyone else come by your house that might have seen something, perhaps a nurse or a cleaner?'

June laughed again. 'I wish. You're the first visitor I've had in months. I might not let you go.'

'You look after yourself and do your own shopping?'

She lifted a gnarled finger. 'I get everything off the internet. What a marvellous invention it is. I wish I'd had it when I was younger. I wouldn't have settled for the first man I met then, I can tell you.'

'What did you mean when you said there were hunters here that didn't only go after animals?'

June's grin was so big, Astrid thought her teeth would fall out as they rattled along with her laugh. 'You're a woman of the world, Astrid Snow; I see it in your eyes. You know what I meant.'

'You meant people preying on other people.'

She flicked her fingers in the air. 'I'm talking about men preying on children and men preying on women. It happens here, and everywhere else. There's no cultural or racial or religious or genetic reason to it. It's all in their heads.' She tapped at her skull. 'My father was like that, so was my husband and his friends. And do you know why it is?'

'No, June.'

Her grin made her look older than ninety-two. 'I don't believe you, Astrid. They do it because they think we're laughing at them. And that's why Adam Church killed those girls, because somebody somewhere laughed at him.'

'Did you see the sisters go into his house?'

'No.'

'Did someone tell you they went into his house?'

'No. It's only what I read on the internet.'

Astrid sighed and stood. 'I'll let myself out, June.'

She turned and left before the woman could move. As she stepped outside, she wondered if there was any point in continuing. If even a ninety-two-year-old recluse thought Adam was guilty, what chance was there of proving his innocence?

She visited the rest of the homes on that side of the street, with no reply from any of them. As she crossed the road, a dog howled and a cat screeched somewhere beyond the cold concrete. It sounded as if they were each chasing their tails, something she could identify with. The first nine houses provided her with only silence, and with the three places she got a response from, it was all hard stares and a few choice curse words.

She approached the last house with a heavy heart. It was the place opposite the Church home, the one with a clear view from one set of windows to another. As she knocked on the door, she considered what had June said about predators and their prey.

What am I missing?

There was no answer after two minutes of waiting. She was about to give up when, from behind her, came the sound of a vehicle pulling up. She turned to see a blonde woman in her twenties get out of the car. She clutched a rucksack to her chest like a birthday present. The car drove off without Astrid seeing who was inside.

The blonde stared at Astrid, her eyes as wide as a frog's. She dropped the bag to the ground and looked as if she was about to faint. Astrid stepped towards her.

'Do you live here?'

The bag rolled on to the road. Astrid reached down and

picked it up. It wasn't heavy, but she felt something rattling around inside. The woman stumbled forward and grasped for the bag.

'This... this... is my parents' house.'

There was panic in her eyes which Astrid recognised from trauma victims. She passed the bag to her.

'Are you okay?'

The blonde lurched past her, fumbling into her pocket and removing house keys. 'I'm fine, thanks. It's been a difficult few days around here.' She rushed up the steps and struggled to get the key in the lock.

'Do you mind if I ask you a few questions?' Astrid said.

The house keys dropped to the ground, bounced down the steps and landed at Astrid's feet. She picked them up and strode next to the nervous woman. She held them out as the blonde faced her.

'Questions about what?' She took the keys in trembling hands.

'About what happened at your neighbour's a few days ago.'

The key clicked in the door and she pushed it open. 'I told the police everything I know.'

'So you know something?'

She stepped inside, still clutching the bag. 'No, I mean, no, I didn't see or hear anything.'

Astrid placed her fingers on the front door. If nothing else, she wanted to get a look around inside. The blonde stumbled back, her eyes moving at a thousand miles a minute.

'I promise I'll be quick. I only want to observe the Church house from here. Is that okay?'

The woman nodded. 'As long as you leave soon because I don't feel well.'

She closed the door. 'Thank you. My name is Astrid Snow. Can I have a look around your living room?'

'It's through there.' She pointed to Astrid's left. 'I'll be right back.' She turned and disappeared into another room.

Astrid marched inside and went to the window. She pulled the curtain aside and peered across the road. She examined the view, but found it impossible to see what was happening in the other house. She could understand why all the neighbours claimed they didn't see anything.

Astrid turned away when the blonde returned.

'Have you seen enough?' she said.

Astrid took two steps towards her. 'You've got blood on your leg.'

'What?'

'Are you sure you're okay?' She pointed at the mark. 'Maybe I should call for a doctor.'

As she spoke, the woman fainted at her feet.

36 TOUCH ME

The drive home was more relaxed than she'd expected, which was surprising considering how much C4 she had nestled between her feet. Conway also continued to do her best at treating her like a long-lost daughter. She found that more terrifying than the explosives between her shoes.

'There's no more teacher/student, principal/teacher barriers between us now, Beverly. From this point forward, we're partners in everything we do. So, you must call me Claudia.'

Her short speech shocked Beverly as much as last night's events. She stared at the principal as they drove through town. The car trundled down the high street and she glanced at Kennedy's bookshop, surprised there was some of it left standing after what she'd heard about the fire damage. Her parents' coffee shop remained intact, but the front was burnt an impressive shade of black. She felt nothing for it, casually noticing they'd temporarily moved a few places down the street.

'Have you planned this for a long time?'

Claudia Conway scratched at her lips as they paused at

a red light. 'Do you mean the reunion party? No, this has been the alignment of several factors falling together at the same point.'

Spots of blood on Beverly's leg mesmerised her, but she dragged her gaze from them. 'You've spent most of your life taking pleasure from watching others suffer. You must have thought of something like this before.'

The light changed from red to green. Conway got them moving again.

'You're the same as me, I know it. People like us, the rare, significant individuals, always seek ways to develop our particular lifestyles. So, yes, I've wondered what it would be like to construct and observe mass suffering, but, as I'm sure you realise, the risks of capture or of revealing my true nature have prevented me from doing such a thing. But, as Robert Zimmerman once sang, the times they are a-changing.'

Beverly laughed. 'If I hadn't broken into your house and tried to kill you, none of this would have happened?'

Claudia grinned. 'Isn't life strange? Perhaps some higher power planned this all along to bring us together.'

The smile disappeared from Beverly's face. 'I don't believe in invisible supernatural beings controlling me. My decisions are my own. I'm in control of what I do, no one else.'

'Have you ever thought about why you're the way you are?'

Beverly placed two fingers in her mouth. They were damp when she tried to rub the blood from her leg. Her eyes twitched as she peered at her new partner.

'What makes a killer a killer?'

'What makes us enjoy the suffering of others?'

'Did you have a difficult childhood?'

A faint curve overtook Claudia's bottom lip, her top row of teeth shining white. 'Oh no, it was quite the contrary. My parents were wonderful to me. They gave me nothing but love. And then I found the love of my life.'

'Your husband?'

She laughed again. 'Robert, no. He was great, but what I'm referring to is the secret pleasure which only you and I understand.' Claudia glanced from the road and at her. 'You had troubles at school, I know that. What was it like for you at home?'

Beverly gazed at the customers trudging into the makeshift coffee shop. 'My parents have always lived to work. They've never had time for anything else. I'm part of a process for them.'

'That sounds terrible.'

'It is what it is, though it didn't prepare me for interacting with others. I don't understand what makes people want to be friends. I have no concept of how to make others like me.' She glanced out the window. 'I have no guilt.'

The car slowed to a halt. Beverly stared beyond Conway towards the Church house opposite them. Her lips glistened at the memory of what she did in there. Claudia put a hand on her arm.

'Get some sleep. I'll text you tonight. And don't forget to remove your virus from Jack's computer. We can't have the police finding that.'

Beverly got out, ready to say goodbye, only to find her attention drawn to the person standing outside her house. She dropped the bag on to the sidewalk, wanting to flee as the car drove away. The woman strode towards her. It was the same one as the other day.

She couldn't remember what happened next, but then they were inside the house and Beverly was stumbling towards the kitchen. She wanted to open the back door, leave the bag behind, and keep on running until she was far away. Tiny explosions burst through her head. One hand was on her throat, her breathing coming in strangled bursts. If she didn't know any better, she would have sworn she was being dragged to the bottom of the ocean.

Get control. Do it now.

She placed the bag on the table and took a drink of water. Every sinew shimmered with electricity as she walked into the living room. The woman was at the window. Then she turned to Beverly.

'You've got blood on your leg.'

They were the words she heard, but her brain translated them into something else.

You're covered in his blood. And I know you killed those girls.

Her legs trembled, and then gave way.

———————

HER FACE WAS PRESSED against the carpet, with bits of the rug sticking to her skin, smelling the chilli her father had dropped there last week. She rolled onto her back and stared at the woman peering at her.

'What?' Beverly said.

'Should I call a doctor?'

Something sprang from her gut, sprinted through her throat and out of her mouth. She laughed liked never before as she sat up.

'I'm sorry, but your accent reminds me of the *Monty Python Show*.' She placed her hand on the carpet and pushed herself up. 'What did you say your name is?'

'I'm Astrid Snow. Are you sure you didn't bang your head on the floor? You seem somewhat giddy.'

'I'm fine, Ms Snow. It's just a lack of sleep. I've been working stupid hours lately.' She brushed at her legs, running her fingers over the dried blood. 'I cut my finger earlier and forgot to wash the stain from my trousers. It's nothing serious.' She held out her hand. 'I'm Beverly.'

Astrid shook her hand. 'What's your job, Beverly?'

'I'm a teacher at the local school. It's not a typical nine-to-five position. I was supposed to work from home today, but I need some sleep first. Have you seen what you wanted here?'

Beverly's heart was back to its normal rhythm, her thinking calm and her body under her control. This woman couldn't hurt her.

'I promise not to keep you much longer, but do you mind if I take a look at the Church house from upstairs?'

Why not? She won't find anything here. If I refuse, she might think it suspicious.

'Of course not. I'll show you up.'

Beverly led her from the living room and upstairs. All her tension had disappeared. She couldn't remember being in this much control of her emotions before. Was it to do with what happened last night? Had Claudia given her this newfound confidence? Or was it to do with the anticipation she felt about the weekend?

They stepped on to the landing and Beverly took Astrid into her bedroom. Her safe computer lay on the bed with the lid up and a screen saver of Tom and Jerry fighting across it. She didn't remember leaving it on before heading to Conway's yesterday. What was open behind that screen saver? Was it her portal into the dark web? Was it the Trojan link into Jack Kennedy's laptop?

Astrid Snow strode towards the window. She stared out of it as Beverly glanced at the computer.

'You didn't see anything the day the Glick girls disappeared?'

Beverly placed her body between the laptop and Snow. 'No. I was working all day. I didn't spend much time away from my desk.'

'How well do you know Adam Church?'

Shadowy fingers clutched at Beverly's mind. 'Not at all. He's a lot older than me.'

She started to move back to sit on the bed, only stopping when she realised any movement could trigger the screen saver to turn off and reveal what was on the computer.

Why would I even leave it on yesterday? And why didn't I set the security to kick in when the screen saver was on?

Because she was lazy and didn't want to go through the process every time the machine sat idle while she went to the toilet or made a sandwich. Inch by inch, the control was slipping away.

'Did the Glick girls attend the school where you work?'

'No. They were too young.' Her leg pushed up against the bed, the insides of her head frazzled as if trapped in the eye of a hurricane. She couldn't move forward or backwards. She stared straight into Snow's face. 'Have you finished here?'

Snow glanced around the bedroom, her eyes moving towards the flickering laptop. 'I guess so. Thanks for your help. I'll see myself out.'

Beverly watched her leave, counted the footsteps as she moved downstairs, and breathed a sigh of relief as the front door opened, then closed. She staggered to the window, eyes fixed on the British woman as she got into the car and drove away. She waited two minutes to make sure she didn't return before turning to her computer. She touched the monitor, and Tom and Jerry stopped hitting each other. The screen was blank. She sat on the bed and turned the machine off. Then she went downstairs and picked up the bag with the explosives and detonator.

Now, where am I going to put you for the night?

She pondered the question for a minute before returning to her room. She placed the bag under the bed. Then, fully clothed, she climbed under the covers. She wasn't tired. She didn't know why, but she just wanted to feel as if she was yet to be born.

And maybe she hadn't been yet.

Perhaps that would come on Saturday.

Astrid spent an hour driving around trying to collect her thoughts. The trip to Elm Street had been a damp squib, and she didn't know what to do next. She waited for Evie's text to say she'd finished with the lawyer and her brother. That came at six o'clock. She was outside the police station by six-fifteen, seeing Evie sitting on the pavement with both hands on her head.

She got out of the car. 'You should have stopped inside for me. You don't know who could be looking for you.' Religious fanatics, failed writers, child killers, or anyone else who feared Evie or her family.

She removed her hands and stared at Astrid. 'I'm done hiding. My life starts here. How was your trip?'

'Wasted. How was your time with your brother?'

Evie stood. 'I'll tell you everything over food. I need something to eat before I shrivel up.'

'You look like you need a drink more.'

'Are you trying to get me drunk?'

Astrid laughed. 'No, but I know the perfect place where we can have both beer and food.'

They got into the car and Astrid drove away. She wanted to quiz Evie about her time in the police station, but recognised the weariness in her. She needed refuelling, and Astrid wasn't opposed to suitable refreshment. She headed out of town and down a dirt road. She grinned at the shock on Evie's face when she parked outside a bar looking like it was from the *Mad Max* movies.

Evie got out of the car. 'Are you trying to corrupt me?'

'After seven years in enforced exile, it's time for you to live a little, and I checked online for the best boozer in Eureka Falls, and this is it.' She stared at the neon sign proclaiming a welcome to the Ducks Deluxe.

They marched up to the bar together. A few middle-aged bikers loitered around with drunken eyes fixed on them as they strode inside. Stale beer and sweat swirled in the air while the jukebox spat out the sounds of New York punk circa 1976. Astrid pointed to an empty spot at the far end. She wanted somewhere she could see the door.

It was like moving through quicksand as they made their way to the table. She scanned the room, assessing the dozen people there. Two burly bearded blokes were serving drinks. Evie sat down first, and Astrid handed her the menu.

'Have a look through that, and I'll get the drinks.'

She left her and went to the bar. The Ramones sang about a blitzkrieg bop as she got the beers and returned to the table. Evie was chewing on her fingers as if she hadn't eaten all day.

'I'll have a chicken burger, fries, onion rings and garlic bread.'

'I'm sure someone will take our order soon.' She pressed a beer towards Evie. 'This might dampen your hunger.

Have a drink, and then tell me what happened this afternoon. You were in there a long time.'

Evie's hands were small and the pint glass wide. She pushed both sets of fingers around it and lifted it to her face, then placed it to her lips and drank. Bits of foam stuck to her mouth as she put the drink onto the table, half of it already gone.

'It's all good news.' She wiped at her face. 'Adam's lawyer, Joan Harris, has a strategy in place to prove his innocence.'

Astrid gulped down her beer. It tasted like hops and she regretted not getting a bottle of cider. She couldn't have much, not when she had to drive back to the hotel, so she didn't want to waste it on that.

'It's going to court, then?'

'According to the lawyer, the police believe they have the right person in my brother. His DNA was on the girls' clothes, so they're not looking for anyone else.'

'What type of DNA?'

'His hair.'

'You don't appear upset by that.'

She watched Evie finish the rest of her drink without stopping to breathe. 'I spent a long time listening to the lawyer. She has a clear plan which convinced me.'

Astrid pushed her unwanted beer towards Evie. 'Tell me all about it.'

'Harris says the prosecution case focuses on two things: the discovery of the bodies in our house and the fact they have Adam's DNA on them.'

Astrid understood what she meant. 'If the police had found the girls in my hotel room, they'd probably have my DNA on them. It wouldn't mean I was their killer. A good defence lawyer would tear that to shreds.'

'And I think Harris is more than a good defence lawyer. She told me several ways his hair could have got on to their clothes without him being there. I also helped out.'

'How so?'

Evie reached into her trouser pocket and removed her key for the family home. 'I told her about this.'

'That would add doubt into the minds of any jury when the prosecution states there was only one way into the house since there was no sign of a break-in.'

'Many people had access to the key during my time at Shady Acres. They could have copied and replaced it at any point without me realising.'

'What about the security code?'

'My parents never changed it in twenty years. Even when they upgraded the system, they always kept the same six numbers.'

'A birthday or anniversary?'

Evie's giggle took a decade and three days of stress from her face. 'Something like that. It's always been 666777.'

'If the Devil is six, then God is seven.'

'Indeed.'

'Did the police mention a motive to the lawyer?'

'They did. They're hung up on Adam's sadomasochistic lifestyle.'

Astrid grinned at her unintentional pun. 'Perhaps we should tell them about Jack Kennedy and what he tried to do to you.'

'I asked one of the officers at the station about him. They don't know where he is. I also got a reply from the literary agent.'

'What did they say?'

'She said they couldn't cancel the book auction without any proof the novel is mine. So I borrowed the lawyer's laptop and emailed the file you rescued from Jack's computer. I'm waiting to hear back from them.'

'How does Adam feel about what his lawyer is doing?'

Evie grabbed the beer with one hand, the glass teetering in her fingers as she sipped from it. 'He's in a much better frame of mind than when we saw him last. I'm not sure he understands that, even if Harris proves his innocence in court, he'll still spend months behind bars.'

'The path of justice is sometimes long and bumpy.'

'Is this what it was like when you were an investigator in Britain?'

'Sometimes. The people I worked for, who your uncle still works for, had their ways of dispensing justice which didn't include wasting time on human rights and the rule of law.'

'Did that bother you?'

Astrid reached for a glass she didn't have. She needed alcohol more than food.

'Not in the slightest. The laws of nature are more important than the laws of man.' She deliberately said man instead of humankind.

'Do you think the end justifies the means?'

She watched as the barmaid stepped into view. Astrid smiled as she walked towards them.

'There is no black and white, only shades of grey.'

'What can I get you, ladies?'

She spoke to them both, but stared straight at Astrid. They ordered their food and another round of drinks, with a bottle of cider for Astrid this time.

'The only way to get your brother out of custody as soon as possible is for me to find the real culprit.'

'Are you making any progress?'

It was a difficult question. She answered it honestly, one eye on the barmaid as she sorted their order.

'No.'

Evie's eyes widened. Astrid couldn't tell if the pain in her heart was guilt or irritation. 'It's not your fault. However long it takes, I know Adam will be proved innocent.' The barmaid brought the drinks to the table. 'The most important thing now is knowing I've regained my faith.'

The bottle was cold in Astrid's hand, the neck of it frozen against her lips, her mind returning to the ragtag bunch who'd taken Evie to that abandoned factory.

'You've returned to religion?'

Evie grinned and took another drink. 'Nothing like that. I've regained my faith in myself. Outside of Adam's situation, I've only got one last thing to do before I move on with my life.'

She put the house key in her pocket and replaced it with a folded piece of paper.

Astrid sipped at the cider and picked up the paper. 'You're going to your school reunion?'

'There are a few things I have to say to certain people, and this is the perfect opportunity for it.'

'Do you want me to come with you?'

'I appreciate the offer, but I need to do this on my own.'

'Jack Kennedy is out there somewhere, and there are others in this town prepared to take their frustrations out on you.'

Evie finished the beer and slipped the paper into her pocket. 'I'm sure you can keep me out of trouble for the next few days. We'll watch old movies on TV and talk about our favourite books.'

The food arrived as Astrid thought about Evie's suggestion. She tried to relax, listening to the music, enjoying the spiced chicken wings, and made the cider last a long time. After they finished eating, they hung around for the live band, a quartet of Stooges-inspired young women called Naked On My Goat. Astrid was pleased to see Evie push her stress away as she had two more beers.

It was close to midnight before they left. Evie had one last surprise for her.

'I want us to stay at Adam's house, to stay at my house. I checked with the police, and they said it's no longer an ongoing crime scene.'

She understood why Evie wanted it, but was also aware of the potential pitfalls. Not many people would fancy sleeping in a place where a killer had murdered two children.

'I'll take us there. Is there anything you need from the hotel?'

Evie considered the question. 'Just the stuff we got from Kennedy's house. I'll need to get up early tomorrow so we can go shopping.'

'Go shopping for what?'

'Well, it's about time I had some new clothes. And maybe we'll buy you something.'

Astrid laughed at the look Evie gave her. 'Don't you like my outfit of leather jacket and jeans?'

'You're my fashion idol. But if I turn up at the reunion looking like you, I might get a few strange looks.'

Astrid started the car. 'What time is it on?'

'It runs from twelve to six. According to the leaflet, the school has set a no-alcohol policy during it so there'll be drinks in town afterwards. I think I'll probably need one by then.'

'You and me both,' Astrid said as she drove away. She was happy to see Evie in a good mood and thinking positively about her life. But all Astrid was thinking about was how she'd let her and her brother down.

Beverly crawled out of bed after her parents had gone to work. She'd had a brief conversation with them last night about the damage to the coffee shop. The insurance would cover the damage to the building and its stock. There should be enough to start again, and in the meantime, they'd continue with their temporary arrangement a few hundred yards from the crispy shell of the old shop.

She pretended to feel happy for them, but felt nothing. She should have moved out years ago, and got her own place, but she'd always made excuses not to. The TV shimmered in silence as she shovelled bits of insipid omelette between her lips. She finished it off with a slice of limp burnt toast.

Beverly pushed the plate to one side and reached for the detonator for the C4. Conway - she still found it hard to think of her as Claudia - had shown her how to set the connector between the explosive and the trigger cradled in her hand. She'd been so excited or nervous, and she couldn't tell which, she'd wanted to do it there and then in Conway's garage.

'Don't be stupid, Beverly.'

That voice had cut right through her, sharp enough to send her spiralling into the past and the time when she was a kid and the other woman was her teacher. She gazed at her then, under no illusions as to what role she played in their partnership.

'I might muck it up at the reunion. I need a test run.'

Conway put her fingers through Beverly's hair like an owner would do with its dog. 'You'll be fine. If we set it today, there's always the possibility of an unfortunate accident between now and then. You have to do it about thirty minutes before setting it off. I'll do the same with mine.'

'What time would that be?'

'People might leave before the finish at six, so let's go out with a bang at five.'

So here she was at ten on Saturday morning with the detonator in hand and the bag on the floor. She'd spent the last two days without leaving the house, expecting a visit from the police at any time, or another one from the British woman hanging around Evie Church. But nobody appeared. She hadn't seen her brother all week, and her parents were too busy with the aftermath of the fire even to wonder why she wasn't at work.

She peered at the bag of explosives. There was a larger carrier next to it, dark black and impossible to see through. This was to ensure no one would later say they saw her carrying Kennedy's backpack.

Beverly thought when she woke, there'd be niggling doubts eating away at her, her mind harassed with fears, but she was the complete opposite, and her determination had strengthened overnight. She stared at the TV while a group of politicians shouted at the screen as demonstrators waved placards at each other.

She spent the rest of the morning in a daze, putting clothes into the washer, including the jeans with the blood on them, and tidying her room. She also considered where she'd move to once it was all over. It was only an hour before the taxi was due that she remembered she had to remove the Trojan from Jack's laptop. How could she have forgotten that?

In her bedroom, she started the safe computer, imagining what was to come and wondering which of her old school friends would be at the reunion. She'd never sent an official reply of attendance to the organisers, so perhaps they wouldn't let her in. She brushed her doubts aside and turned to the screen. Conway had made her delete the Trojan on her computer, but she didn't know Beverly had made a copy of everything on that machine. She'd spend time on that later. Now, she placed the mouse over the connection to Kennedy's laptop. She was about to open it when she noticed someone had accessed his machine since she had.

Fuck!

It was after he'd gone to Conway's house. It was after she'd tortured and killed him. She pulled her hand away and stared at the screen.

Who would use his computer?

It had to be the police. If they did a proper sweep of his laptop, they'd find her Trojan. Would they have people capable of tracing it back to her? In a small-town police force like this one, she doubted it. But it wasn't impossible.

Fuck!

She slammed the lid down. It meant getting rid of the computer and setting up a new safer one. She glanced at the clock on the wall. The taxi would be there soon. She didn't have time to dispose of the computer. She stuffed it under the bed and trudged downstairs. The two bags stood next to each other in the kitchen while the detonator lay on the table.

Beverly removed her jacket from the back of the chair and put it on. She placed the detonator into her pocket. Then she put Kennedy's bag inside the other one, sat down and waited for her lift to arrive.

Twenty minutes later, she was in the car and heading to school. She fought off the temptation to call or message Conway. No contact until after. And only face to face.

The taxi driver made conversation with her. 'How long since you've seen most of these people?'

She forced herself to reply. 'It's nearly ten years.'

He chuckled. 'At least you'll have plenty to talk about.'

She matched his grin, one hand on the bag inside a bag on the seat next to her. Once at the school, she was to go to her office and leave the explosives there. Later on, she would return and set the detonator.

'What will you do in the afternoon?' she'd asked Conway.

'Don't worry; I'll arrive well before anyone else, sometime after breakfast. I'll have a chat with the janitor and make sure he knows what time to lock up. Once he's gone, I'll put the C4 and Kennedy's remains in the boiler room. I'll pop my head in during the day to say hello to my former students, only briefly, and then retire to my office. No one will know, apart from you.'

It all seemed so perfect. But perfect wasn't what she wanted. It was the danger she craved the most: the danger of getting the Glick girls into the house unseen; the danger of stepping into Conway's house to kill her. She'd enjoyed that as much as the violence.

The taxi pulled up outside the school. 'Do you want to book a return?' the driver said as she paid him.

'I'll call when I'm ready.'

The double bag was the glue between her fingers. She carried it up the steps and through the doors. She expected people there, but all she saw were signs and arrows pointing towards the main hall. Beverly ignored them and went the other way, down the corridor and towards her office. She unlocked it and placed the gifts to her former year group inside. As she locked the door, she wondered how many of them would turn up.

She glanced in the opposite direction, tempted to see if Principal Claudia Conway was in her office. She contemplated it for fewer than ten seconds before heading towards the main hall. The closer she got, the more noise she heard.

Twenty yards ahead of her, sitting underneath the banner proclaiming CLASS REUNION, were a man and a woman. As she approached, she didn't need to see their name badges to recognise who they were: Wendy Jones, whose previous short blonde hair had now transformed into shoulder-length raven black locks. Her wide grin told Beverly she'd had her teeth fixed since the two of them were last together at school.

Sitting next to her was Jay Johnson. He'd lost his thick glasses and greasy hair, which had covered most of his face, smiling at her through sea-blue eyes underneath a buzz cut straight from an army training ground. She remembered the two of them from the bottom of the school hierarchy a decade ago.

'Hi there,' the grinning Jay Johnson said to her. 'What's your name?'

They'd changed considerably in the ten years since she'd seen them last, but she knew she hadn't, not physically. That wasn't why they didn't recognise her. They didn't know her now because they'd never known her then. They'd been at the bottom of the social strata, but were still above her.

She placed a hand on her jacket, her fingers close to the detonator resting against her heart. 'Beverly Shaw.'

And I am your death.

39 A FEAST OF FRIENDS

Johnson continued to grin while Jones checked the details. She looked up and shook her head.

'You're not on our list. Did you message the organisers to tell them you were coming?'

'No. I only decided yesterday.'

Once I learnt I could blow most of you into the next world.

She curled her lips at Beverly. 'Well, we've already had a few non-replies turning up, and today's only catered for a hundred.' She shrugged. 'I don't think we can fit anymore in, Bev.'

Beverly dug her nails into her palm, her eyes burning through enough fire to bring down the building without the need of any C4. She was about to comment on Wendy's slapdash makeup when Jay spoke.

'We'll make an exception here, Wendy.' He grinned at Beverly. 'I mean, by the looks of Bev, I don't think she overeats. I'm sure there'll be plenty of *vol-au-vents* left for us, won't there, Bev?'

She removed her fingers from her palm before she started bleeding and gritted her teeth.

'I'll be grateful for anything you could do.'

Wendy let out a huge sigh. 'Oh, all right, but you'll need to wear this at all times.'

She handed her a sticky label with three letters hastily scribbled on to it. Beverly took it and resisted the urge to scratch Wendy's skin.

'Thanks.' She slapped it to the front of her jacket.

She strode towards the main hall. The music had changed to something by Beyoncé. Beverly glanced at her name tag as she pushed the doors open, grimacing at the three letters there.

BEV

A DJ occupied the stage, swaying as jangling pop bounced off the walls. Tables and chairs circled the sides, with food, drink, cutlery and plates on half of them. Something clawed at her stomach, but it wasn't hunger. She looked everywhere, searching for the best spot for the C4. Conway said she'd place her explosives between the boilers in the middle of the room below them. So she had to decide which point would cause maximum damage. And she wondered if Conway's present would achieve what she expected. How many people would get up on the dance floor if there was no alcohol to relax their inhibitions?

She didn't need to worry about that prospect for too long.

'I got you a drink.'

The plastic cup held out to her was as long and dark as the man holding it. It appeared to contain Coke, but it was impossible to ignore the smell of rum. She stared at it as if it was anthrax.

'Isn't this supposed to be a no booze party?'

His eyes sparkled and his teeth gleamed as he spoke. 'Our year group was always rebellious.'

She peered at his name badge: JAMIE.

He was handsome enough for her to consider what might happen between the two of them if there weren't a strong possibility he'd be dead or maimed before the end of the day. She didn't recognise him and guessed he didn't know her. Otherwise, he wouldn't be talking to her.

She took the drink from him.

'I'm sorry, but I don't know who you are.'

He continued to grin. 'I'm not surprised. I only attended the last two months of the final year. I doubt anyone here remembers me.'

His smile was intoxicating. She forgot why she was there and tried to quieten the sound of drums inside her head. Beverly sipped from the drink. It was warm on the lips and made the back of her throat tingle.

'Why were you only here for two months?'

'My father was in the military, and we were always moving around.'

Her instinct was to move away from him, to focus on what she needed to do. And then work out how she was going to get the bag into place without anyone seeing her. It would all be for nothing if some survivor identified her as the one carrying it. Instead, she stepped close enough to smell the musk of his aftershave. It was like standing underneath a tree massed in fresh leaves.

'That must have been difficult for you.'

'No.' He shook his head. 'It was the opposite. I got to travel to loads of interesting places and meet fascinating people. I didn't make any long-lasting friendships, but who does during their schooldays?'

The music changed to Katy Perry. She took another drink. If she kept this up, she'd be drunk in no time.

'So, now you're here trying to find new friends?'

He shrugged. 'Is it working?'

She was starting to like him, and that wasn't good. 'I'll tell you later.'

Beverly moved away as more people entered the hall. No one looked at her as she went to the toilet. She stepped inside and found it empty, throwing the rest of the drink into the sink. She avoided looking into the mirror, going into the first cubicle. She didn't need to pee, only to sit down and gather her thoughts.

Her legs trembled as she sat, her mind racing in a thousand different directions. Five minutes talking to a stranger, and she was already thinking about aborting the plan and going home. He was nice. He was pleasant. And he'd taken an interest in her. Was she prepared to murder him and others?

Before she could answer the question, the door to the restroom slammed open, and a loud voice echoed everywhere.

'Thank God you brought something to drink with you. I'd go mad spending hours in here with these losers without a glass or two.'

'I think you mean a bottle or two.'

Two or three different voices laughed together.

'You're still the hardest of us, Carole.' Beverly didn't recognise the third voice, but she knew who she spoke about: Carole Malone, the blondest blonde girl in their group and the worst bully, male or female, in the school.

'Give me another shot, Tabitha,' Malone said.

Tabitha Cortez, another one of the It girls. 'I don't have much, Carole. We've got to make it last.'

'Don't worry, girls,' Malone said. 'I know a guy who has brought plenty with him.'

'Who?' the unknown voice said.

'Didn't you see Jamie with that skank? He was pouring rum into the Coke earlier.'

'Don't you know who that skank is?' Cortez said.

There was silence, and Beverly imagined the unknown other shaking her dumb head.

Cortez continued. 'That's Bev Shaw. Someone told me she works here as a teacher.'

The laughter started again.

'Shaw the Claw?' Malone said.

'Yeah,' Cortez said. 'Fancy her coming to this.'

One of them turned on a tap, the sound of water matching the vibrations inside Beverly's skull.

'Well, today is going to be more entertaining than I expected. Let's go and find her.'

Their feet trampled out of the restroom, the tap still running as they went. Beverly pushed her legs together and grabbed hold of them with both hands. She struggled to breathe and pushed her head on to her knees.

Shaw the Claw.

She lifted and placed her palm in front of her face. This was her strength now, not a weakness. Beverly regained control and stopped shaking. Power was in her as she stood and left the stall. She walked to the mirror, peered straight into her eyes, and turned off the running tap.

Then she went to find the best place to put the explosives.

40 L'AMERICA

Astrid and Evie spent most of Thursday and Friday shopping and sightseeing in San Antonio. Astrid thought it was best to get Evie away from Eureka Falls for a while and let the lawyer sort out Adam's defence. Apart from the Alamo trip, she spent most of the time waiting around while Evie tried on clothes. She struggled to understand why it would take someone three hours to buy two shirts and a pair of jeans. In the first shop they visited, Astrid had bought a red top within five minutes.

'Don't you want anything else?' Evie said. They'd finished their Saturday outing, and Astrid was readying to drive them back to the Church house. 'I've got a month to pay off my credit card, and Adam gave me his bank details yesterday.'

Astrid provided a polite no, pleased to see the mention of Evie's brother didn't upset her. She ran a finger over her leg.

'You can't get jeans as good as this in America.'

Evie laughed as they drove away. 'I'm reasonably sure they're American made.'

'I doubt it. Hardly any clothes are made in the Western Hemisphere anymore. They're probably from Asia, but I've only ever seen this make for sale in a small tailor in London.'

'From the looks of them, you'll have to go back there soon for a new pair.'

'They'll do for now. What time should I drop you at the school?'

Evie peered out of the window. 'The doors open shortly, but I don't want to be one of the first ones arriving.'

Astrid eased off the pedal. 'You have to be fashionably late in your new clothes.'

'I don't need to spend more than two hours there. Perhaps do three until five, and then I'll take you for something to eat.'

'Do you have somewhere in mind?'

'The bar we went to the other day was cool. And we can have a drink as well.'

Astrid smiled at her. 'That's a good idea, and I think that group are playing as well. We'll get a taxi this time.'

'And maybe you can flirt with that barmaid again?'

'You noticed that, did you?' Astrid laughed.

'I've spent most of my life watching others from a distance, so it wasn't hard. And you weren't that subtle.'

'I thought the drink might have dulled your senses.'

'Not that much.'

It was a pleasant drive to the Church house, only delayed by Astrid stopping at a fast-food takeaway and getting lunch for both of them. They were tucking into it when Astrid approached the subject of the reunion.

'Are you going there to reacquaint yourself with old school friends?'

Evie nearly spat chicken from her sandwich over the kitchen table. 'No, that's not why I'm going.' She pulled a piece of salad from her teeth and dropped it on to her plate. 'I want people to see me, but I don't want to talk to them.'

'So, what's the point of it?'

'Perhaps there's no point to any of it, but I spent five years at that school with nobody taking any notice of me. I was invisible to everyone there. Do you know how it feels when inside you're crying out for someone to like you, but everybody looks right through you?'

'No, I don't.' Astrid tried not to think of her parents. 'A lot of people hurt me when I was younger. Until I hit my teens, I was desperate to be left alone.'

'What happened then?'

She stared at Evie, her mind drifting in and out of her past. 'Then, I stopped caring about what others felt and I took control of my life. No one has hurt me since.'

Was that true?

'You cut yourself off from the world as I did. Only I hid from others behind closed doors while you built barriers inside your head.'

Astrid picked up a can of pop and drank half of it. The sugar was sweet against her lips.

'I guess we're not so different after all.'

'But we can't keep on like this. That's why I'm going to the reunion. This is my new start. What will you do?'

The drink bubbled up from her stomach, parts of it appearing to buzz inside her head. Evie's question was something she'd asked herself numerous times. There was only one answer to it.

'As soon as we get your brother's situation sorted, I'm returning to Britain.'

'Are you going home?'

Astrid pushed the encroaching shadows into their hiding places. 'I don't have a home.'

'Do you have any family?'

She stood and put the empty can in the bin. 'I have a sister who hates me and a niece I rarely see, no matter how much I want to.'

Evie was finishing her food as her cell rang. 'There's always hope, Astrid.'

Astrid left her to it and went into the living room. She grabbed Kennedy's laptop and settled into the sofa. As she waited for it to start, she stared at her mobile. Apart from Evie's, there were only two numbers in her contacts.

If I could only make one call before the world ended, who would it be to?

'What are you going to do with the computer?' Evie stood behind her, emptying the shopping bag of her new clothes.

Astrid slipped the phone into her pocket. 'Kennedy is still on the loose somewhere, so I'm hoping there's something on here to help us find him. If he tried to kill you once to cover up stealing your work, then he might do it again.'

She didn't want to worry Evie, but it had to be said.

'It's funny you mention him. That was his ex-literary agent on the phone.'

'Ex?'

'Yes. The file I sent her was proof of the novel being mine. She said there's a possibility of bringing criminal charges against Jack if I want.'

'We'll have to find him first. What about the auction for your book?'

'They've postponed it. The agent asked to meet me.' Evie's smile lit up the room. 'She still loves the book and wants to represent me.'

'That's great.' The laptop buzzed against her legs. 'You're getting your new life off to a good start.'

Evie grabbed her clothes and headed for the door. 'I'll be back in a couple of hours once I've sorted what I'm wearing. Is that okay?'

'Don't rush on my account.'

Astrid wasn't sure if Evie attending the reunion was appropriate, but it was good to see her happy and confident. Now she focused on Kennedy's computer.

Astrid spent the first hour skipping through his collection of sadomasochist images and videos. It was a tedious affair, a fruitless pursuit trying to find something linking the scene with Adam and anything which might lead her to the murderer of the Glick girls.

Then she searched through his other files, including some of his creative writing. It didn't take her long to understand why he'd become desperate to steal Evie's book. Most of what she found was useless, apart from a dozen or so short stories and poems dedicated to someone called Claudia the Dominatrix. Reading between the lines, Astrid deduced that Claudia was an older woman local to Kennedy.

Perhaps that's where he's hiding.

As fascinating as it was, it was only when Evie returned that she discovered the most interesting thing on the laptop.

Evie strode into the room wearing her new jeans and a shiny, long-sleeved red top.

'What do you think?'

Astrid glanced at her. 'You look fabulous, but not as great as this.'

Evie stood at her side while Astrid showed her the screen. She pointed at a miniature cartoon version of a woman with a shield jumping up and down.

'You're playing one of Jack's computer games?'

'It's nothing so innocent. I downloaded a special type of

security software created by my former employers. And it found this.'

'What is it?'

'It's a Backdoor Trojan, a malicious program which enables a remote hacker to have access to an infected device.'

Evie flopped on to the sofa, her eyes sparkling with fascination. 'How would that get onto his laptop?'

'He could have downloaded it by accident, but I checked the security on his computer, and it's top of the range and was up to date at the point we snatched it from his house.'

'Couldn't he have got it from one of his dodgy sex sites?'

Astrid frowned at her. 'I've gone through his web browsing, and it looks like he kept his sexual tastes to the real world and not online. No, I think the Trojan was installed directly on to this computer.'

'For what purpose?'

'To spy on him.' She watched the truth dawn on Evie.

'So, they'd know about him claiming my book as his?'

'They would, that and everything else on the laptop. And I'd guess it's someone from this town.'

'This is all fascinating, but we've got to go now.' She grabbed hold of Astrid's hand and dragged her off the sofa. The computer slipped on to the empty seat. 'We can talk about this tonight over beer and food.'

Astrid grabbed her jacket as they left, and Evie locked the door behind them. It was a twenty-five-minute drive to the reunion, getting them there just after three-thirty.

'Text me if you need anything,' Astrid said as Evie got out of the car.

'I'll be done by five-thirty.' Evie walked to the entrance of the school.

Astrid watched her go. She was reluctant to return to the Church house and pondered what to do. After twenty seconds, she left and headed towards the Kennedy bookshop. Perhaps there was something in that burnt husk to help find him. She hadn't discounted the possibility there was a connection between his attack on Evie and the framing of Adam.

She drove away as terrible pop music blared out of the school.

41 FIVE TO ONE

Beverly spent most of the afternoon dodging the three women from the bathroom and Jamie with his endless alcohol supply. It didn't take her long to realise most in the main hall had brought booze with them. The good thing about this was they were all using bags or backpacks for their drinks. She'd thought carrying the bag within a bag would make her stand out from the crowd, but there were no worries about that now.

She'd spent time listening to music she disliked, so, encouraged by the knowledge of what she was about to do and ignoring the wide stares and whispered insults, she strode up to the DJ. He wasn't a student from their year group; he looked about eighteen, and she didn't recognise him. Even though they were indoors with little light, he wore wraparound shades and a permanent grimace. She gave him her perfect fake smile.

'Do you take requests?'

'What?' he shovelled his hips to one side as if about to perform a slow-motion jig.

'Can you play some music I might like?'

He grinned and removed his glasses. His eyes were bloodshot and full of liquid as he winked at her.

'Sure, darling; what da ya fancy?'

'Do you have anything by La Roux?'

Eminem was warbling about killing somebody when the DJ gave her the thumbs up. 'I've got plenty of golden oldies in here, sweetheart. I'll find something for ya.'

She wandered away, pondering what the place would look like when two sets of explosives went off, not to mention the contents of the boilers below her feet.

It was dead on half-past three when Principal Claudia Conway entered the fray, making her way around her many ex-students, most of whose enjoyment dissipated when they saw her. She smiled and shook hands while they nodded and forced their lips upwards. Twenty minutes later, she was at Beverly's side at the far end next to some empty tables. She continued smiling while all but one of her former charges looked away from her.

'I've got a present for you.' She placed something in Beverly's hand.

'What is it?'

'It's a short-wave wireless detonator, which works a bit like a Bluetooth device. Put the other detonator in the bag with the C4.'

Ghostly dry nails scratched at the inside of her throat. 'Why do I need this? What's wrong with the other one?'

Conway gripped Beverly's fingers as she spoke. 'Unfortunately, and I only discovered it this morning, the original detonators, mine as well, are that old, they're only fifty per cent reliable. And we can't have that, can we?' She tilted her head to the side and let go of her hand.

'I suppose not.'

'It works on the same signal as the other one, and I've already set it for you. There's just a little problem.'

Rihanna's *Only Girl in the World* burst forth from the speakers.

'What problem?'

'The distance for the connection is shorter. So, you need to get closer to the bag.'

'How close?' In her mind was a scene from some old movie of a man's head exploding.

'Well, make sure you're away from the centre of the room because of the explosives underneath. For your detonation, get at least a hundred yards from it, and you should be okay.'

'I should be okay?'

'It's not an exact science, Beverly. How brave are you prepared to be for your cause?'

She pushed out her cheeks and let out a large gasp of air. 'I haven't worked out where to put the bag yet.' She glanced at the massive clock on the wall showing it was ten to four.

Conway took two steps forward. 'You'll place it under the table you're leaning against, behind that nice white cloth which will cover it. I've ordered a reunion cake to be delivered at half-past four, and it'll go on that table. It's a perfect spot for your surprise package.'

Beverly slipped the detonator into her pocket, her fingers brushing across her face as if to wipe new life into her head.

'And how am I supposed to get it under there without anyone noticing?'

Conway checked the time on her watch. 'At four o'clock, the DJ will stop the music, and I'm going to step on stage, attract everyone's attention, and give a speech telling them how proud of them I am. Nobody will dare take their eyes from me. Go to your office now, get the bag, and be ready to put it under the table when I start talking. Can you do that?'

If their relationship had ever been one of equal partners, it was back to teacher and student now. Beverly nodded and stepped across the floor and out of the hall as the music changed to Kesha. She wanted to run to her office, her legs threatening to take over the rest of her body, but she kept control.

Then she turned the corner and walked straight into Evie Church.

'Ow,' Evie said as they bumped heads.

Beverly raised trembling fingers to her face, her lips quivering. Behind them in the main hall, the music stopped.

'I'm... I'm... sorry.'

The words stumbled out of Beverly's mouth as they stared at each other.

'No,' Evie said. 'It's my fault. I never intended to be this late. Have I missed much?'

Beverly couldn't take her eyes off Evie, the unwanted images in her head coming quickly: the Glick sisters in the Church house; the photos she'd taken of them; two girls in that basement, her fingers around the older girl's throat while the younger one froze in terror. Then the image changed and it was a different two girls in that basement, and the terror was someone else's.

'There's a cake coming soon.'

Beverly blurted the words out and turned towards her office. She marched there without looking back, the key in her hand as she fumbled the door open. The clock on her desk said it was one minute to four.

She fell into the chair, every part of her shaking, but the

tremors were worst in her heart and brain. The bag inside a bag sat at her feet. She reached into her pocket, removed the old charger, and dropped it on top of the explosives.

It was fate. Evie was there. If she'd had doubts about her actions, they were knocked from her by that bump on the head. She grabbed the bag and locked the door behind her. There was no one in the corridor and no sight of Evie. As she reached the main hall entrance and glanced inside, it was five past four. Conway was in the centre of the stage, lording over all those below her.

She scanned the crowd and every eye was on their former teacher. The hall was also darker than when she had been there before. The principal must have turned the lights down to put the spotlight on her. It was clear now for Beverly to get to the table and hide the bag. But there was no sign of Evie, and that worried her.

Her fingers hurt as she clutched on to the bag, her legs throbbed as she made her way around the outside of the hall. She saw Conway holding sway over the group of twenty-somethings. Her lips kept moving, but Beverly didn't hear what she said over the noise of drums beating against the insides of her skull.

It was ten past four when she reached the table. She bent her legs, her bones creaking as she did so, and pushed the bag under it. She made sure the cloth covered it and strode towards the back of the crowd.

'I wish you all the best for the future,' Conway said as the lights came up and the strains of *Bulletproof* by La Roux swirled around the hall. If she'd expected spontaneous applause, she didn't get it. Beverly noticed movement to her right, turning to see delivery people carrying the biggest cake she'd ever seen. It had ten levels to it, with enough sugar to destroy a thousand lives. The crowd started to disperse and watch the cake being carried to the empty tables.

It's too heavy for the table. It'll break, and they'll see what's underneath it.

The muscles in Beverly's legs throbbed to the rhythm of the music. Some people were dancing, their bodies skipping to the beat as the delivery people inched towards the table. There were six of them carrying the cake, and she wondered why they hadn't wheeled the behemoth in. They placed it over two tables, and she was sure she heard the strain of wood about to break until she realised the sound was only in her head.

Somehow, without Beverly seeing how she got there, Conway was next to the cake with a large knife in her hand. The delivery people dumped a load of paper plates on the table, and then left. Conway started slicing into the giant sweet treat and passed the slices out on plates. Beverly could have moved away from all of them, reached the door, and then set the detonator off. The thick plastic was sticking to her leg inside her trouser pocket.

Conway glanced at her as she handed out the cake, and Beverly understood their destinies were linked together. Perhaps they always had been.

'If you don't get some of it, there'll be none left soon.'

Evie Church was at her side. Behind her, looming large on the wall, the clock ticked towards fifteen minutes to five.

Where has all the time gone?

Conway departed the half-drunk crowd swarming around the table and made her way out of the hall.

She's going to the boiler room. I need to get away from this spot.

Beverly turned to Evie. 'There's far too much sugar in that for me. But you should have some.'

'I didn't come here to eat.'

Beverly's fingers went to her pocket, her nails touching the top of the detonator. 'Then why are you here? It can't be to reconnect with all your old friends from our school.'

'I'm guessing it's the same reason why you're here, Beverly.'

She slipped the detonator into her palm so it rested against her scar. Beverly hid behind her fingers as she pulled her hand from her pocket. The music changed as the clock ticked to ten minutes to five. She was fewer than twenty feet from the explosives, perhaps ten from the middle of the main hall. Dozens of people were dancing there; probably thirty more were drinking and chatting near the cake.

'And why am I here, Evie?'

Did she know about the explosives or what happened to Kennedy? Or was she there about the Glick girls?

Evie tilted her head towards the DJ, her eyes narrowing in confusion. 'I know this song, but can't remember what it is.'

'It's *In for the Kill* by La Roux.'

Evie smacked her hands together. 'That's it!'

The hairs on the back of Beverly's hand tingled as if touched by static electricity. 'It was nice to see you again, Evie. I'm glad you finally made it out of that home, but I have to go now.'

She turned to walk towards the exit. Would that be a safe distance and close enough to trigger the explosives?

'You're here because you wanted to look people in the eyes and let them know you survived.'

Beverly froze to the spot. The clock on the wall moved in slow motion to six minutes to five. The whole of her was cold, even though sweat dribbled down her forehead.

'Survived?'

Evie stepped closer to her. 'Yes, you survived their insults and their anger. And you survived your accident.'

Beverly held out her hand and released the grip from her fingers. The detonator lay in the middle of her palm. She couldn't see the clock, but it could have been no more than two minutes to five.

'Accident?'

She was waiting for Evie to reply, her finger close to the trigger, when something crashed into the doors behind them.

42 TEXAS RADIO AND THE
BIG BEAT

The stink of burnt wood and plastic continued to drift from the bookshop. Astrid stood outside and peered through the window. The authorities had plastered DO NOT ENTER and DANGEROUS signs near the front of the building and the coffee shop. They'd also cordoned off the alleyways on both sides of the bookshop with barricades.

She stared at the damage for ten seconds and doubted there would be anything inside to help her find its missing owner. She had two hours to kill and couldn't be bothered to head back to Evie's house; she'd only have to leave again and return to the school to pick her up later. Her stomach grumbled and told her to get something to eat. She watched a customer exit the temporary coffee shop fifty yards away and settled on that.

Astrid pushed the door aside, finding less than half a dozen people inside. She picked an empty table near the window and sat down. As she waited, she removed her phone and went over the list of residents on Elm Street again.

There must be something I've missed. Why would those girls go into the house willingly?

A smiling woman approached with a notepad in her hand. There were more creases on her face than the surface of Mars, and her hair was as white as paper. Her name tag was MARY.

'Hi there. It's always nice to see new customers.' She had a smoker's teeth, discoloured and uneven, and looked tired with dull brown eyes. 'What can I get you?'

Astrid picked up the menu and had a quick look through. 'I thought you'd only serve coffee and maybe a few treats.'

'We had to expand our options to stay open. So, what will you have?'

'I'll have a strawberry milkshake and bacon and eggs, please.'

Mary scribbled it all down, beaming as she did. 'I love your accent. Are you British?'

'Yes, I'm from England.'

'Wow. I don't think we've ever had someone from England here before.'

Astrid smiled. 'I'm surprised you're open, what with the fire at the bookshop.'

A tiny sparkle returned to her face. 'Oh, we got lucky there. This place hadn't been empty long from the previous owners, so everything we needed was still here. Then it was just a case of salvaging what we could from the other shop and borrowing the rest.' She took a cloth from her pocket and wiped a stain from the table. 'It was a shame for Jack, though. I'll put your order in now.'

Mary turned away before Astrid could ask a question. She went through the list on her phone again while she waited for her order. It was a fruitless fifteen minutes staring at the names.

The smell of bacon and eggs drifted through the coffee shop as two more customers entered. An older man, name tag of TOM, brought her order over. She relaxed and took her time, having sips of the milkshake between mouthfuls of food. She went online and searched for the latest news on Adam and found nothing interesting. She was browsing through Jack Kennedy's bookshop website when Mary returned.

'Would you like dessert? We do a fantastic apple pie which I make at home. It's fresh.'

'That sounds great. Can I ask you a few questions first?'

A puzzled look crossed Mary's face. Astrid indicated for her to take the empty seat at the table.

'About what?' She appeared reluctant, but sat down.

'How well do you know Jack Kennedy?'

'You want to know about Jack?'

'He went missing after the fire, and I'm trying to locate him. Anything you tell me could help.'

'Are you a private investigator?'

'Something like that. Have you known him long?'

Mary glanced around the coffee shop, and then put her notebook on the table. 'Well, it's not busy at the moment and, if I can help find Jack....' She placed her pencil on top of the pad. 'We were the first businesses to move into this street nearly twenty years ago. We always helped each other, especially when the recession hit and everyone struggled.'

Astrid noticed the wistful expression on her face. 'Did he tell you he wanted to be a writer?'

She smiled through those nicotine teeth again. 'Oh yes; he'd come in for a coffee, jotting things down in those books of his. Tom and I would ask him about it, but he'd keep most of it to himself. I know he'd had a few disappointments over the years, though he did seem happier about it the last few months and I think he might have been on the verge of something.'

Indeed he was. This would have been the day when he'd have sold Evie's book as his own to a publisher and probably made a shed load of money.

'Did you spend any time with him outside of work?'

Mary raised a hand to her face as her cheeks turned a faint shade of pink. 'What do you mean?'

'Do you know what he did away from his bookshop, if he had any friends or relatives in the town?'

Are you aware he's into sadomasochism? Or who his mysterious Claudia is? Could it be you?

'Oh, he has no family; he did tell me that. I doubt if he had any time for friends.' She turned to watch Tom clearing the table next to them. 'Most of the people still able to run their business are spending all of their waking hours at work. I wish we had time for friends.'

Astrid sank back into her chair, the plastic cutting into her spine. 'Okay.'

'In fact, I think the only time I ever saw him talking to someone else was when Beverly fixed his computer.'

'What?' Astrid shifted forward.

'He had a virus or something, I don't know about this stuff, and he was moaning about it in the shop one day, said he was probably going to lose all his work. She took it off him and fixed it in an hour. And she wouldn't take any money for it, no matter how much he protested.'

Astrid's mind raced away from her. 'Is Beverly a customer of yours?'

Mary burst out laughing. 'No, nothing like that; she's our daughter.'

'Is she a computer specialist, a technician?' Who better to place a Trojan horse on an unsuspecting person?

'Well, she's always been good with computers even when she was young, and we did think after university, she'd end up at one of those tech companies. I mean, she finds it easier to be around machines than people, so we were both surprised when she landed a job teaching at the school.'

Astrid nearly fell from the chair. 'Does she teach at the elementary school?' Did she know the Glick girls?

'No. Beverly works with middle and high school kids. Tom and I hoped she might have started a family of her own by now, but, well, with the problems she's had...' Her eyes glanced upwards as her voice faded out.

Astrid gave no thought for pressing this tired and stressed-out woman about her personal life, her brain stitching together a map inside her head which showed how Adam was innocent after all.

'What sort of problems does your daughter have, Mary?'

She laughed nervously. 'Oh, she's fine now, just a little quiet and reserved. We try and talk to her, but it's hard with the hours we work.' She glanced at her husband as he served a customer at the front of the shop. 'But she had a difficult childhood, after the... after the accident.'

'Do you want to talk about the accident?'

Mary's face relaxed, distant light flickering at the back of her eyes. 'It's funny, really.' She wasn't laughing anymore. 'We tried several therapists, counsellors, and psychiatrists with her over the years, you know, to get her to talk about what happened, but I don't think we've ever spoken to anyone about it.'

Astrid reached across the table and touched Mary's hand. 'It must have been a great strain on you. Sometimes it's better to get everything out and not hold it in.'

Mary patted her on the fingers. 'I believe you're right.' She took another deep breath. 'She was five years old when it happened. We never called her Beverly then; it was Bev. Our little Bev.' Her voice trembled. 'We'd just taken over the shop and were working every hour we could; nothing's changed much there.' The nervous laugh returned. 'So we left her at a friend's house whose older brother babysat them both. That's when it happened.'

All the pieces came together inside Astrid's head. 'Was that friend Evie Church?'

Mary nodded. 'Yes, and her brother Adam was looking after them.'

'But something happened?'

'We don't blame Adam; we never have. But he was playing video games upstairs when the girls snuck into the basement. It should have been locked. Their dad was always working on something for the church and had tools and bits of metal and wood stored down there. And that's when it happened.'

'The accident?'

Mary let go of Astrid's hand and wiped a tear from her eye. 'The girls must have been playing down there, running around after each other, when Bev fell and... and...' she struggled to finish the sentence.

'She injured herself?'

'Bev fell on to a metal pole. We were lucky. It could have been so much worse; it could have gone through her heart or her head. Instead, she put her hand out, and it cut right through her palm. Adam heard the screams and ran into the basement.'

'It sounds terrible, but not life-threatening. It was traumatic for Beverly, though?'

'It left a large circular wound in the middle of her hand, and around the edges were lots of smaller scars shaped like an octopus's tentacles. But that wasn't the worst of it.'

'That was how she reacted to it?'

Mary put a finger to her mouth, then let go when her lips stopped trembling. 'She hated the scars in her hand, having to look at them every day, thinking what the other kids would say to her. You know how cruel they can be.'

Astrid nodded. 'I do.'

'She couldn't bear to leave the house looking like that, so she began curling her fingers forward to cover up the damage. Beverly held them like that all the time, never moving them, never using that hand for anything. She stopped cutting her nails until... until... well, it resembled a crooked branch ready to spring open and claw your eyes out. It took years for her to relax her hand. When she left school and went to university, we thought she'd put it all behind her.' Mary stared at her husband. 'If you wait long enough, you can adjust to anything.'

Astrid placed money on the table and got up. 'You and Beverly live in the house across from Adam Church and your surname is Shaw?'

Everything had clicked into place, and she'd completed the murder map for the Glick girls.

'That's correct.'

'Is it okay if I go to your home and have a word with her?'

There was no point worrying this poor woman by telling her it was likely her daughter was a child murderer. Mary got out of her seat, looking happier.

'You were right; it was good to talk about it. I know

Beverly is better because she's leaving town soon to find a new job, but she won't be at home now. She left us a note saying she had to go to school today.'

'She's gone to work?'

'No, she's there for the reunion. She said she had one final thing to take care of before she leaves.'

Astrid didn't say goodbye, didn't wait for her change. She was out of the door and running as the clocks struck four-thirty all over town. She jumped into the car and drove off without checking the traffic. It was fewer than forty seconds before the other vehicle plunged into her side, and both cars tumbled off the road.

43   WHEN THE MUSIC'S OVER

The crashing sounds behind her made Beverly jump. A long-forgotten switch flicked inside her mind. Her fingers sprang out uncontrollably, bending forward like a claw. She dropped the detonator on to the ground. It must have been one minute to five. The detonator tumbled and rolled on to the dancefloor, and disappeared between a tangle of feet and legs.

She threw herself into the middle of them, pushing people aside. They laughed at her as she dropped to her knees and scooped it up. There couldn't have been more than thirty seconds left before Claudia Conway flicked her switch. Beverly ran towards the door, looking for Evie Church but finding an empty spot where she'd been.

The detonator was in her good hand as the clock struck five. She stared at her other hand, unable to get it to return to normal no matter how many buttons she pushed inside her mind.

Transfer the pain.

She placed one finger over the detonator and got ready to press. Fewer than ten seconds now.

'Don't do it, Beverly.' The voice was behind her. And it was British.

She turned to face Astrid Snow. Evie stood next to her as Beverly glanced at the time. It was five o'clock and the Black Eyed Peas bounced off every wall.

The British woman was there to stop her; she knew that. Did it mean there was someone else in the boiler room stopping Conway? Was that why she hadn't set off her explosives? Were the police down there arresting her right now?

It's all down to me, then. But they know it's me. I won't get away.

She stared at Snow. 'Don't do what?'

Snow scanned the room, but kept her eye on the detonator. 'I've just had a conversation with your mother, Beverly. She told me how good you are with computers.'

'What?' Beverly said.

'You must be very good. I wouldn't have found the Trojan you placed on Jack Kennedy's laptop without some specialist tracking software.'

'I don't know what you're talking about.'

The music and the dancing continued.

I shouldn't be having this conversation with her. I should blow the explosives now. But something has gone wrong. It was obvious when Conway didn't detonate the C4. I don't want to die. But I don't want to go to jail either. What does this woman want?

'There's always a problem for someone placing a Trojan on a computer, though, isn't there, Beverly? I bet you know what it is.'

The DJ put *Poker Face* on his digital turntable.

'You open a backdoor connection to whoever - not me - installed the Trojan.'

Snow stood in front of Evie. 'It was hard to do, but, with a bit of help, I made the link run both ways. I saw everything on your computer, looked through all your files, read all your messages.' Beverly let the information sink in. 'Found all your photos.' She paused again. 'Even the ones you took for trophies.'

Evie pushed her way forward. 'What are you two talking about?'

Snow ignored her and stared straight at Beverly. 'Is this because of the accident you had in the Church basement twenty years ago? Is that why you killed the Glick girls there, to get back at Adam?'

Evie gasped and turned to Beverly. 'What is this?'

Snow answered. 'Do you remember the night your brother babysat for the two of you and Beverly had an accident in the basement?'

'It wasn't an accident. It was his fault.' Beverly's voice was like steel as she walked towards them. The clock on the wall said ten past five. She knew there'd be no explosion below them now.

But I can still do it.

Evie stared at Beverly, her eyes wide, her lips trembling. 'You did this to get back at Adam? You murdered those poor girls?'

'I didn't do anything. Your British friend is crazy.'

'It was an accident, Beverly, don't you remember? We were playing hide and seek when you fell over.'

Beverly's fingers were still crunched over like a claw. The music had stopped and people were staring at them. The girls who'd hated her, the boys who'd laughed at her, were all there, gazing at her again. It wasn't too late to pay them all back.

'It wasn't an accident. Adam should have been looking after us. That was his job.'

She raised her voice, the blood throbbing inside her veins. Had she left any fingerprints on the bags or the explosives, or the other detonator? She probably had, thinking they would have been blown to bits by now.

Prison or death. What should I choose?

Snow stepped forward. 'I was lying about reversing the Trojan connection. There's no proof you killed those girls. You can walk away from this a free woman. No one would know but us three.'

Evie turned to Snow, her nostrils flaring and her eyes bulging. 'Are you mad? We have to get Adam out of custody.'

'Adam will be fine, Evie. You said yourself his lawyer is good enough to get him off at trial.'

'But people will still believe he's guilty, will still call him a child murderer.'

'I'm sure he'd take that over having his sister, and who knows how many others, blown to bits in this hall.'

The gravity of Snow's words appeared to hit Evie for the first time, her gaze turning to Beverly and her hand.

'I wish we'd stayed friends, Beverly.' She held out her fingers to her. 'There's still time to rectify that.'

Beverly's shoulders relaxed, her hand returning to normal. She didn't care about Evie Church's pitiful attempt at friendship. It was far too late for that, but she could still escape this situation. She could leave and continue somewhere else where she wouldn't get sucked into someone else's stupid plans. The police would trace the explosives to Conway's garage, Beverly would deny all knowledge of it, and now she was sure she'd worn gloves when handling them. She could do it. She was smarter than all of them, even Conway.

And definitely smarter than this Astrid Snow.

Beverly slipped the detonator into her trouser pocket and moved around them as the lights came up and the reunion finished. 'Well, it was a fun imaginary conversation we had, but I'm going home.' There was a skip in her step and relief in her heart. She knew everything was going to be okay.

She kept on believing that right up until the moment she strode into the police standing behind Snow and Evie.

Astrid was standing behind Shaw when the teacher froze in front of the police. She watched the surprise in Shaw's eyes transfer to her hand as she relaxed her fingers. It was enough for Astrid to snatch the detonator from her. Then Detective Hicks stepped forward with a policewoman at his side holding handcuffs.

'One of my colleagues will read you your rights, Ms Shaw.'

Astrid handed him the detonator. 'You need to get everyone out of here as quick as possible and check the whole building, not just the hall, for explosives.'

Beverly twisted her neck to stare at Astrid as the policewoman took her out of the school.

Evie gazed at Astrid. 'You've got a bruise on your head.'

Astrid raised her hand to the injury. 'You can thank Hicks for that. He drove his car into mine when I was on my way here.'

The detective looked at her. 'I apologise again, Ms Snow. But at least we got you here quicker than you would have without being chauffeur driven by the police with all sirens blaring.'

'Is it true?' Evie said. 'Did she kill those girls to frame my brother?'

Officers swarmed into the hall as ex-students piled out. Astrid grabbed Evie and dragged her outside. She looked at the staff photos on the reception wall as they left, finding Shaw on the first row, her blank face peering out from the picture. She glanced at all the others and wondered how many would be shocked once they discovered Shaw's murderous nature. Lights flashed everywhere as she answered Evie's question.

'It looks like Beverly murdered the Glick girls in your house.'

'This was to get back at my brother for when she had her accident?'

'That's probably only part of it. After speaking to her mother, I think Shaw has stored her resentment for several years, but it could be she just enjoys killing. The police will have a grand time interviewing her.'

'How did you know she intended to blow up the school?'

'I didn't until I turned up and saw the detonator in her hand. I came here because I thought she was going to hurt you.'

'I bumped into her when I stepped into the corridor. I think she was as surprised to see me as I was her. How does a small-town teacher have explosives?'

'That's up to the police to find out.' Astrid noticed Detective Hicks stride out of the school. 'We'll get a lift to the station with him and ask when they'll release Adam.'

'There's evidence of his innocence and Beverly's guilt?'

'I told them Shaw had photographs of the murdered girls on her computer.'

'The story of the reverse Trojan horse was true?'

'Nope, that was a complete bluff.'

Evie's face turned a pale shade of white. 'What... so how...?'

Astrid pulled on her arm and they headed towards Hicks. 'I was at her house yesterday, inside her bedroom. A laptop was switched on in the room, a swirling screensaver hiding what was on the machine. She was desperate for me not to see what was on it.'

'That's it? That's your reason to think there's incriminating photos on her computer?' Evie's volume increased so much, Astrid thought she'd explode like a pricked balloon.

'She's a killer, I know it, and killers like her always take trophies of their crimes. They can't help themselves.'

Hicks stepped towards them. 'We found explosives under a table in the main hall.'

'There's nothing else?'

'Not yet, but we'll keep looking. Uniformed officers are at her house, collecting her electronic devices. Where did you say you saw the crime photos?'

'Get your tech people to search through everything and you'll find what you need. Give us a lift to the station, and I'll give you a statement.'

He nodded and they climbed into the back of a police car. Evie didn't speak all the way there, and Astrid assumed she was both nervous and a little mad at her. She'd trusted her instincts, and if nothing else, they'd stopped Shaw blowing up that hall.

Adam's lawyer was waiting for them when they got there. Astrid left Evie and the lawyer to it, sitting at Hicks's desk. She removed the phone from her pocket and wondered again who she'd ring if she were only allowed one call.

Perhaps I should ring George.

SHE'D SAT THERE for an hour before a uniformed officer asked her if she wanted a drink. He brought her a can of Coke while she was checking the latest news online. There was no official statement from the police, but plenty of rumours were running around about a potential terrorist attack at the school.

There was one particular convoluted conspiracy theory circulating about what happened, which amused Astrid. She was tempted to leave a comment on the webpage when Hicks returned. He pulled up a chair opposite her and dropped a folder on to his desk.

'You were more than right about the photos.'

She kept her relief hidden. 'How so?'

'Well, we had to break through her security first, but once we did, we hit the jackpot. Along with many disturbing images of the Glick sisters, she'd written a full manifesto of how she planned the whole thing.'

'Let me guess: she stole a spare key from the house when she was there with Evie as kids.'

Hicks pointed at her. 'You're spot on, Snow. She's been spilling her guts since we brought her in.'

'Even though the Glick girls weren't old enough to attend Shaw's school, they must have known her, recognised and trusted her to enter the house.'

He nodded. 'Apparently, she and some of the other high

school teachers regularly went to the elementary school to give the kids lessons on how to use the internet safely.' He rubbed at the palm of his hand, and Astrid thought of Shaw's childhood scar, long since healed, which still lived inside her mind. 'What we don't know yet is how she knew the girls would be there that day or if it was a random attack.'

Astrid shook her head. 'She knew. I'm guessing Shaw was planning this for a long time. She must have seen the sisters playing in the woods before and memorised their routine.'

'Well, I guess we'll know soon enough. She seems keen to tell us everything.'

'Did you find anything else useful on her machine, like where she got the explosives?'

'No, we're still working on that. It's the one thing she doesn't want to talk about. But we did get these.' He opened the folder and removed two bits of A4 paper covered in colour photographs. Astrid picked them up and looked through them.

'These are body parts?'

'Indeed they are, and just before I returned here, I got a call from the team at the school.'

'They found more explosives?'

He pointed at the photos. 'They discovered these in four bags in the boiler room under the main hall. There's a head in there as well, which one of our guys recognised.'

'Who is it?'

'Jack Kennedy.'

Astrid relaxed into the chair. Her mouth was dry. She reached for the can of Coke and drained it.

'When will you release Adam?'

'Look over there.'

She turned and saw Adam, Evie, and the lawyer enter the room. She got up as Evie ran towards her. They hugged and, on this rare occasion, Astrid didn't want it to end.

They had an interesting conversation on the journey back to the Church house.

45 END OF THE NIGHT

It was distressing for Claudia to empty everything from the garage, but she knew it was coming once she'd convinced Shaw to blow up the school. She'd left no prints or DNA evidence on the bags containing the explosives and Kennedy's body parts. She thought the police would turn up after they arrested Shaw, but it had been twenty-four hours since then, and they hadn't appeared. She was ready to deny anything Shaw claimed.

She entered her house and went to the kitchen; the occasion deserved the best champagne she had. She opened the fridge and got the bottle. It was hard to keep the grin from her face as she poured a glass. It was incredible how little Bev Shaw, Shaw the Claw, had fallen into her lap.

Shaw is easily manipulated.

Conway had written those words ten years ago and how prophetic she'd been. She took her drink and went into the living room. She was two steps inside and close to slumping into her favourite seat when she realised someone was sitting there.

'Ever get the feeling you've been cheated?' The woman leant forward, her British accent stinging Conway's ears.

'How... how did you get in here?'

'You're wondering why your camera alarms didn't trigger? I cut the electricity to the house before I picked the lock on the back door.'

'What do you want?'

'It's impressive how quickly you've emptied the place of anything linking you to Beverly Shaw's crimes. The garage is particularly sparse.'

'I don't know what you're talking about.'

Conway's heart rate didn't increase. She felt no fear or pressure, her initial surprise having vanished in a flash. She strode past the intruder and placed the glass of champagne on her writing desk. Then she moved to the other side and sat down.

'You were her teacher when she was a student at the school, and now you're her boss, but I still can't work out your murder connection. I don't think you're long-time partners. This has to be a recent thing.'

Conway picked up her glass and sipped at it. This was a game, and she liked playing games; the more dangerous, the better.

'I suppose you're about to tell me what this is all about, Ms...?'

'You can call me Astrid.' She crossed her legs and settled into the sofa. 'Did you get sick of the sado-masochistic scene, or did it lose its edge for you? I've been down that route, and it gets dull very quickly.'

Conway's interest was piqued. 'Is that where you're from? Are you someone I spurned a long time ago?'

A rejected lover, just like Jack. How quaint.

Astrid shook her head and smiled. 'No, that wasn't me. That was Kennedy. Having read his work, I can see why he was a failed writer, but he liked to wax lyrical about you. Were you aware he called you Claudia Dominatrix? Not exactly original, but he poured his heart out in those pages. Is that your link to Beverly Shaw and Adam Church?' She twisted her gaze around the room. 'Is this where you killed him?'

'I've never killed anyone.'

'Do you know, I believe you. I think you enjoy the manipulation, the watching, while others do your work and people suffer. What I don't understand is how you tricked Shaw into believing you'd help her. I know she's afraid of you. It's a mixture of hatred and terror, which is why she's keeping quiet about your involvement so far. Once I tell her about my visit here, I'm sure she'll change her mind. She won't trust you then.'

Claudia Conway pushed the glass to one side and opened a drawer in the writing desk. She stood and removed a gun from it.

'Trust is good, but control is better.'

'Do you think you can end all this by shooting me?'

'You broke into my house and attacked me. I can kill you without batting an eyelid. This isn't Britain. We do things differently in America.'

Astrid placed a hand on her knee. 'I read your hidden school reports; that's two decades of fascinating stuff you've written.'

Conway stepped from the desk, the revolver still pointing forward. 'How did you see those?'

'Shaw copied everything on your computer. It was on an external hard drive I found in her house. They are very detailed, very dedicated. Have you been manipulating her for a decade or more? That's some long-time grooming if you have.'

Conway's laugh was low. 'No, of course not. She was barely on my radar until she returned to the school as a teacher, and even then, she was nothing to me. It was only when she came here to kill me that I took a real interest in her.'

'You wanted to control her again like you did when she was your student.'

Conway continued to grin. 'It was effortless; there was no challenge to it. I convinced her to torture and kill Kennedy. I even gave her the videos and photos I'd taken, making sure there was nothing to connect me to them, knowing it would be another piece of evidence to convict her once I'd finished.'

Astrid uncrossed her legs and got up. 'Shaw came here to murder you. She hated you and read the horrible things you'd written about her, yet you managed to convince her to kill Kennedy and join you in blowing up the building. I've met plenty of killers in my time, but that's impressive.'

'I have to admit, I enjoyed it more than I thought I would. It was a disappointment she didn't destroy the school, but you coming here now, giving me the chance to talk to someone nearly my equal, has just about made up for it. And I'll be able to visit Bev in prison. That will be fun, but confusing for her.'

'Confusing?'

She was only a few feet from Astrid, the gun aimed at her head. 'I told her I was dying, which was a lie, and that I was going to blow up the boiler room in the school, another lie, while she destroyed the main hall. Of course, I never placed any explosives there, only what remained of poor Jack, plus the tools Bev used to torture and kill him.' Conway's eyes sparkled. 'It's a shame we can't play this game any longer, and I do usually hate having to do stuff like this, but I'm afraid it's time for me to send you to meet your British ancestors, Astrid.'

Conway was grinning as she pulled the trigger.

For the second time in successive days, she was disappointed when an explosion didn't happen. She pulled the trigger again and again, with the same results.

Astrid smiled at her. 'Do you think I'd come here without checking the place for weapons?' She reached into her pocket and removed six bullets. She used her free hand to lift her arm and speak into the cuff of her jacket. 'You can come in now.'

Detective Hicks and three armed officers marched through the living room door. Conway stood there like a victim of Medusa.

'You set me up?'

Astrid walked to her. 'You were right, Claudia; manipulating people into doing things against their best interests is fun.'

<hr>

FORTY-EIGHT HOURS LATER, Astrid was on a plane back to England. Her phone was in her hand, her sister's number on the screen. There was no point calling, she wouldn't be able to get a signal, but as soon as she'd left Conway's house, she'd made a promise to herself: go home and speak to Courtney. She was ready to sort out the thorny problem of getting regular access to Olivia.

And no more trips abroad.

Evie squeezed past her and took the window seat. 'You

need to show me the sights of London when we get there. I've always wanted to explore Hampton Court.'

Astrid gripped on to the phone. 'There'll be plenty of time for that later. You've got your first meeting with your literary agent, and then the rearranged auction.'

She was surprised the publishers had agreed to it once Evie told her agent she was off to London for a month.

Evie grinned in acquiescence. 'You're in control, Snow.'

We'll travel across the country when Evie's book auction is over. And once I've finally put my past behind me.

She continued to stare at her sister's phone number as the plane climbed above the clouds and the temperature dropped.

ABOUT THE AUTHOR

Andrew French lives amongst faded seaside glamour on the North East coast of England. He likes gin and cats but not together, new music and old movies, curry and ice cream. Slow bike rides and long walks to the pub are his usual exercise, as well as flicking through the pages of good books and the memoirs of bad people.

Find out more at www.andrewsfrench.com

Facebook:

https://www.facebook.com/A-S-French-Author-150145625006018

Twitter:

www.twitter.com/andrewfrench100

Instagram:

www.instagram.com/andrewfrench100

And replies to all his email at mail@andrewsfrench.com

If you have the time, please leave a review at Amazon or Goodreads

Thank you!

ACKNOWLEDGMENTS

Many thanks to my wonderful wife for all her support and patience.

Gone to Texas edited by Alison Jack.

Cover design by James, GoOnWrite.com

www.ingramcontent.com/pod-product-compliance
Lightning Source LLC
Chambersburg PA
CBHW010551170726
48285CB00011B/2854